The Autocracy
of Mr Parham

BY THE SAME AUTHOR
ALL PUBLISHED BY HOUSE OF STRATUS

The Autocracy
of Mr Parham

H G WELLS

**HOUSE OF
STRATUS**

This edition published in 2002 by House of Stratus, an imprint of House of Stratus Ltd, Thirsk Industrial Park, York Road, Thirsk, North Yorkshire, YO7 3BX, UK.
Also at: House of Stratus Inc., 2 Neptune Road, Poughkeepsie, NY 12601, USA.

www.houseofstratus.com

Typeset, printed and bound by House of Stratus.

A catalogue record for this book is available from the British Library and The Library of Congress.

ISBN 0-7551-0391-2

CONTENTS

BOOK ONE

THE HOPEFUL FRIENDSHIP

CHAPTER ONE

Introduces Mr Parham and Sir Bussy Woodcock

For a time Mr Parham was extremely coy about Sir Bussy Woodcock's invitation to assist at a séance.

Mr Parham did not want to be drawn into this séance business. At the same time he did not want to fall out of touch with Sir Bussy Woodcock.

Sir Bussy Woodcock was one of those crude plutocrats with whom men of commanding intelligence, if they have the slightest ambition to be more than lookers-on at the spectacle of life, are obliged to associate nowadays. These rich adventurers are, under modern conditions, the necessary interpreters between high thought and low reality. It is regrettable that such difficult and debasing intervention should be unavoidable, but it seems to be so in this inexplicable world. Man of thought and man of action are mutually necessary – or, at any rate, the cooperation seems to be necessary to the man of thought. Plato, Confucius, Machiavelli had all to seek their princes. Nowadays, when the stuffing is out of princes, men of thought must do their best to use rich men.

Rich men amenable to use are hard to find and often very intractable when found. There was much in Sir Bussy, for example, that a fine intelligence, were it not equipped with a magnificent self-restraint, might easily have found insupportable. He was a short ruddy freckled man with a nose sculptured in the abrupt modern style and a mouth like a careless gash; he was thickest, a thing irritating in itself to an associate of long slender lines, and he moved with an impulsive rapidity of movement that was startling often and testified always to a total lack of such inhibitions as are inseparable from a cultivated mind. His manners were – voracious. When you talked to him he would jump suddenly into your pauses, and Mr Parham, having long been accustomed to talk to muted undergraduates, had, if anything, developed his pauses. Half the good had gone from Mr Parham if you robbed him of these significant silences. But Sir Bussy had no sense of significant silences. When you came to a significant silence, he would ask, "Meantersay?" in an entirely devastating manner. And he was always saying, "Gaw." Continually he said it with a variety of intonations, and it never seemed to be addressed to anyone in particular. It meant nothing, or, what was more annoying, it might mean anything.

The fellow was of lowly extraction. His father had driven a hansom cab in London, while his mother was a nurse in a consumption hospital at Hampstead – the "Bussy" came from one of her more interesting patients – and their son, already ambitious at fourteen, had given up a strenuous course of Extension Lectures for an all-time job with a garrulous advertisement contractor, because, said he, there was "no *go* in the other stuff." The other "stuff," if you please, was Wordsworth, the Reformation, Vegetable Morphology and Economic History as interpreted by fastidious-minded and obscurely satirical young gentlemen from the elder universities.

Mr Parham, tolerant, broad-minded, and deliberately quite modern, was always trying to forget these things. He never really forgot them, but whenever he and Sir Bussy were together he was always trying very hard to so. Sir Bussy's rise to wealth and power from such beginnings was one of the endless romances of modern business. Mr Parham made a point of knowing as little about it as possible.

There the man was. In a little less than a quarter of a century, while Mr Parham had been occupied chiefly with imperishable things – and marking examination papers upon them – Sir Bussy had become the master of a vast quantity of transitory but tangible phenomena which included a great advertising organization, an important part of the retail provision trade, a group of hotels, plantations in the tropics, cinema theatres, and many other things felt rather than known by Mr Parham. Over these ephemerons Sir Bussy presided during those parts of his days that were withdrawn from social life, and occasionally even when he was existing socially he was summoned to telephones or indulged in inaudible asides to mysterious young men who sprang from nowhere on their account. As a consequence of these activities, always rather obscure to Mr Parham, Sir Bussy lived in the midst of a quite terrific comfort and splendour surrounded by obedience and a dignified obsequiousness that might have overawed a weaker or a vulgarer mind than Mr Parham's altogether. He appeared in a doorway at night, and marvellous chauffeurs sprang out of the darkness to the salute at his appearance; he said "Gaw," and great butlers were ashamed. In a more luminous world things might have been different, but in this one Sir Bussy's chauffeurs plainly regarded Mr Parham as a rather unaccountable parcel which Sir Bussy was pleased to send about, and though the household menservants at Buntincombe, Carfex House, Marmion House, and the Hanger treated Mr Parham as a gentleman, manifestly they did so rather through training than perception. A continual miracle, Sir Bussy was. He had acquired a colossal power of ordering people about, and it was evident to Mr Parham that he had not the slightest idea what on the whole he wanted them to do. Meanwhile he just ordered them about. It was natural for Mr Parham to think, "If I had the power he has, what wonderful things I could achieve."

For instance, Sir Bussy might make history.

Mr Parham was a lifelong student and exponent of history and philosophy. He had produced several studies – mainly round and about Richelieu and going more deeply into the mind of Richelieu than anyone has ever done before – and given short special courses upon historical themes; he had written a small volume of essays; he was general editor of Fosdyke's popular "Philosophy of History" series, and he would sometimes write reviews upon works of scholarly distinction, reviews that appeared (often shockingly cut and mutilated) in the *Empire,* the *Weekly Philosopher*, and the *Georgian Review*. No one could deal with a new idea struggling to take form and wave it out of existence again more neatly and smilingly than Mr Parham. And loving history and philosophy as he did, it was a trouble to his mind to feel how completely out of tune was the confusion of current events with anything that one could properly call fine history or fine philosophy. The Great War he realized was History, though very lumpish, brutalized, and unmanageable, and the Conference of Versailles was history also – in further declination. One could still put that Conference as a drama between this power and that, talk of the conflict for "ascendancy," explain the "policy" of this or that man or this or that foreign office subtly and logically.

But from about 1919 onward everything had gone from bad to worse. Persons, events, had been deprived of significance more and more. Discordance, a disarray of values, invaded the flow of occurrence. Take Mr Lloyd George, for example. How was one to treat a man like that? After a climax of the Versailles type the proper way was to culminate and let the historians get to work, as Woodrow Wilson indeed had done, and as Lincoln or Sulla or Cæsar or Alexander did before him. They culminated and rounded off, inconvenient facts fell off them bit by bit, and more and more surely could they be treated *historically*. The reality of history broke through superficial appearance; the logic of events was made visible.

But now, where were the powers and what were the forces? In the face of such things as happen today this trained historian felt like a skilled carver who was asked to cut up soup. Where were the bones? – any bones? A man like Sir Bussy ought to be playing a part in a great struggle between the New Rich and the Older Oligarchy; he ought to be an Equestrian pitted against the Patricians. He ought to round off the Close of Electoral Democracy. He ought to embody the New Phase in British affairs – the New Empire. But did he? Did he stand for anything at all? There were times when Mr Parham felt that if he could not make Sir Bussy stand for something, something definitely, formally and historically significant, his mind would give way altogether.

Surely the ancient and time-honoured processes of history were going on still – surely they were going on. Or what could be going on? Security and predominance – in Europe, in Asia, in finance – were gravely discussed by Mr Parham and his kindred souls in the more serious weekly and monthly reviews. There were still governments and foreign offices everywhere, and they went through the motions of a struggle for world ascendancy according to the rules, decently and in order. Nothing of the slightest importance occurred now between the Powers that was not strictly confidential. Espionage had never been so universal, conscientious, and respected, and the double cross of Christian diplomacy ruled the skies from Washington to Tokio. Britain and France, America, Germany, Moscow cultivated navies and armies and carried on high dignified diplomacies and made secret agreements with and against each other just as though there had never been that stupid talk about "a war to end war." Bolshevik Moscow, after an alarming opening phase, had settled down into the best tradition of the Czar's Foreign Office. If Mr Parham had been privileged to enjoy the intimacy of statesmen like Sir Austen Chamberlain and Mr Winston Churchill or M. Poincaré, and if he could have dined with some of them, he felt sure that after dinner, with the curtains drawn and the port and cigars moving with a pensive irregularity like chess pieces upon the reflective mahogany, things would be said, a tone would be established that would bring him back warmly and comfortably again into his complete belief in history as he had learnt it and taught it.

But somehow, in spite of his vivid illuminating books and able and sometimes quite important articles, such social occasions did not come to his assitance.

Failing such reassurances, a strange persuasion in his mind arose and gathered strength, that round and about the present appearances of historical continuity something else quite different and novel and not so much menacing as dematerializing these appearances was happening. It is hard to define what this something else was. Essentially it was a vast and increasing inattention. It was the way everybody was going on, as if all the serious things in life were no longer serious. And as if other things were. And in the more recent years of Mr Parham's life it had been, in particular, Sir Bussy.

One night Mr Parham asked himself a heart-searching question. It was doubtful to him afterwards whether he had had a meditation or a nightmare, whether he had thought or dreamt he thought. Suppose, so it was put to him, that statesmen, diplomatists, princes, professors of economics, military and naval experts, and in fact all the present heirs of history, were to bring about a situation, complex, difficult, dangerous, with notes, counter notes, utterances – and even ultimatums – rising towards a declaration of war about some "question." And suppose – oh, horror! – suppose people in general, and Sir Bussy in particular, just looked at it and said, "Gaw," or "Meantersay?" and turned away. Turned away and went on with the things they were doing, the silly things unfit for history? What would the heirs of history do? Would the soldiers dare to hold a pistol at Sir Bussy, or the statesmen push him aside? Suppose he refused to be pushed aside and resisted in some queer circumventing way of his own. Suppose he were to say, "Cut all this right out – now." And suppose they found they had to cut it out!

Well, what would become then of our historical inheritance? Where would the Empire be, the Powers, our national traditions and policies? It was an alien idea, this idea that the sawdust was running out of the historical tradition, so alien indeed that it surely never entered Mr Parham's mind when it was fully awake.

There was really nothing to support it there, no group of concepts to which it could attach itself congenially, and yet, once it had secured its footing, it kept worrying at Mr Parham's serenity like a silly tune that has established itself in one's brain. "They won't obey – when the time comes they won't obey"; that was the refrain. The generals would say, "Haw," but the people would say, "Gaw!" And Gaw would win! In the nightmare, anyhow, Gaw won. Life after that became inconceivable to Mr Parham. Chaos!

In which somehow, he felt, Sir Bussy might still survive, transfigured, perhaps, but surviving. Horribly. Triumphantly.

Mr Parham came vividly and certainly awake and lay awake until dawn.

The muse of History might tell of the rise of dynasties, the ascendancy of this power or that, of the onset of nationalism with Macedonia, of the Decline and Fall of the Roman Empire, of the age-long struggles of Islam and Christendom and of Latin and Greek Christianity, of the marvellous careers of Alexander and Cæsar and Napoleon, unfolding the magic scroll of their records, seeking to stir up Sir Bussy to play his part, his important if subservient part in this continuing drama of hers, and Sir Bussy would reflect almost sleepily over the narrative, would seem to think nothing of the narrative, would follow some train of thought of his own into regions inaccessible to Mr Parham, and would say, "Gaw."

Gaw!

Mr Parham was becoming neurasthenic…

And then, to add to his troubles, there was this damned nonsense now about going to a séance and taking mediums seriously, them and their nasty, disreputable, and irritatingly inexplicable phenomena.

About dawn Mr Parham was thinking very seriously of giving up Sir Bussy. But he had thought of that several times before and always with a similar result. Finally he went to a séance, he went to a series of séances with Sir Bussy, as this narrative will in due course relate.

CHAPTER TWO

Tells how Sir Bussy and Mr Parham Became Associated

When five years or more ago Mr Parham had met Sir Bussy for the first time, the great financier had seemed to be really interested in the things of the mind, modestly but seriously interested.

Mr Parham had talked of Michael Angelo and Botticelli at a man's dinner given by Sebright Smith at the Rialto. It was what Mr Parham called one of Sebright Smith's marvellous feats of mixing and what Sebright Smith, less openly, called a "massacre." Sebright Smith was always promising and incurring the liability for hospitality in a most careless manner, and when he had accumulated a sufficiency of obligations to bother him he gave ruthless dinners and lunches, machine-gun dinners and lunches, to work them off. Hence his secret name for these gatherings. He did not care whom he asked to meet whom, he trusted to champagne as a universal solvent, and Mr Parham, with that liberal modern and yet cultivated mind of his, found these feasts delightfully catholic.

There is nothing like men who are not at their ease, for listening, and Mr Parham, who was born well informed, just let himself go. He said things about Botticelli that a more mercenary man might have made into a little book and got forty or fifty pounds for. Sir Bussy listened with an expression that anyone who did not know him might have considered malignant. But it was merely that when he was interested or when he was occupied with an idea for action he used to let the left-hand corner of his mouth hang down.

When there came a shift with the cigars and Negro singers sang Negro spirituals, Sir Bussy seized an opportunity and slipped into one of the two chairs that had become vacant on either side of Mr Parham.

"You know about those things?" he asked, regardless of the abounding emotional richness of "Lat my people go-o."

Mr Parham conveyed interrogation.

"Old masters, Art and all that."

"They interest me," said Mr Parham, smiling with kindly friendliness, for he did not yet know the name or the power of the man to whom he was talking.

"They might have interested *me* – but I cut it out. D'you ever lunch in the city?"

"Not often."

"Well, if ever you are that way – next week, for example – ring me up at Marmion House."

The name conveyed nothing to Mr Parham.

"I'll be delighted," he said politely.

Sir Bussy, it seemed, was on his way to depart. He paused for a moment. "For all I know," he said, "there may be a lot in Art. Do come. I was really interested." He smiled, with a curious gleam of charm, turned off the charm, and departed briskly, in

14

an interlude while Sebright Smith and the singers decided noisily about the next song.

Later Mr Parham sought his host. "Who is the sturdy little man with a flushed face and wiry hair who went early?"

"Think I know everybody here?" said Sebright Smith.

"But he sat next to you!"

"Oh, *that* chap! That's one of our conq – conquerors," said Sebright Smith, who was drunk.

"Has he a name?"

"Has he not?" said Sebright Smith. "Sir Blasted Bussy Bussy Buy-up-the-Universe Woodcock. He's the sort of man who buys up everything. Shops and houses and factories. Estates and pot houses. Quarries. Whole trades. Buys things on the way to you. Fiddles about with them a bit before you get 'em. You can't eat a pat of butter now in London before he's bought and sold it. Railways he buys, hotels, cinemas and suburbs, men and women, soul and body. Mind he doesn't buy you."

"I'm not on the market."

"Private treaty, I suppose," said Sebright Smith, and realizing from Mr Parham's startled interrogative face that he had been guilty of some indelicacy, tried to tone it down with, "Have some more champagne?"

Mr Parham caught the eye of an old friend and did not answer his host's last remark. Indeed, he hardly saw any point to it, and the man was plainly drunk. He lifted a vertical hand to his friend as one might hail a cab and shouldered his way towards him.

In the course of the next few days Mr Parham made a number of discreet inquiries about Sir Bussy, he looked him up in *Who's Who,* where he found a very frank and rather self-conscious half column, and decided to accept that invitation to Marmion House in a decisive manner. If the man wanted tutoring in Art he should have tutoring in Art. Wasn't it Lord Rosebery who said, "We must educate our masters?"

They would have a broad-minded, friendly tête-à-tête, Mr Parham would open the golden world of Art to his host and incidentally introduce a long-cherished dream that it would cost Sir Bussy scarcely anything to make into a fine and delightful reality.

This dream, which as destined to hold Mr Parham in resentful vassalage to Sir Bussy through long, long years of hope deferred, was the vision of a distinguished and authoritative weekly paper, with double columns and a restrained title heading, of which Mr Parham would be the editor. It was to be one of those papers, not vulgarly gross in their circulation, but which influence opinion and direct current history throughout the civilized world. It was to be all that the *Spectator*, the *Saturday Review*, the *Nation*, and the *New Statesman* have ever been and more. It was to be largely the writing of Mr Parham and of young men influenced and discovered by him. It was to arraign the whole spectacle of life, its public affairs, its "questions," its science, art, and literature. It was to be understanding, advisory, but always a little aloof. It was to be bold at times, stern at times, outspoken at times, but never shouting, never vulgar. As an editor one partakes of the nature of God; you are God with only one drawback, a Proprietor. But also, if you have played your cards well, you are God with a definite Agreement. And without God's responsibility for the defects and errors of the universe you survey. You can smile and barb your wit as He cannot do. For He would be under suspicion of having led up to His own jokes.

16

Writing "Notes of the Week" is perhaps one of the purest pleasures life offers an intelligent, cultivated man. You encourage or you rebuke nations. You point out how Russia has erred and Germany taken your hint of the week before last. You discuss the motives of statesmen and warn bankers and colossal business adventures. You judge judges. You have a word of kindly praise or mild contempt for the foolish multitude of writers. You compliment artists, sometimes left-handedly. The little brawling Correspondents play about your feet, writing their squabbling, protesting letters, needing sometimes your reproving pat. Every week you make or mar reputations. Criticizing everyone, you go uncriticized. You speak out of a cloud, glorious, powerful and obscure. Few men are worthy of this great trust, but Mr Parham had long felt himself among that elect minority. With difficulty he had guarded his secret, waiting for his paper as the cloistered virgin of the past waited for her lover. And here at last was Sir Bussy, Sir Bussy who could give this precious apotheosis to Mr Parham with scarcely an effort.

He had only to say "Go" to the thing. Mr Parham knew just where to go and just what to do. It was Sir Bussy's great opportunity. He might evoke a God. He had neither the education nor the abilities to be a God, but he could bring a God into being.

Sir Bussy had bought all sorts of things but apparently he had never yet come into the splash and excitement of newspaper properties. It was time he did. It was time he tasted Power, Influence, and Knowledge brimming fresh from the source. His own source.

With such thoughts already pullulating in his mind Mr Parham had gone to his first lunch at Marmion House.

Marmion House he found a busy place. It had been built by Sir Bussy. Eight and thirty companies had their offices there, and in the big archway of the Victoria Street entrance Mr Parham was jostled by a great coming and going of swift-tripping clerks and stenographers seeking their midday refreshment. A populous lift shed passengers at every floor and left Mr Parham alone with the lift boy for the top.

It was not be the pleasant little tête-à-tête Mr Parham had expected when he had telephoned in the morning. He found Sir Bussy in a large dining room with a long table surrounded by quite a number of people who Mr Parham felt from the very outset were hangers-on and parasites of the worst description. Later he was to realize that a few of them were in a sense reputable and connected with this or that of the eight and thirty companies Sir Bussy had grouped about him, but that was not the first impression. There was a gravely alert stenographer on Sir Bussy's left-hand side whom Mr Parham considered much too dignified in her manner and much too graceful and well dressed for her position, and there were two very young women with grossly familiar manners who called Sir Bussy "Bussy dear" and stared at Mr Parham as though he were some kind of foreigner. Later on in the acquaintanceship Mr Parham was to realize that these girls were Sir Bussy's pet nieces by marriage – he had no children of his own – but at the time Mr Parham thought the very worst of them. They were painted. There was a very, very convex, buoyant man wearing light tweeds and with an insinuating voice who asked Mr Parham suddenly whether he didn't think something ought to be done about Westernhanger and then slipped off into an obscure joke with one of the nieces while Mr Parham was still wondering who or what Westernhanger might be. And there was a small, preoccupied looking man with that sort of cylinder forehead one really ought to take off before sitting down to lunch, who Mr Parham learnt was Sir Titus Knowles of Harley Street. There was no serious conversation at lunch but only a throwing about of remarks. A quiet man sitting between Mr Parham and Sir Bussy asked Mr Parham whether he did not find the architecture of the city abominable.

"Consider New York," he said.

Mr Parham weighed it. "New York is different."

The quiet man after a pause for reflection said that was true but still...

Sir Bussy had greeted Mr Parham's arrival with his flash of charm and had told him to "sit down anywhere." Then after a little obscure badinage across the table with one of the pretty painted girls about the possibility of her playing "real tennis" in London, the host subsided into his own thoughts. Once he said, "Gaw!" – about nothing.

The lunch had none of the quiet orderliness of a West-End lunch party. Three or four young men, brisk but not dignified, in white linen jackets did the service. There were steak-and-kidney pudding and roast beef, celery for everyone in the American fashion, and a sideboard with all manner of cold meat, cold fruit tarts, and bottles of drink thereon. On the table were jugs of some sort of cup. Mr Parham thought it best became a simple scholar and a gentleman to disdain the plutocrat's wines and drink plain beer from a tankard. When the eating was over half the party melted away, including the graceful secretary whose face Mr Parham was beginning to find interesting, and the rest moved with Sir Bussy into a large low lounge where there were cigars and cigarettes, coffee and liqueurs.

"We're going to this tennis place with Tremayne," the pretty girls announced together.

"Not Lord Tremayne!" thought Mr Parham and regarded the abdominal case with a new interest. The fellow had been at C.C.C.

"If he tries to play tennis with clubs and solid balls after the lunch he's eaten, he'll drop dead," said Sir Bussy.

"You don't know my powers of assimilation," said the very convex gentleman.

"Have some brandy, Tremayne, and make a job of it," said Sir Bussy.

"Brandy," said Tremayne to a passing servitor. "A double brandy."

"Get his lordship some old brandy," said Sir Bussy.

So it was really Lord Tremayne! But how inflated! Mr Parham was already a tutor when Lord Tremayne had come up, a beautifully slender youth. He came up and he was sent down. But in the interval he had been greatly admired.

The three departed, and Sir Bussy came to Mr Parham.

"Got anything to do this afternoon?" he asked.

Mr Parham had nothing of a compelling nature.

"Let's go and look at some pictures," said Sir Bussy. "I want to. D'you mind? You seem to have ideas about them."

"There's so *many* pictures," said Mr Parham in a rather jolly tone and smiling.

"National Gallery, I mean. And the Tate, perhaps. Academy's still open. Dealer's shows if necessary. We ought to get around as much as we need to in the afternoon. It's general idea I want. And how it looks to you."

As Sir Bussy's Rolls-Royce went its slick, swift way westward through the afternoon traffic, he made their objective clearer. "I want to *look* at this painting," he said, with his voice going up at the "look." "What's it all *about?* What's it all *for?* How did it get there? What does it all amount to?"

The corner of his mouth went down and he searched his companion's face with an extraordinary mixture of hostility and appeal in his eyes.

Mr Parham would have liked to have had notice of the question. He gave Sir Bussy profile.

"What is Art?" questioned Mr Parham, playing for time. "A big question."

"Not Art – just this painting," corrected Sir Bussy.

"It's Art," said Mr Parham. "Art in its nature. One and Indivisible."

"Gaw," said Sir Bussy softly and became still more earnestly expectant.

"A sort *quintessence*, I suppose," Mr Parham tried. He waved a hand with a gesture that had earned him the unjust and unpleasant nickname of "Bunch of Fingers" among his undergraduates. For his hands were really very beautifully proportioned. "A kind of getting the concentrated quality of loveliness, of beauty, out of common experience."

"That we certainly got to look for," injected Sir Bussy.

"And fixing it. Making it permanent."

Sir Bussy spoke again after a pause for reflection. He spoke with an air of confiding thoughts long suppressed. "Sure these painters haven't been putting it over us a bit? I thought – the other night – while you were talking…just an idea…,"

21

Mr Parham regarded his host slantingly. "No," he said slowly and judiciously, "I don't think they've been putting it over us." Just the least little stress in the last four words – imperceptible to Sir Bussy.

"Well, that's what we got to see."

A queer beginning for a queer afternoon – an afternoon with a Barbarian. But indisputably, as Sebright Smith had said, "one of our conquerors." He wasn't a Barbarian to be sniffed away. He fought for his barbarism like a bulldog. Mr Parham had been taken by surprise. He wished more and more that he had had notice of the question that was pressed upon him as the afternoon wore on. Then he could have chosen his pictures and made an orderly course of it. As it was he got to work haphazard, and instead of fighting a set battle for Art and the wonder and sublimity of it, Mr Parham found himself in the position of a commander who is called upon with the enemy already in his camp. It was a piecemeal discussion.

Sir Bussy's attitude so far as Mr Parham could make it out from his fragmentary and illiterate method of expressing himself, was one of sceptical inquiry. The man was uncultivated – indeed, he was glaringly uncultivated – but there was much natural intelligence in his make-up. He had evidently been impressed profoundly by the honour paid to the names of the great Princes of pictorial art by all men of taste and intelligence, and he could not see why they were exalted to such heights. So he wanted it explained to him. He had evidently vast curiosities. Today it was Michael Angelo and Titian he questioned. Tomorrow it might be Beethoven or Shakespeare. He wasn't to be fobbed off by authority. He didn't admit authority. He had to be met as though the acquiescence and approval of generations to these forms of greatness had never been given.

He went up the steps from the entrance to the National Gallery with such a swift assurance that the thought occurred to Mr Parham that he had already paid a visit there. He made at once for the Italians.

"Now, here's pictures," he said, sweeping on through one room to another and only slowing down in the largest gallery of all. "They're fairly interesting and amoosing. The most part. A lot of them are bright. They might be brighter, but I suppose none of them are exactly fast colour. You can see the fun the chaps have had painting them. I grant all that. I wouldn't object to having quite a lot of them about in Carfex House. I'd like to swipe about with a brush myself a bit. But when it comes to making out they're something more than that and speaking of them in a sort of hushed religious way as though those chaps knew something special about heaven and just let it out, I don't get you. I don't for the life of me get you."

"But here, for instance," said Mr Parham, "this Francesca – the sweetness and delicacy – surely *divine* isn't too much for it."

"Sweetness and delicacy! Divine! Well, take a spring day in England, take the little feathers on a pheasant's breast, or bits of a sunset, or the morning light through a tumbler of flowers on a window sill. Surely things of that sort are no end sweeter and more delicate and more divine and all the rest of it than this – this *pickled* stuff."

"Pickled!" For a moment Mr Parham was overcome.

"Pickled prettiness," said Sir Bussy defiantly. "Pickled loveliness, if you like… And a lot of it not very lovely and not so marvellously well pickled."

Sir Bussy continued hitting Mr Parham while he was down. "All these Madonnas. Did they *want* to paint them or were they obliged? Who ever thought a woman sitting up on a throne like that was any catch?"

"Pickled!" Mr Parham clung to the main theme. *"No!"*

Sir Bussy, abruptly expectant, dropped the corner of his mouth and brought his face sideways towards Mr Parham.

Mr Parham waved his hand about and found the word he wanted. "Selected."

He got it still better. "Selected and fixed. These men went about the world seeing – seeing with all their might. Seeing with gifts. Born to see. And they tried – and I think succeeded – in seizing something of their most intense impressions. For us. The Madonna was often – was usually – no more than an excuse..."

Sir Bussy's mouth resumed its more normal condition, and he turned with an appearance of greater respect towards the pictures again. He would give them a chance under that plea. But his scrutiny did not last for long.

"That thing," he said, returning to the object of their original remarks.

"Francesca's Baptism," breathed Mr Parham.

"To my mind it's not a selection: it's an assembly. Things he liked painting. The background is jolly, but only because it reminds you of things you've seen. I'm not going to lie down in front of it and worship. And most of this – "

He seemed to indicate the entire national collection.

" – is just painting."

"I must contest," said Mr Parham. "I must contest."

He pleaded the subtle colouring of Filippo Lippi, the elation and grace and classic loveliness of Botticelli; he spoke of richness, anatomical dexterity, virtuosity, and culminated at last in the infinite solemnity of Leonardo's Madonna of the Rocks. "The mystery, the serene mystery of that shadowed woman's face; the sweet wisdom of the Angel's self-content," said Mr Parham. "Painting! It's Revelation."

"Gaw," said Sir Bussy, head on one side.

He was led from picture to picture like an obstinate child. "I'm not saying the stuff's *bad*," he repeated; "I'm not saying it isn't interesting; but I don't see the call for superlatives. It's being reminded of things, and it's you really that has the things. Taking it altogether," and he surveyed the collection, "I'll admit it's clever, sensitive work, but I'm damned if I see anything divine."

Also he made a curiously ungracious concession to culture. "After a bit," he said, "one certainly gets one's eye in. Like being in the dark in a cinema."

But it would be tedious to record all his crude reactions to loveliness that have become the dearest heritage of our minds. He said Raphael was "dam' genteel." He rebelled at El Greco. "Byzantine solemnity," he repeated after Mr Parham, "it's more like faces seen in the back of a spoon." But he came near cheering Tintoretto's Origin of the Milky Way. "Gaw," he said warmly. "Now *that!* It isn't decent but it's damn fine."

He went back to it.

It was in vain that Mr Parham tried to beguile him past the Rokeby Venus.

"Who did that?" he asked, as if he suspected Mr Parham.

"Velazquez."

"Well, what's the essential difference between that and a good big photograph of a naked woman tinted and posed to excite you?"

Mr Parham was little ashamed to find himself arguing an issue so crude in a public place and audibly, but Sir Bussy was regarding him with that unconscious menace of his which compelled replies.

"The two things aren't in the same world. The photograph is material, factual, personal, individual. Here the beauty, the long delightful lines of a slender human body, are merely the theme of a perfect composition. The body becomes transcendental. It is sublimated. It is robbed of all individual defect and individual coarseness.

"Nonsense! that girl's individualized enough for – anybody."

"I do *not agree*. Profoundly I do *not* agree."

"Gaw! I'm not quarrelling with the picture, only I don't see the force of all this transcending and sublimating. I like it – just as I like that Tintoretto. But a pretty naked young woman is beautiful anywhere and anyhow, especially if you're in the mood, and I don't see why a poor little smut seller in the street should be run in for selling just exactly what anyone in the world can come here to see – and buy photographs of in the vestibule. It isn't Art I'm objecting to, but the Airs Art gives itself. It's just as if Art had been asked to dinner at Buckingham Palace and didn't want to be seen about with its poor relations. Who got just as much right to live."

Mr Parham moved on with an expression of face – as if the discussion had decayed unpleasantly.

"I wonder if there is time to get on to the Tate," he considered. "There you'll find the British school and the wild

26

uncharted young." He could not refrain from a delicate, almost imperceptible sneer. "Their pictures are newer. You may find them brighter and more pleasing on that account."

They did go on to the Tate Gallery. But Sir Bussy found no further objections to art there nor any reconciliation. His chief judgment was to ascribe "cheek" to Mr Augustus John. As he and Mr Parham left the building he seemed to reflect, and then he delivered himself of what was evidently his matured answer to his self-posed question for that afternoon.

"I don't see that this Painting gets you out to anything. I don't see that it gets you out of anything. It's not discovery and it's not escape. People talk as if it was a door out of this damned world. Well – *is* it?"

"It has given colour and interest to thousands – myriads – of quietly observant lives."

"Cricket can do that," said Sir Bussy.

Mr Parham had no answer to such a remark. For some brief moments it seemed to him that the afternoon had been a failure. He had done his best, but this was an obdurate mind, difficult to dominate, and he had, he felt, failed completely to put the idea of Art over to it. They stood side by side in silence in the evening glow, waiting for Sir Bussy's chauffeur to realize that they had emerged. This plutocrat, thought Mr Parham, will never understand me, will never understand the objectives of a true civilization, never endow the paper I need. I must keep polite and smiling as a gentleman should, but I have wasted time and hope on him.

In the car, however, Sir Bussy displayed an unexpected gratitude, and Mr Parham realized his pessimism had been premature.

"Well," said Sir Bussy, "I got a lot out of this afternoon. It's been a Great Time. You've interested me. I shall remember all sorts of things you've said about this Art. We held on fine. We looked and we looked. I think I got your point of view; I really think I have. That other evening I said, 'I must get that chap's point of view. He's amazing.' I hope this is only the first of quite a lot of times when I'm going to have the pleasure of meeting you and getting your point of view... Like pretty women?"

"Eh?" said Mr Parham.

"Like pretty women?"

"Man is mortal," said Mr Parham with the air of a confession.

"I'd love to see you at a supper party I'm giving at the Savoy. Thursday next. Supper and keep on with it. Everything fit to look at on the London stage and most of it showing. Dancing."

"I'm not a dancing man, you know."

"Nor me. But *you* ought to take lessons. You've got the sort of long leg to do it. Anyhow, we might sit in a corner together and you tell me something about Women. Like you've been telling me about Art. I been so busy, but I've always wanted to know. And you can take people down to supper whenever you feel dullish. Any number of them ready to be taken down to supper. Again and again and again and again, as the poem says. We don't stint the supper."

CHAPTER THREE

Mr Parham Among the Gayer Rich

It was not clear to Mr Parham that he would get his
newspaper, but it was quite clear that he had a reasonable
prospect of becoming a sort of Mentor to Sir Bussy. Just
what sort of Mentor it was still too early to guess. If you will
imagine Socrates as tall and formally good-looking and
Alcibiades as short and energetic, and if you will suppose that
unfortunate expedition to Syracuse replaced under sound advice
by a masterful consolidation of Greece; if indeed you will flatten
that parallel to the verge of extinction without actually
obliterating it, you will get something of the flavour of Mr
Parham's anticipations. Or perhaps Aristotle and Alexander will
better serve our purpose. It is one of the endless advantages of a
sound classical education that you need never see, you can never
see, a human relationship in its vulgar simplicity; there is always
the enrichment of these regurgitated factors. You lose all sense of
current events; you simply get such history as you have
swallowed repeating itself.

In this party at the Savoy Mr Parham saw Sir Bussy seriously
engaged in expenditure for the first time. A common mind would
have been mightily impressed by the evident height, width,

depth, and velocity of the flow, and even Mr Parham found himself doing little sums and estimates to get an idea of what this one evening must be costing his new acquaintance. It would, Mr Parham reckoned, have maintained a weekly of the very highest class for three years or more.

Mr Parham made it his rule to dress correctly and well for every social occasion. He did not believe in that benefit of clergy which is used as an excuse by men of learning and intellectual distinction for low collars on high occasions and antiquated smoking jackets at dances. He thought it better to let people understand that on occasion a philosopher is fully equal to being a man of the world. His tallness permitted a drooping urbanity, a little suggestive of Lord Balfour, and on the whole he knew himself with his fine and fastidious features to be anything but ill-looking. His Gibus hat, a trifle old-fashioned in these slovenly times, kept his bunch of fingers within bounds, and his fine gold chain was plainly ancestral.

The entire Savoy had placed itself at the disposal of Sir Bussy. Its servants were his servants. In their grey plush breeches and yellow waistcoats they looked like inherited family servitors. In the cloakroom he found Sir Titus Knowles of the stupendous brow divesting himself of an extremely small black hat and a huge cloak.

"Hullo!" said Sir Titus. "*You* here!"

"Apparently," said Mr Parham taking it in good part.

"Ah," said Sir Titus.

"No need for a ticket, Sir Titus," said the receiver of cloaks. "Too well known, sir."

Sir Titus disappeared, smiling faintly.

But Mr Parham received a ticket for his overcoat.

THE AUTOCRACY OF MR PARHAM

He drifted past the men waiting for their womankind towards a dazzling crowd of lovely and extremely expensive-looking ladies with shining arms and shoulders and backs and a considerable variety of men. There was talk like a great and greatly fluctuating wind blowing through tin-leaved trees. A sort of reception was in progress. Sir Bussy appeared abruptly.

"Good," he said with gusto. "We must have a talk. You know Pomander Poole? She's dying to meet you."

He vanished, and that evening Mr Parham never had an opportunity to exchange more than two or three missile sentences with him, though he had endless glimpses of him at a distance, moodily active or artificially gay.

Miss Pomander Poole began very seriously by asking Mr Parham his name, which Sir Bussy, through inadvertency or a momentary forgetfulness, had never mentioned. "Parham is the name of the man you are dying to meet," said Mr Parham, and did a dazzling smile with all his excellent teeth, except, of course, the molars at the back.

"Bussy's more like a flea than ever tonight," said Miss Pomander Poole. "He ought to be called the Quest. Or the little wee Grail. I've seen six people trying to catch him,"

She was a dark, handsome lady with tormented-looking eyes and more breadth than is fashionable. Her voice was rich and fine. She surveyed the long room before them. "Why in heaven he gives these parties I can't imagine," she said, and sighed and became still, to show she had finished her part in the conversation.

Mr Parham hung fire. The name of Pomander Poole was very familiar to him, but for the life of him at that moment he could not connect it with books, articles, plays, pictures, scandals, society gossip, or the music-hall stage with any of the precision necessary if he was to talk in the easy, helpful, rather amused way becoming to a philosopher in his man-of-the-world mood. So he had to resort to what was almost questioning.

"I've known our host only very recently," said Mr Parham, plainly inviting comment.

"He doesn't exist," she said.

Apparently we were going to be brilliant, and if so Mr Parham was not the man to miss his cues. "We've met a sort of simulacrum," he protested.

She disregarded Mr Parham's words altogether. "He doesn't exist," she sighed. "So not only can no one else catch him, he can't catch himself. He's always turning back the bedclothes and having a good look for himself, but it's never any good."

The lady certainly had breadth.

"He acquires wealth," said Mr Parham.

"Nature abhors a vacuum," she said with the weariness of one who answers a familiar catechism. She was looking about her with her sombre, appealing eyes as she spoke, as if she were looking for someone to relieve her of Mr Parham.

"Tonight the vacuum is full of interesting people."

"I don't know a tithe of them."

"I'm sufficiently unworldly to find their appearances interesting."

"I'm sufficiently worldly to build no hopes on that."

A second phase of awkwardness hung between Mr Parham and his companion. He wished she could be just wiped out of existence and somebody easier put in her place. But she it was who saved the situation. "I suppose it's too early to begin going down to supper," she said; "down or up or wherever it is. These vacuum parties provoke feelings of extraordinary emptiness in me."

"Well, let's explore," said Mr Parham, doing his smile again and taking the lady in tow.

"I'm sure I've heard you lecture at the Royal Institution," she opened.

"Never been there," said Mr Parham.

"I've seen you there. Usually two or three of you. You're a man of science."

"Classical, dear lady. Academic. With a few old and tested ideas like favourite pipes that I brood over again and again – and an inky forefinger."

Now that wasn't so bad. Miss Poole looked at him as though she had just observed his existence for the first time. A ray of interest shone and then dissolved into other preoccupations.

When we say that Mr Parham took the lady in tow and found the supper room we defer rather to the way in which he would have liked to have put it. But in fact, as they made their way through the brilliant multitude, she was usually leading in a distraught yet purposive manner by anything between two yards and six. Supper had indeed begun noisily and vigorously, and Miss Poole, still leading, was hailed by a group of people who seemed to be not so much supping as laying in provisions. "What are you saying tonight, Pomander?" cried a handsome young man, and she melted into the centre of the group without any attempt to introduce Mr Parham. "I'm doubting Bussy's real existence," answered Miss Poole, "and craving for his food."

"Like a modern Christian and his God," said someone.

Mr Parham travelled round the outskirts of the group and came to the glittering tablecloth. The board was bountiful, and the only drink, it seemed to Mr Parham, was champagne, poured from glass jugs. He tried to get a drink for Miss Poole, but she was already supplied, so he drank himself, pretended to participate in the conversation of the backs that were turned towards him, looked amused, and ate a couple of chicken sandwiches with an air of careless ease. Miss Poole had brightened considerable. She smacked a large ham-faced Jew on the cheek with a *pâté de foie gras* sandwich – for no apparent reason. Perhaps she liked him. Or perhaps it was just playfulness. She led up to and repeated her picture of Sir Bussy looking for himself in the bedclothes, and it was hailed with wild delight. Amidst the applause a small blond youth turned round with every appearance of extreme caution, repeated the delightful invention carefully to Mr Parham, and then forgot him again instantly.

Mr Parham tried not to feel that the group had – as Mr Aldous Huxley, in that physiological manner of his, might say – excreted him, but that was very much his feeling, and he was bearing up against it with a second glass of champagne when he discovered Sir Titus Knowles close beside him and evidently also undergoing elimination from an adjacent group of bright young things, "Hullo," he said. "*You* here?"

"Rather fun," said Sir Titus insincerely, and then out of nowhere came the most ravishing of youthful blondes, all warmth and loveliness, pretending to be out of breath and addressing herself particularly to the great consultant.

"Gentleman of the name of Parham, Sir Titus," she said in a warm husky voice. "Meanwhile something to eat, please."

Her immediate need was supplied. "When I asked Bussy what's he like, he said, 'Oh, you'll know him when you see him.'

34

I got to find him, take him, and make him dance. He bet me.
Parham. Shall I round singing it? I suppose there's about a
million people here. I'll be thrown out for accosting."

She glanced at Sir Titus, detected a directive grimace, became
alert to the situation, and faced Mr Parham. "Of course!" she
said with her mouth full. "Right in one. My name's Gaby
Greuze. You're the handsomest man here. I might have known
Bussy wouldn't put me off with anything cheap."

Mr Parham's expression mingled delight and candid
disavowal. "You'll never make me dance," he said.

The accidental pressures of the crowd about them brought
her extremely close to him. What a lovely face it was, seen so
nearly! Impudent, blue eyed! The modelling of the eyelids was
exquisite. The little soft corner of the drooping mouth! "I'll
make you dance. I c'd make you do no end of things. Cause
why?"

She took a healthy mouthful of ham and munched.

"I like you."

She nodded confirmation. Mr Parham's brilliant smile came
unbidden. "I'm not going to resist for a moment, I can assure
you," he said and added with the air of a redoubtable character,
"Trust me." Like her! He could have eaten her. Yes, this was
something better than the apparently premeditated brilliance of
Miss Pomander Poole. He forgot that disconcerting person
ostentatiously there and then. She might hit them all with
sandwiches and dig everybody in the ribs with chocolate éclairs
for all he cared.

Miss Gaby Greuze addressed herself to her task with
deliberation and intelligence. There is nothing so private and
intimate in the world as a duologue in a crowd engaged in eating

and talking. The sounds of Sir Bussy's party have already been compared to a wind in a forest of metallic leaves. Plates, knives, and dishes were added now to the orchestra. These woven sounds, this metallic tissue in the air seemed to make an arbour, a hiding place for Mr Parham and his lovely companion. From this secret bower he had but to thrust an arm and get more champagne, salads of diverse sorts in little dishes, everything nice in aspic and fruits in their season and out of it. Then he held out his winnings to her and she smiled her thanks at him with those incredibly lovely eyes and partook. Afterwards they went off with arms entwined, roguishly seeking a "quiet corner" where she could teach him his elements before he made his début on the dancing floor. They got on together wonderfully. His fine classical face bending down to say airy nothings was caressed by the natural silk of her hair.

There was something in this experience that reminded Mr Parham of Horace and the naughtier side of the Latin poets, and anything that reminded him of Horace and the naughtier side of the Latin poets could not, he felt, be altogether vulgar or bad. And there was a moment or so when nothing but his classical training, his high literary and university standing, his sense of the extraordinary number of unexpected corners, casual mirrors, and observant attendants in the Savoy, and also, we must add, something stern and purposeful in himself, restrained him for seizing this most provocative young woman and showing her what a man of learning and spirit could do in the way of passionate pressure with his lips. He was flushed now and none the worse looking for that.

"Don't forget what I've told you," said Miss Gaby Greuze, guiding him back towards the more frequented regions of the party; "keep your head – best keep it in your heels – and the next dance is ours. Let's go and sit and look at them, and I'll have a lemonade."

Mr Parham smiled to think what some of his undergraduates would make of it if they could see him now. He sat by his partner with his hand just a little familiarly on the back of her chair and talked like an intimate.

"I find Sir Bussy a marvel," he said, blinking at the throng.

"He's a very Teasing Marvel," she said. "One of these days he'll get his little face smacked."

"I hope not."

"It won't get that damned grin of his off. He ought to find something better in life than pulling people's legs – all the money he's got."

"I've only just been drawn into the vortex."

But something missed fire in that remark, because she said, "It's one of the selectest clubs in London, I believe," and seemed to respect him more.

"And *now*," she said, standing up, and prepared to carry Mr Parham into the dance so soon as sufficient couples had accumulated to veil the naked bareness of the floor. She had strong arms, Mr Parham realized with amazement, a strong will, and her instructions had been explicit. Mr Parham had got as near as he was ever likely to get to modern dancing. "Bussy's over there," she said and cut a corner towards their host.

He was standing quite alone near the gesticulating black and brown band, concentrated, it would seem, upon their elusive transitions. His hands were deep in his pockets and his head swayed dreamily. Mr Parham and his partner circled smiling about him before he became aware of them.

"Gaw!" said Sir Bussy, looking up at last. "It hasn't taken you an hour!"

"This him?" she demanded triumphantly.

"That's him!" said Sir Bussy.

"You've lost."

"No. It's you have won. I'm quite content. I congratulate you on your dancing, Parham. I knew you'd make a dancer directly I saw you. Given a proper dancing mistress. Life's full of lessons for all of us. How d'you like her? Puts old Velazquez in his place. A young mistress is better than an old master, eh?"

"After that insult I'll go and eat you out of house and home," Miss Greuze retorted, missing the point of a remark for the second time that night, and she made Mr Parham take her down to supper again without completing the dance. He would have liked to go on dancing with her forever, but apparently the dance had served her purpose.

She became curiously angry. "Bussy never leaves you with the feel of winning," she said, "even when you've won. I'll do him down one of these days – if I have to bust everything to do it. He puts ideas into one's head."

"What ideas?" asked Mr Parham.

"I wonder if I told you…she speculated with a strange sudden expression in her eyes, and she seemed to measure Mr Parham.

"You can tell me anything," said he.

"Sometimes telling means a lot. No – not just yet, anyhow. Very likely never."

"I can hope," said Mr Parham, feeling that might mean anything or nothing.

At supper Mr Parham lost her. He lost her while he was thinking over this queer little passage. He was not to learn what this idea of hers was for quite a long time. A sudden tide of young things like herself but not so perfectly beautiful, poured round and over her and submerged and took possession of her, caressing her most intimately and calling her pet names: Gaby Sweet! Gaby Perfect! Gaby Darling! some sort of professional sisterhood of dancers or young actresses. He drifted off and was almost entangled again with Miss Pomander Poole, before he realized his danger.

For a time he was lonely, seeking but failing to restore contact with his all too popular Gaby. By some fatality during this period he seemed always to be drifting towards Pomander Poole, and an equal fatality drove her towards him. At unconscious dramatic urge in her, a mechanical trick of thinking in gestures, made it all too plain to him how little she wanted to resume their conversation. It looked as if she talked to herself also, but happily he was never quite close enough to hear. Then Lord Tremayne turned up, bright and hearty, with "You never told me what you thought about Westernhanger."

Mr Parham's momentary tension was relieved when the young man added, "It's too late now, so don't let's bother about it. I call it a Disgrace... I doubt if you know many people in this shallow, glittering world. Eh? Ask me for anyone you fancy. I know the blessed lot."

He then proceeded to introduce Mr Parham to two countesses and his sister-in-law, Lady Judy Percival, who happened to be handy, and so departed upon some quest of his own. The introductions, as people say of vaccinations, didn't "take" very well, the three ladies fell into a talk among themselves, and Mr Parham had a quiet, thoughtful time for a while, surveying the multitude. The elation of his success with Gabrielle Greuze had a little abated. Later on perhaps he would be able to detach her again and resume their talk. He noted Sir Titus in the distance wearing his forehead, he thought, just a trifle too much over one eye and with his arm manifestly about the waist of a slender, dark lady in green. It helped to remind Mr Parham of his own dignity. He leant against a wall and became observantly still.

Strange to reflect that physically this night party given by a London plutocrat in a smart hotel was probably ten times as luminous, multitudinous, healthy, and lovely as any court pageant of Elizabethan or Jacobean days. Twenty times. How small and dusky such an occasion would seem if it could be trailed across this evening's stirring spectacle! Brocades and wired dresses, none of them too fresh and clean, lit by candles and torches. Astounding, the material exuberance of our times. Yet that dim little assembly had its Shakespeare, its Bacon, its Burleigh, and its Essex. It had become history through and through. It was an everlasting fount of book writing, "studies," comments, allusions. The lightest caresses of the Virgin Queen were matters now for the gravest of scholars. Narrow rooms, perhaps, but spacious times.

But all this present thrust and gaiety − where did it lead? Could it ever become history in any sense of the word? In the court of Queen Elizabeth they moulded the beginnings of America, they laid the foundations of modern science, they forged the English language which these people here with their slang and curt knowingness of phrase were rapidly turning to dust. A few artists there might be here, a stripling maker of modern comedies. Mr Parham would grant something for the people who might be unknown to him, and still the balance against this parade was terrible.

The jazz music came out of the background and began to pound and massage his nerves. It beat about the gathering monstrously, as though it were looking for him, and then it would seem to discover him and come and rock him. It smote suddenly into his heart with jungle cries of infinite melancholy and then took refuge in dithering trivialities and a pretence of never having been anything but trivial. It became intimate; it became suggestively obscene. Drums and bone clappers and buzzers. He realized how necessary it was to keep on dancing or talking here, talking fast and loud, to sustain one's self against that black cluster of musicians. How alien they were, almost of another species, with their shining exultant faces, their urgent gestures! What would the Virgin Queen, what would her dear and most faithful Burleigh have made of that bronze-faced conductor?

Queer to think it was she who had, so to speak, sown the seed of that Virginia from which in all probability he came. He seemed now to be hounding on these whites to some mysterious self-effacement and self-destruction. They moved like marionettes to his exertions...

Such exercises of an observant, thoughtful, well-stored mind were interrupted by the reappearance of Lord Tremayne, encumbered with one of the countesses he had already once introduced to Mr Parham.

"Here's the very man," he cried joyously. "You know my cousin Lady Glassglade! If anyone can tell you all about Westernhanger, *he* can. He talked about it *marvellously* the other day. Marvellously!"

Mr Parham was left with Lady Glassglade.

The Glassglades had a place in Worcestershire and were decidedly people to know. Though what the lady could be doing here was perplexing. Sir Bussy's social range was astonishing. She was a little smiling lady with slightly bleached hair and infinite self-possession. Mr Parham bowed gracefully. "We are too near the band for talking," he said. "Would you care to go down to the supper room?"

"There was such a crowd. I couldn't get anything," said the lady.

Mr Parham intimated that all that could be changed.

"And I came on here because I was hungry!"

Charming! They got on very well together, and he saw that she had all she needed. He was quietly firm about it. They talked of the place in Worcestershire and of the peculiar *English* charm of Oxfordshire, and then they talked of their host. Lady Glassglade thought Sir Bussy was "simply wonderful." His judgments in business, she was told, were instinctive, so swift he was able to seize on things while other men were just going about and asking questions. He must be worth eight or ten millions.

"And yet he strikes me as a *lonely* figure," said Mr Parham. "Lonely and detached."

Lady Glassglade agreed that he was detached.

"We haven't assimilated him," said Mr Parham, using his face to express a finely constituted social system suffering from indigestion.

"We have not," said Lady Glassglade.

"I've met him quite recently," said Mr Parham. "He seems strangely typical of the times. All this new wealth, so sure, so bold and so incomparably lacking in *noblesse oblige*."

"It *is* rather like that," said Lady Glassglade.

They both replenished their glasses with more of Sir Bussy's champagne.

"When one considers the sense of obligation our old territorial families displayed…"

"Exactly," said Lady Glassglade sadly.

And then recovering her spirits, "All the same, he's rather fun."

Mr Parham looked wider and further. He glanced down the corridors of history and faced the dark menace of the future. "I wonder," he said.

It was quite a time before he and Lady Glassglade got disassociated. Mr Parham was wistfully humorous about a project of Oxford offering "post graduate courses" for the *nouveau riche*. Lady Glassglade seemed to be greatly amused by the idea.

"With tennis, table manners, grouse shooting and professional golf."

Lady Glassglade laughed that well-known merry laugh of hers. Mr Parham was encouraged to elaborate the idea. He invented a Ritz College and a Claridge's College and a Majestic all competing against each other. Loud speakers from the lecture rooms by each bedside.

As the night drew on Mr Parham's memories of Sir Bussy's party lost the sharp distinctness of his earlier impressions. In some way he must have lost Lady Glassglade, because when he was talking of the duty under which even a nominal aristocracy lay to provide leadership for the masses, he looked round to see if she appreciated his point, and she had evidently been gone some time. A sort of golden gloom, a massive and yet humorous solemnity, had slowly but surely replaced the rhythmic glittering of his earlier mental state. He talked to strange people about their host. "He is," said Mr Parham, "a lonely and leaderless soul. Why? Because he has no tradition."

He remembered standing quite quite still for a very long time, admiring and pitying a very beautiful tall and slender woman with a quiet face, who was alone and who seemed to be watching for someone who did not come. He was moved to go up to her and say very softly and clearly to her, "Why so pensive?"

Then, as startled and surprised she turned those lovely violet eyes to him, he would overwhelm her with a torrent of brilliant conversation. He would weave fact and fancy together. He would compare Sir Bussy to Trimalchio. He would give a brief but vivid account of the work of Petronius. He would go on to relate all sorts of curious impish facts about Queen Elizabeth and Cleopatra and people like that, and she would be fascinated.

"Tell me," he said to a young man with an eye-glass who had drifted near him, and repeated, "Tell me."

He found something queer and interesting had happened to his fingers as he gesticulated, and for a time this held his attention to the exclusion of other matters.

The young man's expression changed from impatience to interest and sympathy. "Tell you *what?*" he asked, getting first Mr Parham's almost autonomous hand and then Mr Parham himself well into the focus of the eye-glass.

"Who is that perfect lovely lady in black and — I think they are called sequins, over there?"

"That, sir, is the Duchess of Hichester."

"Your servant," said Mr Parham.

His mood had changed. He was weary of this foolish, noisy, shallow, nocturnal, glittering great party. Monstrous party. Party outside history, beginning nowhere, going nowhere. All mixed up. Duchesses and dancers. Professors, plutocrats, and parasites. He wanted to go. Only one thing delayed him for a time; he had completely lost his Gibus hat. He patted his pockets; he surveyed the circumjacent floor. It had gone.

Queer!

Far off he saw a man carrying a Gibus hat, an unmistakable Gibus. Should he whip it out of his hand with a stern "Excuse me?"

But how was Mr Parham to prove it was his Gibus hat?

Chapter Four

Nocturne

M r Parham woke up with a start. He remembered now quite clearly that he had put down his Gibus hat on the table in the supper room. Some officious attendant had no doubt whisked it aside. He must write to the Savoy people about it in the morning.

"Sir" or "Dear Sirs" or "Mr Parham presents his compliments." Not too austere. Not too familiar…Ta ra ra ra – ink a-poo poo.

If he had left his Gibus he seemed to have brought home the greater part of the jazz band. He had got it now in his head, and there, with all the irrepressible vigour of the Negro musician, it was still energetically at work. It had a large circular brassy headache for a band stand. Since it rendered sleep impossible and reading for some reason undesirable, Mr Parham thought it best to lie still in the dark – or rather the faint dawn – abandoning himself to the train of thought it trailed after it.

It had been a *silly* evening.

Oh! a silly evening!

Mr Parham found himself filled with a sense of missed opportunities, of distractions foolishly pursued, of a lack of continuity and self-control.

47

That girl Gaby Greuze – she had been laughing at him. Anyhow, she might have been laughing at him. *Had* she been laughing at him?

The endocranial orchestra had evoked the figure of Sir Bussy, alone and unprotected, standing, waving his head to its subtropical exuberances. Moody he had seemed, mentally vacant for the moment. It would of course have been perfectly easy to catch him in that phase, caught him and got hold of him. Mr Parham could have gone up to him and said something pregnant to him, quietly but clearly.

"Vanitas vanitatum," he could have said, for example, and, since one never knows where one may not strike upon virgin ignorance in these new men, a translation might have been added tactfully and at once: "Vanity of vanities."

And why? Because he had no past. Because he had lost touch with the past. A man who has no past has no future. And so on to the forward-looking attitude – and the influential weekly.

But instead of telling this to Sir Bussy himself, straight and plain, Mr Parham had just wandered about telling it to Gaby Greuze, to Lady Glassglade, to casual strangers, any old people. "I am not used to action," groaned Mr Parham to his God. "I am not direct. And opportunity passes me by."

For a time he lay and wondered if it would not be good for all scholars and men of thought to be *obliged* to take decisive action of some sort at least once a day. Then their wills would become nervous and muscular. But then – ? Would they lose critical acuteness? Would they become crude?

After a time he was back arguing in imagination with Sir Bussy.

"You think this life is pleasure," he would say. "It is not. It is nothing. It is less than nothing. It is efflorescence."

"Efflorescence." A good word. This was an Age of Efflorescence. If a parallel was wanted one must read Petronius. When Rome was still devouring the world. That too was an Age of Efflorescence. Everywhere a hastening from one meretricious pleasure to another. Old fashions abandoned for the mere love of novelty. These ridiculous little black evening hats, for instance, instead of the stately Gibus. (Come to think of it, it was hardly worthwhile to recover that Gibus. He would have to get one of these evening slouches.) No precedence. No restriction. Duchesses, countesses, diplomatists, fashionable physicians, rubbing shoulders with pretty chorus girls, inky adventuresses, artists, tradesmen, actors, movie stars, coloured singers, Casanovas and Cagliostros – *pleased* to mingle with them – no order, no sense of function. One had to say to fellows like Sir Bussy. "Through some strange dance of accident power has come to you. But beware of power that does not carry on and develop tradition. Think of the grave high figures of the past: Cæsar, Charlemagne, Joan of Arc, Queen Elizabeth, Richelieu (you should read my little book), Napoleon, Washington, Garibaldi, Lincoln, William Ewart Gladstone, kings, priests and prophets, statesmen and thinkers, builders of Powers; the increasing purpose, the onward march! Think of great armoured angels and beautiful intent symbolic faces! Our Imperial Destinies! The Destiny of France! Our Glorious Navy! Embattled flags! Here now is the sword of power in your hands! Is it to do nothing more than cut innumerable sandwiches for supper?"

Again Mr Parham spoke aloud in the night. "Nay!" he said.

He was suddenly reminded of the champagne.

Efflorescence was really a very good word. No, *not* effervescence, efflorescence. If only one had a weekly, what a scathing series of articles reviewing modern tendencies might there not be under that general title! People would ask, "Have you seen 'Efflorescence' again in the *Paramount Weekly?* Pitiless!"

It was a bother that the band inside his headache did not know when to leave off. It went so and it went so... What a lot of champagne there had been! Efflorescence and effervescence.

He saw himself giving a little book to Sir Bussy almost sacramentally. "Here," he would say, "is a book to set you thinking. I know it is too much to ask you to read it through, short though it is, but at least read the title, *The Undying Past.* Does that convey nothing to you?"

He saw himself standing gravely while Sir Bussy tried uneasily to get past him.

After all efflorescence, as the chemists had taught us to use the word nowadays, implies a considerable amount of original stuff still undecayed. Beneath this glittering froth, this levity, this champagne drinking and jazz dancing, this careless mixing of incompatible social elements, far beneath was the old enduring matter of human life, the toil, the sustained purpose, the precedences, the loyalties, the controls. On the surface the artist of life might seem to be a slightly negroid Fragonard, but below stern spirits were planning the outline of stupendous destinies. Governments and foreign offices were still at their immemorial work; the soldiers gathered in their barracks and the great battleships ploughed remorselessly the vainly slapping waves. Religious teachers inculcated loyalty and obedience; the businessmen ordered their argosies across the oceans, and the social conflicts muttered about the factories. There was likely to be grave economic trouble this winter. "The grim spectre of want." Sir Bussy indeed lived in a dream world of uninterrupted indulgence. But all dreams come to an end.

The spirit of Carlyle, the spirit of the Hebrew prophets entered into Mr Parham. It was like some obscure stern sect coming to a meeting in a back street chapel. One by one they came. High above the severe lines of that little back street façade, the red planet Mars ruled his sky. The band in his headache played wilder, more threatening airs.

"Verily," he whispered and "Repent...Yesss."

The real stern things of life gathered unobtrusively but surely, prepared when the time came to blow their clarions, prepared to rouse this trivial world again to fresh effort and grim resolve, to unbend the fluttering flag, to exalt and test the souls of men, to ennoble them by sacrifice and suffering.

The wailing multitude would call for guidance. What could men like Sir Bussy give it?

"And yet I would have stood by your side," Mr Parham would say. "I would have stood by your side."

For a time Mr Parham's mind seemed to be full of marching troops, host by host, corps by corps, regiment after regiment, company upon company. They marched to the rhythm of the Negro band, and as they marched they receded. Down a long vista they receded and the music receded.

The face of Mr Parham became firm and hard and calm in the darkness. Stern resolve brooded over the troubled frothing of his thoughts and subdued them. The champagne made one last faint protest.

Presently his lips relaxed. His mouth fell a little open...
A deep, regular, increasing sawing of his breath told the
mouse behind the skirting that Mr Parham was asleep.

CHAPTER FIVE

The Devious Pursuit

Such were the opening phases of the friendship of Mr Parham and Sir Bussy Woodcock. It was destined to last nearly six years. The two men attracted and repelled each other in about equal measure, and in that perhaps lay the sustaining interest of their association. In its more general form in Mr Parham's mind, the relationship was a struggle to subdue this mysteriously able, lucky adventurer to the Parham conception of the universe, to involve him in political affairs and advise and direct him when these affairs became perplexing, to build him up into a great and central figure (with a twin star) in the story of the Empire and the world. In its more special aspect the relationship was to be one of financial support for Mr Parham and the group of writers and university teachers he would gather round him, to steer the world – as it had always been steered. When the history of the next half-century came to be written people would say, "There was the finger of Parham," or, "He was one of Parham's Young Men." But how difficult it was to lead this financial rhinoceros, as Mr Parham, in the secrecy of his own thoughts, would sometimes style his friend, towards any definite conception of a role and a policy outside the now almost automatic process of buying up everything and selling it for more.

At times the creature seemed quite haphazard, a reckless spendthrift who could gain more than he spent. He would say, "Gaw! I'm going to have a lark," and one had either to drop out of the world about him or hang on to him into the oddest and strangest of places.

There were phases of passionate resentment in Mr Parham's experience, but then again there were phases of clear and reasonable hope. Sir Bussy would suddenly talk about political parties with a knowledge, a shrewdness that amazed his friend. "Fun to push 'em all over," he would say. And once or twice he talked of Rothermere, Beaverbrook, Burnham, Riddell, with curiosity and something like envy. Late at night on each occasion it was, other people, people one suspected, were present, and Mr Parham could not bring him to the point of a proposal.

Then off went everything like dead leaves before a gale, a vast hired yacht to the Baltic, to Maine, Newfoundland, and the Saint Lawrence River, and the strangest people packed aboard. Or Mr Parham found himself surveying the Mediterranean from a Nice hotel of which Sir Bussy had taken a floor for Christmas. Once or twice he would come most unexpectedly to his Mentor, so full of purpose in his eyes, that Mr Parham felt the moment had come. Once he took him suddenly, just they two, to see Stravin-sky's *Noces* at Monte Carlo and once in London a similar humility of approach preluded a visit to hear the Lener Quartette.

"Pleasant," said Sir Bussy, coming away. "Pleasant sounds. It cleans and soothes. And more. It's – " his poor untrained mind, all destitute of classical precedents, sought for an image – "it's like putting your head down a rabbit hole and hearing a fairy world going on. A world neither here nor there. Is there anything more to it than that?"

"Oh!" said Mr Parham, as though he cried to God; "windows upon heaven!"

"Gaw!"

"We went there – we went there *sailcloth*. It turned us to silk."

"Well – *did* it? It sounds as if it was telling you something, but does it tell you anything? This music. It gets excited and joyous, for no reason, just as you get excited and joyous in dreams; it's sad and tender – about nothing. They're burying a dead beetle in fairyland. It stirs up appropriate memories. Your mind runs along according to the rhythm. But all to no effect. It doesn't give you anything real. It doesn't let you out. Just a finer sort of smoking," said Sir Bussy.

Mr Parham shrugged his shoulders. No good to get this savage books on "How to Listen to Music." He did listen, and this was what he made of it.

But one sentence lingered in Mr Parham's mind: "It doesn't," said Sir Bussy, "*let you out.*"

Did he want to be let out of this gracious, splendid world of ours, built foursquare on the pillars of history, with its honours, its precedences, its mighty traditions? Could he mean that?

Mr Parham was reminded of another scene when Sir Bussy had betrayed very much that same thought. They were recrossing the Atlantic to the Azores after visiting Newfoundland. The night was gloriously calm and warm. Before turning in Mr Parham, who had been flirting rather audaciously with one of the pretty young women who adorned Sir Bussy's parties so abundantly, came out on the promenade deck to cool his nerves and recall some lines of Horace that had somehow got bent in his memory and would return to him only in a queerly distorted form. He had a moment of daring, and the young thing had pretended fright and gone to bed. Fun – and essentially innocent.

At the rail Mr Parham discovered his host, black and exceedingly little against the enormous deep blue sky.

"Phosphorescence?" asked Mr Parham in an encouraging tenor.

Sir Bussy did not seem to hear. His hands were deep in his trouser pockets. "Gaw," he said. "Look at all this wet – under that *ghastly* moon!"

At times his attitudes took Mr Parham's breath away. One might think the moon had just appeared, that it had no established position, that it was not Diana and Astarte, Isis and a thousand sweet and lovely things.

"Curious," this strange creature went on. "We're half outside the world here. We are. We're actually on a bulge, Parham. That way you go down a curve to America, and *that* way you go down a curve to your old Europe – and all that frowsty old art and history of yours."

"It was 'frowsty old Europe,' as you call it, sent this yacht up here."

"No fear! it got away."

"It can't stay here. It has to go back."

"This time," said Sir Bussy after a pause.

He started for a moment or so at the moon with, if anything, an increasing distaste, made a gesture of his hand as if to dismiss it, and then, slowly and meditatively, went below, taking no further notice of Mr Parham.

But Mr Parham remained.

What was it this extravagant little monster wanted, in this quite admirable world? Why trouble one's mind about a man who could show ingratitude for that gracious orb of pale caressing light? It fell upon the world like the silver and gossamer robes of an Indian harem. It caressed and provoked the luminosities that flashed and flickered in the water. It stirred with an infinite gentleness. It incited to delicately sensuous adventure.

Mr Parham pushed his yachting cap back from his forehead in a very doggish manner, thrust his hands into the pockets of his immaculate ducks and paced the deck, half hoping to hear a rustle or a giggle that would have confessed that earlier retreat insincere. But she really had turned in, and it was only when Mr Parham had done likewise that he began to think over Sir Bussy and his ocean of "wet – under that *ghastly* moon.".…

But this work, it is well to remind ourselves and the reader, is the story of a metapsychic séance and its stupendous consequences, and our interest in these two contrasted characters must not let it become a chronicle of the travels and excursions of Sir Bussy and Mr Parham. They went once in a multitudinous party to Henley, and twice they visited Oxford together to get the flavour. How Mr Parham's fellow-dons fell over each other to get on good terms with Sir Bussy, and how Mr Parham despised them! But bringing Sir Bussy down made a real difference to Mr Parham's standing in Oxford. For a time Sir Bussy trifled with the Turf. The large strange parties he assembled at the Hangar and at Buntincombe and Carfex House perpetually renewed Mr Parham's amazement that he should know so many different sorts of people and such queer people and be at such pains to entertain them and so tolerant of some of the things they did.

They got up to all sorts of things, and he let them. It seemed to Mr Parham he was chiefly curious to know what they got out of what they got up to. Several times they discussed it together.

"Not a horse on the Turf," said Sir Bussy, "is being run absolutely straight."

"But surely – "

"Honourable men there, certainly. They keep the rules because there'd be no fun it if they didn't. It would just go to pieces, and nobody wants it to go to pieces. But do you think they run a horse all out to win every time? Nobody dreams of such a thing."

"You mean that every horse is pulled?"

"No. No. *No*. But it isn't allowed to strain itself unduly at the beginning. That's quite a different thing."

Mr Parham's face expressed his comprehension of the point. Poor human nature!

"Why do you bother about it?"

"My father the cab driver used to drive broken-down racehorses," he said, "and was always backing Certs. It interfered with my education. I've always wanted to see this end of it. And I inherit an immense instinct for human weakness from my mother."

"But it's costly?"

"Not a bit of it," said Sir Bussy, with a sigh. "I seem always to see what they are up to. Before they see I see it. I make money on the Turf. I *always* make money."

His face seemed to accuse the universe, and Mr Parham made a sympathetic noise.

When Mr Parham went to Newmarket or a race meeting with Sir Bussy he saw to it that his own costume was exactly right. At

Ascot he would be in a silky grey morning coat and white spatterdashes and a grey top hat with a black band; the most sporting figure there he was; and when they went to Henley he was in perfect flannels and an Old Arvonian blazer, not a new one but one a little faded and grubby and with one patch of tar. He was a perfect yachtsman on yachts, and at Cannes he never failed to have that just-left-the-tennis-round-the-corner touch, which is the proper touch for Cannes. His was one of those rare figures that could wear plus fours with distinction. His sweaters were chosen with care, for even a chameleon can be correct. Never did he disfigure a party; often, indeed, he would pull one together and define its place and purpose.

The yachtsman ensemble was the hardest to preserve because Mr Parham had more than an average disposition towards seasickness. There he differed from Sir Bussy, who was the better pleased the rougher the water and the smaller the boat. "I can't help it," said Sir Bussy. "It's the law of my nature. What I get I keep."

But if Mr Parham's reactions were prompt they were cheerful. "Nelson," he would say, after his time of crisis. "He would be sick for two or three days every time he went to sea. That consoles me. The spirit indeed is unwilling but the flesh is weak."

Sir Bussy seemed to appreciate that.

By thus falling into line with things, by refusing to be that social misfit, the intractable and untidy don, Mr Parham avoided any appearance of parasitism in his relations with Sir Bussy and kept his own self-respect unimpaired. He was "*right there*"; he was not an intrusion. He had never dressed well before, though he had often wanted to do so, and this care for his costume made rather serious inroads upon his modest capital, but he kept his aim steadily in view. If one is to edit a weekly that will sway the world one must surely look man of the world enough to do it. And there came a phase in his relations with Sir Bussy when he had to play the role of a man of the world all he knew how.

It has to told, though for some reasons it would be pleasanter to omit it. But it is necessary to illuminate the factors of antagonism and strife within this strange association with its mutual scrutiny, its masked and hidden criticisms.

Perhaps – if the reader is young...

Yet even the young reader may want to know.

Let us admit that this next section, though illuminating, is not absolutely essential to the understanding of the story. It is not improper, it is not coarse, but frankly – it envisages something – shall we call it "Eighteenth Century"? – in Mr Parham's morals. If it is not an essential part of the story it is at any rate very necessary to our portrait of Mr Parham.

Chapter Six

An Indiscretion

Happily we need not enter into details. The method and manner of the affair are quite secondary. We can draw a veil directly the latchkey of Miss Gaby Greuze clicks against the latch of Miss Gaby Greuze's sumptuous flat, and it need not be withdrawn again until Mr Parham re-emerges from that same flat looking as respectable as a suburban embezzler going to church. As respectable? Except for a certain glory. An exaltation. Such as no mere thief of money ever knew.

Fragments of a conversation follow, a conversation it is undesirable to locate.

"I've always liked you since first we met," said Gaby...

"It was a sort of promise."...

"How quick you were to understand. You *are* quick! I see you watching people – summing them up."...

"It must be wonderful to know all you know," said Gaby, "and think all you think. You make me feel – so shallow!"

"What need have *you* for the helm of Athene?" Mr Parham exclaimed.

"Well, a woman likes to feel at the helm now and then," said Gaby, with her usual infelicity of apprehension, and for a time she seemed moody.

But she said Mr Parham was very beautifully made. His smile when she said it lit the flat. And so strong. Did he take much exercise? Tennis. She would play tennis if she wasn't afraid of muscles in the wrong place. Exercise, she said, was ever so much better than taking exercises except for that. Of course, there *were* exercises one took. Some that made one supple and were good for one's carriage and figure. Had Mr Parham ever seen her sort of exercises? Well...

They were lovely exercises.

She patted his cheek and said, "*Nice* man!" She said that several times.

And she said, "You are what I should call simple."

"Delicate," she added, noting a question in his face, "but not complex."

She said this with a distant, pensive look in her eyes. She was admiring the sheen on her beautiful arm and wrist, and then she said, "And when one is being as lovely as one can be to you, whatever else you do or say, anyhow, you don't say 'Gaw!' "

She compressed her lips and nodded. "Gaw!" she repeated; "as though he had found you out in something that not for a minute you had ever felt or intended.

"Making you feel – like some insect."

She began to weep unrestrainedly, and suddenly she threw herself once more into Mr Parham's arms.

Poor, poor little woman, sensitive, ardent, generous, and so misunderstood!...

When Mr Parham met the unsuspecting Sir Bussy again after this adventure a great pride and elation filled him. Touched with a not unpleasant remorse. He had to put an extra restraint upon his disposition towards condescension. But afterwards he found Sir Bussy looking at him curiously, and feelings of a less agreeable kind, a faint apprehension, mingled with his glory.

When Mr Parham encountered Gaby Greuze once more, and it is notable how difficult it became to meet her again except in the most transitory way, this glory of his glowed with a passionate warmth that called for the utmost self-control. But always a man of honour respects a modest woman's innate craving for secrecy. Not even the roses in her bosom must suspect. She was evasive; she wished to be evasive. Delicately and subtly Mr Parham came to realize that for him and his fellow-sinner it was best that it should be as if this bright, delicious outbreak of passion had never occurred.

Nevertheless, there it was; he was one up on Sir Bussy.

BOOK TWO

HOW THE MASTER SPIRIT ENTERED THE WORLD

CHAPTER ONE

Disputes and Tension over Sir Bussy's Dinner Table

This mutual frequentation of Sir Bussy and Mr Parham necessarily had intermissions, because of Mr Parham's duty to his university and his influence upon the rising generation, and because also of perceptible fluctuations in Sir Bussy's need of him. And as time went on and the two men came to understand each other more acutely, clashes of opinion had to be recognized. Imperceptibly Sir Bussy passed from a monosyllabic reception of Mr Parham's expositions of the state of the world and the life of man to more definitely sceptical comments. And at times Mr Parham, because he had so strong a sense of the necessity of dominating Sir Bussy and subduing his untrained ignorance to intelligible purposes, became, it may be, a little authoritative in his argument and a trifle overbearing in his manner. And then Sir Bussy would seem almost not to like him for a time and would say "Gaw," and turn away.

For a few weeks, or even it might be for a month or so, Mr Parham would have no more abnormal social adventures, and then quite abruptly and apropos of any old thing Sir Bussy would manifest a disposition to scrutinize Mr Parham's point of view again, and the excursions and expeditions would be renewed. A hopeful friendship it was throughout on Mr Parham's side, but at no time was it a completely harmonious one. He found Sir Bussy's choice of associates generally bad and often lamentable. He was constantly meeting people who crossed and irritated him beyond measure. With them he would dispute, even acrimoniously. Through them it was possible to say all sorts of things at Sir Bussy that it might have been undesirable to say directly to him.

There were times when it seemed almost as if Sir Bussy invited people merely to annoy Mr Parham, underbred contradictory people with accents and most preposterous views. There was a crazy eclecticism about his hospitality. He would bring in strange Americans with notions rather than ideas about subjects like currency and instalment buying, subjects really more impossible than indecency, wrong sorts of Americans, carping and aggressive, or he would invite Scandinavian ideologists, or people in a state of fresh disillusionment or fresh enthusiasm from Russia, even actual Bolsheviks, Mr Bernard Shaw and worse, self-made authors, a most unpleasant type, wild talkers like Mr J B S Haldane, saying the most extravagant things. Once there was a Chinaman who said at the end of a patient, clear exposition of the British conception of self-government and the part played by social and intellectual influence in our affairs, "I see England at least is still looled by mandolins," whatever that might mean. He nodded his gold spectacles towards Mr Parham, so probably he imagined it did mean something. Most subtly and insidiously Sir Bussy would sow the seeds of a dispute amid such discordant mixtures and sit in a sort of intellectual rapture, mouth dropping, while Mr Parham, sometimes cool but sometimes glowing, dealt with the fallacies, plain errors, misconceptions, and misinformation that had arisen. "Gaw!" Sir Bussy would whisper.

No support, no real adhesion, no discipleship; only that colourless "Gaw." Even after a quite brilliant display. It was discouraging. Never the obvious suggestion to give this fount of sound conviction and intellectual power its legitimate periodic form.

But the cumulative effect of these disputes upon Mr Parham was not an agreeable one. He always managed to carry off these wrangles with his colours flying, for he had practised upon six generations of undergraduates; he knew exactly when to call authority to the aid of argument and, in the last resort, refer his antagonist back to his studies effectively and humiliatingly, but at bottom, in its essence, Mr Parham's mental substance was delicate and fine, and this succession of unbelieving, interrogative, and sometimes even flatly contradictory people left their scars upon him – scars that rankled. It was not that they produced the slightest effect upon his essential ideas of the Empire and its Necessary Predominance in World Affairs, of the Historical Task and Destiny of the English, of the Roles of Class and Law in the world and of his Loyalties and Institutions, but they gave him a sense of a vast, dangerous, gathering repudiation of these so carefully shaped and established verities. The Americans, particularly since the war, seemed to have slipped away, mysteriously and unawares, from the commanding ideas of his world. They brought a horrible tacit suggestion to Sir Bussy's table that these ideas were now queer and old-fashioned.

Renegades! What on earth had they better? What in the names of Queen Elizabeth, Shakespeare, Raleigh, the *Mayflower*, Tennyson, Nelson, and Queen Victoria had these people better? Nowadays more and more they seemed to be infected with an idea that they were off and away after some new and distinctive thing of their own.

There they were, and there were a hundred and twenty million of them with most of the gold in the world – out of hand. It was not that they had any ideas worth considering to put in the place of Mr Parham's well-wrought and tested set. Positive suggestions he could deal with. One foolish visitor breathed the words "World State." Mr Parham smiled all his teeth at him and waved his fingers.

"My *dear* sir," said Mr Parham, with a kind of deep richness in his tone. And it sufficed.

Another said, "League of Nations."

"Poor Wilson's decaying memorial," said Mr Parham.

All the time, behind his valiant front this gnawing away of Mr Parham's confidence went on, his confidence that these ideas of his, right though they certainly were, would be honestly and properly endorsed and sustained, at home and abroad, when next they were put to the test. In 1914 they had been tested; had they been overstrained? Imperceptibly he drifted into that state of nervous uncertainty we have attempted to convey in our opening section. Was history keeping its grip? Would the game still be played? The world was going through a phase of moral and intellectual disintegration; its bonds relaxed; its definite lines crumbled. Suppose, for example, a crisis came in Europe and some strong man at Westminster flashed the sword of Britannia from the scabbard. Would the ties of Empire hold? Suppose the

Dominions cabled "This is not our war. Tell us about it." They had already done something of the sort when the Turks had returned to Constantinople. They might do it again and more completely. Suppose the Irish Free State at our backs found our spirited gesture the occasion for ungracious conduct. Suppose instead of the brotherly applause and envious sympathy of 1914, a noise like the noise of skinners sharpening their knives came from America. Suppose once again in our still unconscripted land Royal Proclamations called for men and that this time instead of another beautiful carnival of devotion like that of 1914 – how splendid that had been! – they preferred to remain interrogative. Suppose they asked, "Can't it be stopped?" or, "Is the whole thing worth while?" The Labour Movement had always a left wing nefariously active, undermining the nation's forces, destroying confidence, destroying pride in service, willingness to do and die. Amazing how we tolerated it! Suppose, too, the businessmen proved even more wicked than they were in 1914.

For Mr Parham knew. They had been wicked; they had driven a bargain. They were not the patriots they seemed.

An after-dinner conversation at Carfex House crystallized these floating doubts. When it took place Sir Bussy had already embarked upon those psychic experiments that were to revolutionize his relations to Mr Parham. But this dinner was an interlude. The discussion centred upon and would not get away from the topic of the Next War. It was a man's dinner, and the most loquacious guest was an official from Geneva, Sir Walter Atterbury, a figure of importance in the League of Nations Secretariat, an apparently unassuming but really very set and opinionated person. But there was also an American banker, Mr

Hamp, a grey-faced, elderly, spectacled man, who said strange things in a solemn manner, and there was Austin Camelford, the industrial chemist, who was associated with Sir Bussy in all sorts of business enterprises and who linked with him the big combinations of Romer Steinhart Crest & Co. He it was who recalled to Mr Parham's mind the cynicism of the businessmen in 1914. He was a lank and lean creature with that modern trick of saying the wildest nonsense as though it was obvious and universally recognized fact. There was also a young American from one of these new-fangled Western universities where they teach things like salesmanship and universal history. He was too young to say very much, but what he said was significant.

At first it was Atterbury did most of the talking and he talked evidently with the approval of the others. Then Mr Parham was moved to intervene and correct some of the man's delusions – for delusions they plainly were. The talk became more general, and certain things that came from Camelford and Hamp brought home to Mr Parham's mind the widening estrangement of industry and finance from the guiding concepts of history. Towards the end, Sir Bussy by some fragmentary comments of an entirely hostile sort, set the seal to a thoroughly disconcerting evening.

Sir Walter, trailing clouds of idealism from this Geneva of his, took it for granted that everyone present wanted to see war staved off forever from the world. Apparently he could conceive no other view as possible in intelligent company. And yet, oddly enough, he realized that the possibility of fresh wars was opening wider every year. He showed himself anxious and perplexed, as well he might, distressed by a newborn sense of the inadequacy of his blessed League to ward off the storms he saw gathering about it. He complained of the British government and the French government, of schools and colleges and literature, of armaments and experts, of a worldwide indifference to the accumulating stresses that made for war. The Anglo-American naval clash had distressed him particularly. It was the "worst thing that had happened for a long time." He was facty and explicit after the manner of his type. Four or five years ago one did not get these admissions of failure, these apprehensions and heart sinkings, from Geneva.

Mr Parham let him run on. He was all for facts from well-informed sources, and so far from wanting to suppress Sir Walter, his disposition was to give him all the rope he wanted. If that weekly had been in existence he would have asked him to write a couple of articles for it. At the normal rates. And then flicked aside his pacificist implications with a bantering editorial paragraph or so.

At this dinner he resorted to parallel tactics. For a time he posed as one under instruction, asking questions almost respectfully, and then his manner changed. His intelligent interrogations gave place to a note of rollicking common-sense. He revealed that this official's admissions of the impotence of the League had been meat and drink to him. He recalled one or two of Sir Walter's phrases and laughed kindly with his head a little on one side. "But what did you *expect?*" he said. "What *did* you expect."

And after all was said and done, asked Mr Parham, was it so bad? Admittedly the extravagant hopes of some sort of permanent world peace, some world Utopia, that had run about like an epidemic in 1918, were, realized now, mere fatigue phenomena, with no force of will behind them. The French, the

73

Italians, most lucid-minded and realistic of peoples, had never entertained such dreams. Peace, now, as always, rested on an armed balance of power.

Sir Walter attempted contradiction. The Canadian boundary?

"The pressure in that case lies elsewhere," said Mr Parham, with a confidence that excluded discussion of what these words might mean.

"Your armed balance of power is steadily eating up every scrap of wealth industrial progress can produce," said Sir Walter. "The military force of France at present is colossal. All the European budgets show an increase in armaments, and people like Mussolini jeer at the Kellogg Pact even as they sign it. The very Americans make the clearest reservation that the Pact doesn't mean anything that matters. They won't fight for it. They won't let it interfere with the Monroe doctrine. They sign the Pact and reserve their freedom of action and go on with the armament race. More and more the world drifts back to the state of affairs of 1913.

"The most serious thing," Sir Walter went on, "is the increasing difficulty of keeping any counter movement going. It's the obstinate steadiness of the drive that dismays me. It's not only that the accumulation of wealth is being checked and any rise in the standard of living prevented by these immense preparations, but the intellectual and moral advance is also slowing down on account of it. Patriotism is killing mental freedom. France has ceased to think since 1919, and Italy is bound and gagged. Long before actual war returns, freedom of speech may be held up by the patriotic censorship in every country in Europe. What are we to do about it? What is there to do?"

"I suggest that there is nothing to do," said Mr Parham. "And I don't in the least mind. May I speak with the utmost frankness – as one man to another – as a realist in a world of human beings, very human beings? Frankly, I put it to you that we do not want this pacificist movement of yours. It is a dream. The stars in their courses fight against it. The armed man keepeth his house until a stronger cometh. Such is the course of history, my dear sir. So it has ever been. What is this free speech of yours but the liberty to talk nonsense and set mischief afoot? For my own part I would not hesitate for a moment in the choice between disorganizing babble and national necessity. Can you really mourn the return of discipline and order to countries that were in a fair way to complete social dissolution?"

He recalled one of those striking facts that drive reality home to the most obdurate minds. "In 1919, when my niece went to Italy for her honeymoon, she had two handbags stolen from the train, and on her return her husband's valise went astray from the booked luggage and never turned up again. That was the state of affairs before the strong hand took hold.

"No," said Mr Parham in a clear, commanding tone, so as to keep the rostrum while he returned to the general question. "As to the facts I see eye to eye with you. Yet not in the same spirit. We enter upon a phase of armament mightier than that which preceded the Great War. Granted. But the broad lines of the struggle shape themselves, they shape themselves – rationally and logically. They are in the nature of things. They cannot be evaded."

Something almost confidential crept into his manner. He indicated regions of the tablecloth by gestures of his hands, and his voice sank. Sir Walter watched him, open-eyed. His brows wrinkled with something like dismay.

"Here," said Mr Parham, "in the very centre of the Old World, illimitably vast, potentially more powerful than most of the rest of the world put together – " he paused as if fearing to be overheard – "is *Russia*. It really does not matter in the least whether she is Czarist or Bolshevik. She is the final danger – the overwhelming enemy. Grow she must. She has space. She has immense resources. She strikes at us, through Turkey as always, through Afghanistan as always, and now through China. Instinctively she does that – necessarily. I do not blame her. But preserve ourselves we must. What will Germany do? Cleave to the East? Cleave to the West? Who can tell? A student nation, a secondary people, a disputed territory. We win her if we can, but I do not count on her. The policy imposed upon the rest of the world is plain. *We must circumvent Russia;* we must encircle this threat of the Great Plains before it overwhelms us. As we encircled the lesser threat of the Hohenzollerns. In time. On the West, here, we outflank her with our ally France and Poland her pupil; on the East with our ally Japan. We reach at her through India. We strive to point the spearhead of Afghanistan against her. We hold Gibraltar on her account; we watch Constantinople on her account. America is drawn in with us, necessarily our ally, willy-nilly, because she cannot let Russia strike through China to the sea. There you have the situation of the world. Broadly and boldly seen. Fraught with immense danger – yes. Tragic – if you will. But fraught also with limitless possibilities of devotion and courage."

Mr Parham paused. When it was evident he had fully paused, Sir Bussy whispered his habitual monosyllable. Sir Walter cracked a nut and accepted port.

"There you are," he said with a sigh in his voice, "if Mr –?"

"Parham, Sir."

"If Mr Parham said that in any European capital from Paris to Tokio, it would be taken quite seriously. Quite seriously. That's where we are, ten years from the Armistice."

Camelford, who had been listening hitherto, now took up the discourse. "That is perfectly true," he said. "These governments of ours are like automata. They were evolved originally as fighting competitive things and they do not seem able to work in any other way. They prepare for war and they prepare war. It is like the instinctive hunting of a pet cat. However much you feed the beast, it still kills birds. It is made so. And they are made so. Until you destroy or efface them that is what they will do. When you went to Geneva, Sir Walter, I submit with all respect you thought they'd do better than they have done. A lot better?"

"I did," said Sir Walter. "I confess I've had a lot of disillusionment – particularly in the last three or four years."

"We live in a world of the wildest paradox today," said Camelford. "It's like an egg with an unbreakable shell, or a caterpillar that has got perplexed and is half a winged insect and the other half crawler. We can't get out of our governments. We grow in patches and all wrong. Certain things become international – cosmopolitan. Banking, for instance" – he turned to Hamp.

"Banking, sir, has made immense strides in that direction since the war," said Hamp. "I say without exaggeration, immense strides. Yes. We have been learning to work together. As we never thought of doing in pre-war days. But all the same, don't you imagine we bankers think we can stop war. We know better than that. Don't expect it of us. Don't put too much on us. We can't fight popular clamour, and we can't fight a mischievous politician who stirs it up. Above all, we can't fight the printing press. While these sovereign governments of yours can turn paper into money we can be put out of action with the utmost ease. Don't imagine we are that mysterious unseen power, the Money Power, your parlour Bolsheviks talk about. We bankers are what conditions have made us and we are limited by our conditions."

"*Our* position is fantastic," said Camelford. "When I say 'our' I mean the chemical industries of the world, my associates, that is, here and abroad. I'm glad to say I can count Sir Bussy now among them."

Sir Bussy's face was a mask.

"Take one instance to show what I mean by 'fantastic,'" Camelford went on. "We in our various ramifications, are the only people able to produce gas on the scale needed in modern war. Practically now all the chemical industries of the world are so linked that I can say '*we*.' Well, we have perhaps a hundred things necessary for modern warfare more or less under our control, and gas is the most important. If these sovereign Powers which still divide the world up in such an inconvenient way, contrive another war, they will certainly have to use gas, whatever agreements they may have made about it beforehand. And we, our great network of interests, are seeing to it that they will have plenty of gas, good reliable gas at reasonable business rates, all and more than they need. We supply all of them now and probably if war comes we shall still supply all of them – both sides. We may break up our associations a bit for the actual war, but that will be a mere incidental necessity. And so far we haven't been able to do anything else in our position than what we are doing. Just like you bankers, we are what circumstances have made us. There's nothing sovereign about *us*. We aren't governments with the power to declare war or make peace. Such influence as we have with governments and war offices is limited and indirect. Our position is that of dealers simply. We sell gas just as other people sell the Army meat or cabbages.

"But see how it works out. I was figuring at it the other day. Very roughly, of course. Suppose we put the casualties in the next big war at, say, five million and the gas ones at about three – that, I think, is a very moderate estimate; but then you see I'm convinced the next war will be a gas war – every man gassed will have paid us, on the average, anything between fourpence and three-and tenpence, according to the Powers engaged, for the manufacture, storage, and delivery of the gas he gets. My estimate is naturally approximate. A greater number of casualties will, of course, reduce the cost to the individual. But each of these predestined gasees – if I may coin a word – is now paying something on that scale year by year in taxation – and we of the big chemical international are seeing that the supply won't fail him. We're a sort of gas club. Like a goose-club. Raffle at the next great war. *Your* ticket's death in agony, *yours* a wheezing painful lung and poverty, *you're* a blank, luck chap! You won't get any good out of it, but you won't get any of the torture. It seems crazy to me, but it seems reasonable to everybody else, and what are we to fly in the face of the Instincts and Institutions of Mankind?"

Mr Parham played with the nutcrackers and said nothing. This Camelford was an offensive cynic. He would rob even death in battle of its dignity. Gasees!

"The Gasees Club doesn't begin to exhaust the absurdities of the present situation," Camelford went on. "All these damned war offices, throughout the world, have what they call secrets. Oh! – Their *secrets!* The fuss. The precautions. Our people in England, I mean our war office people, have a gas, a wonderful gas – L. It's General Gerson's own pet child. His only child. Beastly filth. Tortures you and then kills you. He gloats over it. It needs certain rare earths and minerals that we produce at Cayme in Cornwall. You've heard of our new works there – rather a wonderful place in its way. Some of our young men do astonishing work. We've got a whole string of compounds that might be used for the loveliest purposes. And in a way they are coming into use. Only unhappily you can also get this choke stink out of one of our products. Or *they* can – and we have to pretend we don't know what they want it for. Secret, you know. Important military secret. The scientific industrial world is keeping secrets like that for half a dozen governments... It's childish. It's insane."

Mr Parham shook his head privately as one who knows better.

"Do I understand," said Hamp, feeling his way cautiously, "that you know of that new British gas – I've heard whispers –?"

He broke off interrogatively.

"We have to know more or less. We have to sit on one side and look on and pretend not to see or know while your spies and experts and our spies and experts poke about trying to turn pure science into pure foolery... Boy scout spying and boy scout chemists... It can't go on. And yet it *is* going on. That is the situation. That is where the world's persistence in independent sovereign governments is taking us. What can we do? You say you can do nothing. I wonder. We might cut off the supply of this pet gas for the British; we might cut off certain high explosives and other material that are the darling secrets of the Germans and your people. There'd have to be a tussle with some of our own associates. But I think we could do it now... Suppose we did make the attempt. Would it alter things much? Suppose they had the pluck to arrest us. The Common Fool would be against us."

"The Common Fool!" cried Mr Parham, roused at last. "By that, sir, you mean that the whole tenor of human experience would be against you. What else can there be but these governments at which you cavil? What do they stand for? The common life and thought of mankind. And – forgive me if I put you in difficulties – who are *you*? Would you abolish government? Would you set up some extraordinary super-government, some freemasonry of bankers and scientific men to rule the world by conspiracy?"

"*And* scientific men! Bankers *and* scientific men! Oh, we *try* to be scientific men in our way," protested Hamp, seeking sympathy by beaming through his spectacles at Sir Bussy.

"I think I would look for some new way of managing human affairs," said Camelford answering Mr Parham's question. "I think sooner or later we shall have to try something of the sort. I think science will have to take control."

"That is to say Treason and a new International," flashed Mr Parham. "Without even the social envy of the proletariat to support you!"

"Why not?" murmured Sir Bussy.

"And how are you superior people going to deal with the Common Fool – who is, after all, mankind?"

"You could educate him to support you." said Atterbury. "He's always been very docile when you've caught him young."

"Something very like a fresh start," said Camelford. "A new sort of world. It's not so incredible. Modern political science is in its infancy. It's a century or so younger than chemistry or biology. I suppose that to begin with we should have a new sort of education, on quite other lines. Scrap all these poisonous national histories of yours, for example, and start people's minds clean by telling them what the world might be for mankind."

Sir Bussy nodded assent. Mr Parham found his nod faintly irritating. He restrained an outbreak.

"Unhappily for your idea of fresh starts," he said, "the Days of Creation are over, and now one day follows another."

He liked that. It was a good point to make.

In the pause Sir Walter addressed himself to Camelford. "That idea of yours about the gasees club is very vivid. I could have used that in a lecture I gave, a week ago."

The young American, who had taken no part in the discussion hitherto, now ventured timidly, "I think perhaps you Europeans, if I might say so, are disposed to underestimate the sort of drive there was behind the Kellogg Pact. It may seem fruitless – who can tell yet? – but mind you there was something made that gun. It's in evidence, even if it's no more than evidence. The Kellogg Pact isn't the last proposition of that sort you'll get from America."

He reddened as he said his piece, but clearly he had something definite behind what he said.

"I admit that," said Sir Walter. "In America there is still an immense sentiment towards world peace, and you find something of the same sort in a less-developed form everywhere. But it gets no organized expression, no effective development. It remains merely a sentiment. It isn't moving on to directive action. That's what's worrying my mind more and more. Before we can give that peace feeling real effectiveness there has to be a tremendous readjustment of ideas."

Mr Parham nodded his assent with an air of indifference and consumed a few grapes.

And then it seemed to him that these other men began to talk with a deliberate disregard of what he had been saying. Or, to be more precise, with a deliberate disregard of the indisputable correctness of what he had been saying. It was not as if it had not been said, it was not as if it had been said and required answering, but it was as if a specimen had been laid upon the table.

In the later stages of Sir Bussy's ample and varied dinners Mr Parham was apt to experience fluctuations of mood. At one moment he would be solid and strong and lucidly expressive, and then he would flush, and waves of anger and suspicion would wash through his mind. And now suddenly, as he listened to the talk – and for a while he did no more than listen – he had that feeling which for some time had been haunting him more and more frequently, that the world, with a sort of lax malice, was slipping away from all that was sane and fine and enduring in human life. To put it plainly, these men were plotting, openly and without any disguise, the subordination of patriotism, loyalty, discipline, and all the laboured achievements of statecraft to some vague international commonweal, some fantastic organization of cosmopolitan finance and cosmopolitan industrialism. They were saying things every whit as outrageous as the stuff for which we sent the talkative Bolshevik spinning back to his beloved Russia. And they were going on with this after all he had said so plainly and clearly about political realities. Was it any good to speak further?

Yet could he afford to let it go unchallenged? There sat Sir Bussy, drinking it in!

They talked. They talked.

"When first I went to Geneva," said Sir Walter, "I didn't realize how little could be done there upon the basis of current mentality. I didn't know how definitely existing patriotisms were opposed to the beginnings of an international consciousness. I thought they might fade down in time to a generous rivalry in the service of mankind. But while we try to build up a permanent world peace away there in Geneva, every schoolmaster and every cadet corps in England and every school in France is training the next generation to smash anything of the sort, is doing everything possible to carry young and generous minds back to the exploded delusions of wartime patriotism... All over the world it seems to be the same."

The young American, shy in the presence of his seniors, could but make a noise of protest like one who stirs in his sleep. Thereby he excepted his native land.

"Then," said Mr Parham, doing his smile but with a slight involuntary sneer of his left nostril, "you'd begin this great new civilization that is to come, by shutting up our schools?"

"He'd *change* 'em," corrected Sir Bussy.

"Scrap schools, colleges, churches, universities, armies, navies, flags, and honour, and start the millennium from the ground upwards," derided Mr Parham.

"Why not?" said Sir Bussy, with a sudden warning snarl in his voice.

"That," said Hamp, with that profundity of manner, that air of marking an epoch by some simple remark, of which only Americans possess the secret, "is just what quite a lot of us are hesitating to say? *Why not?* Sir Bussy, you got right down to the bottom of things with that 'Why not?' "

The speaker's large dark grey eyes strongly magnified by his spectacles went from face to face; his cheeks were flushed.

"We've scrapped carriages and horses, we're scrapping coal fires and gas lighting, we've done with the last big wooden ships, we can hear and see things now on the other side of the world and do a thousand – miracles, I call them – that would have been impossible a hundred years ago. What if frontiers too are out of date? What if countries and cultures have become too small? Why should we go on with the schools and universities that served the ends of our great-grandfathers, and with the governments that were the latest fashion in constitutions a century and a half ago?"

"I presume," said Mr Parham unheeded, addressing himself to the flowers on the table before him, "because the dealings of man with man are something entirely different from mechanical operations."

"I see no reason why there shouldn't be invention in psychology, just as much as in chemistry or physics," said Camelford.

"Your world peace, when you examine it," said Mr Parham, "flies in the face of the fundamental institutions – the ancient and tested institutions of mankind – the institutions that have made man what he is. That is the reason."

"The institutions of mankind," contradicted Camelford, with tranquil assurance, "are just as fundamental and no more fundamental than a pair of trousers. If the world grows out of them and they become inconvenient, it won't kill anything essential in man to get others. That, I submit, is what he has to set about doing now. He grows more and more independent of the idea that his pants are him. If our rulers and teachers won't attempt to let out or replace the old garments, so much the worse for them. In the long run. Though for a time, as Sir Walter seems to think, the tension may fall on us. In the long run we shall have to get a new sort of management for our affairs and a new sort of teacher for our sons – however tedious and troublesome it may be to get them – however long and bloody the time of change may be."

"Big proposition," said Mr Hamp.

"Which ought to make it all the more attractive to a citizen of the land of big propositions," said Camelford.

"Why should we be so confoundedly afraid of scrapping things?" said Sir Bussy. "If the schools do mischief and put back people's children among the ideas that made the war, why not get rid of 'em? Scrap our stale schoolmasters. We'd get a new sort of school all right."

"And the universities?" said Mr Parham, amused, with his voice going high.

Sir Bussy turned on him and regarded him gravely.

"Parham," he said slowly, "you're infernally well satisfied with the world. I'm not. You're afraid it may change into something else. You want to stop it right here and now. Or else you may have to learn something new and throw away the old bag of tricks. Yes – I know you. That's your whole mind. You're afraid that a time will come when all the important things of today will just not matter a rap; when what that chap Napoleon fancied was his Destiny or what old Richelieu imagined to be a fine forward foreign policy, will matter no more to intelligent people than – " he sought for an image and drew it slowly out of his mind – "the ideas of some old buck rabbit in the days of Queen Elizabeth."

The attack was so direct, so deliberately offensive in its allusion to Mr Parham's masterly studies of Richelieu, that for the moment that gentleman had nothing to say.

"Gaw," said Sir Bussy, "when I hear talk like this it seems to me that this Tradition of yours is only another word for Putrefaction. The clean way with Nature is dying and being born. Same with human institutions – only more so. How can we live unless we scrap and abolish? How can a town be clean without a dust destructor? What's your history really? Simply what's been left over from the life of yesterday. Eggshells and old tin cans."

"Now *that's* a thought," said Hamp and turned appreciative horn spectacles to Sir Bussy.

"The greatest of reformers, gentlemen," said Hamp, with a quavering of the voice, "told the world it had to be born again. And that, as I read the instruction, covered everybody and everything in it."

"It's a big birth we want this time," said Camelford.

"God grant it isn't a miscarriage," said Sir Walter.

He smiled at his own fancy. "If we *will* make the birth chamber an arsenal, we may have the guns going off – just at the wrong moment."

Mr Parham, still and stiff, smoked his excellent cigar. He knocked off his ash into his ash tray with a firm hand. His face betrayed little of his resentment at Sir Bussy's insult. Merely it insisted upon dignity. But behind that marble mask the thoughts stormed. Should he get up right there and depart? In silence? In contemptuous silence? Or perhaps with a brief bitter speech: "Gentlemen, I've heard enough folly for tonight. Perhaps you do not realize the incalculable mischief such talk as this can do. For me at least international affairs are grave realities."

He raised his eyes and found Sir Bussy, profoundly pensive but in no way hostile, regarding him.

A moment – a queer moment, and something faded out in Mr Parham.

"Have a little more of this old brandy," said Sir Bussy in that persuasive voice of his.

Mr Parham hesitated, nodded gravely – as it were forgivingly – seemed to wake up, smiled ambiguously, and took some more of the old brandy.

But the memory of that conversation was to rankle in Mr Parham's mind and inflame his imagination like a barbed and poisoned arrowhead that would not be removed. He would find himself reprobating its tendencies aloud as he walked about Oxford, his habit of talking to himself was increased by it, and it broke his rest of nights and crept into his dreams. A deepening hatred of modern scientific influences that he had hitherto kept at the back of his mind, was now, in spite of his instinctive resistance, creeping into the foreground. One could deal with the financial if only the scientific would leave it alone. The banker and the merchant are as old as Rome and Babylon. One could deal with Sir Bussy if it were not for the insidious influence of such men as Camelford and their vast materialistic schemes. They were something new. He supplied force, but they engendered ideas. He could resist and deflect, but they could change.

That story about an exclusive British gas...!

With Camelford overlooking it like a self-appointed God. Proposing to cut off the supply. Proposing in effect to stand out of war and make the game impossible. The strike, the treason, of the men of science and the modern men of enterprise. Could they work such a strike? The most fretting it was of all the riddles in our contemporary world. And while these signs of Anglo-Saxon decadence oppressed him, came Mussolini's mighty discourse to the Italian nation on the eve of the General Elections of 1929. That ringing statement of Fascist aims, that assertion of the paramount need of a sense of the state, of discipline and energy, had a clarity, a nobility, a boldness and power altogether beyond the quality of anything one heard in English. Mr Parham read it and re-read it. He translated it into Latin and it was even more splendid. He sought to translate it, but that was more difficult, into English prose. "This is a man," said Mr Parham. "Is there no other man of his kind?"

And late one evening he found himself in his bedroom in Pontingale Street before his mirror. For Mr Parham possessed a cheval glass. He had gone far in his preparation for bed. He had put on his dressing gown, leaving one fine arm and shoulder free for gesticulation. And with appropriate movements of his hand, he was repeating these glorious words of the great dictator.

"Your Excellencies, Comrades, Gentlemen," he was saying.

"Now do not think that I wish to commit the sin of immodesty in telling you that all this work, of which I have given a summarized and partial résumé, has been activated by my mind. The work of legislation, of putting schemes into action, of control and of the creation of new institutions, has formed only a part of my efforts. There is another part, not so well known, but the existence of which will be manifest to you through the following figures which may be of interest: I have granted over 60,000 audiences; I have dealt with 1,887,112 cases of individual citizens, received directly by my private secretary...

"In order to withstand this strain I have put my body in training; I have regulated my daily work; I have reduced to a minimum any loss of time and energy and I have adopted this rule, which I recommend to all Italians. The day's work must be methodically and regularly completed within the day. No work must be left over. The ordinary work must proceed with an almost mechanical regularity. My collaborators, whom I recall with pleasure and whom I wish to thank publicly, have imitated me. The hard work has appeared light to me, partly because it is varied, and I have resisted the strain because my will was sustained by my faith. I have assumed – as was my duty – both the small and the greater responsibilities."

Mr Parham ceased to quote. He stared at the not ungraceful figure in the mirror.

"Has Britain no such Man?"

CHAPTER TWO

How Sir Bussy Resorted to Metapsychics

But the real business we have in hand in this book is to tell of the Master Spirit. A certain prelude has been necessary to our story, but now that we are through with it we can admit it was no more than a prelude. Here at the earliest possible moment the actual story starts. There shall be nothing else but story telling now right to the end of the book.

Mr Parham's metapsychic experiences were already beginning before the conversation recorded in the previous section. They began, or at least the seed of them was sown, in a train bringing Sir Bussy and a party of friends back to London from Oxford after one of Mr Parham's attempts to impose something of the ripeness and dignity of that ancient home of thought upon his opulent friend. It was the occasion of Lord Fluffingdon's great speech on the imperial soul. They had seen honorary degrees conferred upon a Royal Princess, an Indian Rajah, the expenditure secretary of a wealthy American millionaire and one of the most brilliant and successful collectors of honours in the world, three leading but otherwise undistinguished conservative politicians, and a Scotch comedian. It had been a perfect day in the sunshine, rich late Gothic, old gardens, robes, smiles, and mellow compliments. The company had been the picked best of *Who's Who* dressed up for the occasion, and Lord Fluffingdon had surpassed expectation. In the compartment with Sir Bussy and Mr Parham were Hereward Jackson, just in the enthusiastic stages of psychic research, and Sir Titus Knowles, and the spacious open-mindedness of Sir Oliver Lodge, slow, conscientious, and lucid, ruled the discussion.

Hereward Jackson started the talk about psychic phenomena. Sir Titus Knowles was fiercely and vulgarly sceptical and early lost his always very thin and brittle temper. Sir Bussy said little.

Nearly six years of intermittent association had lit no spark of affection between Sir Titus and Mr Parham. For Mr Parham Sir Titus combined all that is fearful in the medical man, who at any moment may tell you to take off everything and be punched about anywhere, and all that is detestable in the scientist. They rarely talked, and when they did contradictions flew like sparks from the impact.

"The mediums as a class are rogues and tricksters," said Sir Titus. "It's common knowledge."

"Ah, *there!*" said Mr Parham cutting in, "there you have the positivism and assurance of − if you will pardon the adjective − old-fashioned science."

"Precious few who haven't been caught at it," said Sir Titus, turning from Hereward Jackson to this new attack upon his flank.

"On some occasions, but not on *all* occasions," said Mr Parham. "We have to be logical even upon such irritating questions as this."

Normally he would have kept himself smilingly aloof and sceptical. It was his genuine hatred for the harsh mentality of Sir

Titus that had drawn him in. But there he was, before he knew it taking up a position of open-minded inquiry close to Sir Oliver's, and much nearer to Jackson's omnivorous faith, than to doubt and denial. For a time Sir Titus was like a baited badger. "Look at the facts!" he kept barking, "Look at the actual facts!"

"That's just what I *have* looked at," said Hereward Jackson...

It did not occur to Mr Parham that he had let himself in for more than a stimulating discussion until Sir Bussy spoke to him and the others, but chiefly to him, out of his corner.

"I didn't know Parham was open-minded like this," he said.

And presently: "Have you ever seen any of this stuff, Parham? We ought to go and see some, if you think like that."

If Mr Parham had been alert he might have nipped the thing in the bud then and there, but he was not alert that afternoon. He hardly realized that Sir Bussy had pinned him.

And so all that follows followed.

CHAPTER THREE

Metapsychics in Buggins Street

For a month or so Mr Parham opposed and evaded Sir Bussy's pressure towards psychic research. It wasn't at all the sort of thing to do, nowadays. It had been vulgarized. Their names were certain to be used freely in the most undignified connections. And at the bottom of his heart Mr Parham did not believe that there was the shadow of an unknown reality in these obscure performances.

But never had he had such occasion to appreciate the force and tenacity of Sir Bussy's will. He would lie awake at nights wondering why his own will was so inadequate in its resistance. Was it possible, he questioned, that a fine education and all the richness and subtlety that only the classics, classical philosophy, and period history can impart, were incompatible with a really vigorous practical thrust. Oxford educated for quality, but did it educate for power?

Yet he had always assumed he was preparing his Young Men for positions of influence and power. It was a disagreeable novelty for him to ask if anything was wrong with his own will, and if so, what it was that was wrong. And it seemed to him that if only he had believed in the efficacy of prayer, he would have

prayed first and foremost for some tremendous affluence of will that would have borne away Sir Bussy's obstinacy like a bubble in a torrent. So that it would not be necessary to evade and oppose it afresh day after day. And at last, as he perceived he must, yield to it.

All the private heart searchings of this period of resistance and delay were shot with the reiteration of what had been through all the six years of intercourse an unsettled perplexity. What was Sir Bussy doing this for? Did he really want to know that there was some sort of chink or retractile veil that led out of this sane world of ours into worlds of that unknown wonder, and through which that unknown wonder might presently break into our common day? Did he hope for his "way out of it" here? Or was he simply doing this – as he seemed to have done so many other queer things – to vex, puzzle, and provoke queer reactions in Mr Parham, Sir Titus, and various other intimates? Or was there a confusion in that untrained intelligence between both sets of motives?

Whatever his intentions, Sir Bussy got his way. One October evening after an exceptionally passoverish dinner at Marmion House, Mr Parham found himself with Sir Titus, Hereward Jackson, and Sir Bussy in Sir Bussy's vast smooth car, in search of 97 Buggins Street, in the darker parts of the borough of Wandsworth, Mr Hereward Jackson assisting the chauffeur spasmodically, unhelpfully, and dangerously at the obscurer corners. The peculiar gifts of a certain Mr Carnac Williams were to be studied and considered.

The medium had been recommended by the best authorities, and Hereward Jackson had already visited this place before. Their hostess was to be old Mrs Mountain, a steadfast pillar in

the spiritualist movement in dark days and prosperous days alike, and this first essay would, it was hoped, display some typical phenomena, voices, messages, perhaps a materialization, nothing very wonderful, but a good beginner's show.

Ninety seven Buggins Street was located at last, a dimly lit double-fronted house with steps up to a door with a fanlight.

Old Mrs Mountain appeared in the passage behind the small distraught domestic who had admitted her guests. She was a comfortable, shapeless old lady in black, with a mid-Victorian lace cap, lace ruffles, and a lace apron. She was disposed to be nervously affable and charming. She welcomed Hereward Jackson with a copious friendliness. "And here's your friends," she said. "Mr Smith, shall we say? And Mr Jones and Mr Brown. Naming no names. Welcome all! Last night he was *wonderful.*"

Hereward Jackson explained over his shoulder: "Best to be pseudonymous," he said.

She ushered them into a room of her own period, with a cottage piano topped with a woollen mat on which were a pot of some fine-leaved fern and a pile of music, a mantel adorned with a large mirror and many ornaments, a central table with a red cloth and some books, a gas pendant, hanging bookshelves, large gilt-framed oleograph landscapes, a small sofa, a brightly burning fire, and a general air of comfort. Cushions, small mats, and antimacassars abounded, and there was an assemblage of stuffed linnets and canaries under a glass shade. It was a room to eat muffins in. Four people, rather drawn together about the fire and with something defensive in their grouping, stood awaiting the new inquirers. An overgrown-looking young man of forty with a large upturned white face and an expression of strained indifference was "my son Mr Mountain." A little blonde woman was "Miss – something or other"; a tall woman in mourning with thin cheeks, burning eyes, and a high colour was "a friend who joins us," and the fourth was Mr Carnac Williams, the medium for the evening.

"Mr Smith, Mr Jones, Mr Brown," said Mrs Mountain, "and this gentleman you know."

The little blonde woman glowed the friendliness of a previous encounter at Hereward Jackson, and Mr Mountain hesitated and held out a flabby hand to shake Sir Bussy's.

Mr Parham's first reaction to the medium was dislike. The man was obviously poor, and the dark, narrow eyes in his white face were quick and evasive. He carried his hands bent at the wrist as if he reserved the palms, and his manner was a trifle too deferential to Sir Bussy for that complete lack of information about the visitors attributed to the home team.

"I can't answer for anything," said Mr Williams in flat, loud tones. "I'm merely a tool."

"A wonderful tool last night," said Mrs Mountain.

"I knew nothing," said Mr Williams.

"It was very wonderful to *me*," said the tall woman in a soft musical voice – and seemed restrained by emotion from saying more.

There was a moment's silence.

"Our normal procedure," said Mr Mountain, betraying a slight lisp in his speech, "is to go upstairs. The room on the first floor is prepared – oh! you'll be able to satisfy yourselves it's not been prepared in any wrong sense. Recently we have been so fortunate as to get actual materializations – a visitant. Our atmosphere has been favourable... If nothing happens to change it... But shall we go upstairs?"

The room upstairs seemed very bare in comparison with the crowded cosiness of the room below. It had been cleared of bric-à-brac. There was a large table surrounded by chairs. One of them was an armchair, destined for Mrs Mountain, and by it stood a small occasional table bearing a gramophone; the rest were those chairs with bun-like seats so characteristic of the Early Maple period. A third table carried some loose flowers, a tambourine, and a large slate, which was presently discovered to be painted with phosphorescent paint. One corner had been curtained off. "That's the cabinet," said Mrs Mountain. "You're quite welcome to search it."

On a small table inside it there were ropes, a candle, sealing wax, and other material.

"We aren't for searching tonight," said Sir Bussy. "We're just beginners and ready to take your word for almost anything. We want to get your point of view and all that. It's afterwards we'll make trouble."

"A very fair and reasonable way of approaching the spirits," said Williams. "I feel we'll have a good atmosphere."

Mr Parham looked cynically impartial.

"If we're not to apply any tests..." began Sir Titus, with a note of protest.

"We'll just watch this time," said Sir Bussy. "I'll let you have some tests all right later."

"We don't mind tests," said Williams. "There's a lot about this business I'd like to have tested up to the hilt. For I understand it no more than you do. I'm just a vehicle."

"Yaa," said Sir Titus.

Mr Mountain proceeded with his explanations. They had been working with a few friends at spirit appearances. Their

99

recent custom had been to get the most sceptical person present to tie up Williams in his chair as hard and firmly as possible. Then hands were joined in the normal way. Then, in complete darkness, except for the faint glimmer of phosphorescence from the slate, they waited. Mrs Mountain would keep the gramophone going and had a small weak flashlight for the purpose. The person next her could check her movements. The thread of music was very conducive to phenomena, they found. They need not wait in silence, for that sometimes produced a bad atmosphere. They might make light but not frivolous conversation or simple comments until things began to happen.

"There's nothing mysterious or magical about it," said Mr Mountain.

"*You'll* do the tying up," said Hereward Jackson to Sir Titus.

"I know a knot or two," said Sir Titus ominously. "Do we strip him first?"

"Oo!" said Mr Mountain reproachfully and indicated the ladies. The question of stripping or anything but a superficial searching was dropped.

Mr Parham stood in unaffected boredom studying the rather fine lines of the lady in mourning while these preliminaries were settled. She was, he thought, a very sympathetic type. The other woman was a trifle blowsy and much too prepossessed by the medium and Hereward Jackson. The rest of these odd people he disliked, though he bore himself with a courtly graciousness towards old Mrs Mountain. What intolerable folly it all was!

After eternities of petty fussing the medium was tied up, the knots sealed, and the circle formed. Mr Parham had placed himself next to the lady in black, and on the other side he fell into contact with the flabby Mountain. Sir Bussy, by a sort of natural precedence, had got between the medium and the old lady. Sir Titus, harshly vigilant, had secured the medium's left. The lights were turned out. For several dreary centuries nothing happened except a dribble of weak conversation and an uneasy rustling from the medium. Once he moaned. *"He's going off!"* said Mrs Mountain. The finger of the lady in mourning twitched, and Mr Parham was stirred to answering twitches, but it amounted to nothing, and Mr Parham's interest died away.

Sir Bussy began a conversation with Hereward Jackson about the prospects of Wildcat for the Derby.

"Darling Mummy," came in a faint falsetto from outside the circle.

"What was that?" barked Sir Titus sharply.

"Ssh!" from Sir Bussy.

The lady beside Mr Parham stirred slightly, and the pressure of her hand beside his intensified. She made a noise as though she wanted to speak, but nothing came but a sob.

"My *dear* lady!" said Mr Parham softly, deeply moved.

"Just a fla, Mummy. I can't stop tonight. The's others want to come."

Something flopped lightly and softly on the table; it proved afterwards to be a chrysanthemum. There was a general silence, and Mr Parham realized that the lady beside him was weeping noiselessly. "Milly – sweetheart," she whispered. "Goodnight, dear. Goodnight."

Mr Parham hadn't reckoned on this sort of thing. It made his attention wander. His fine nature responded too readily to human feeling. He hardly noticed at first a queer sound that grew louder, a slobbering and slopping sound that was difficult to locate.

"That's the ectoplasm," said old Mrs Mountain, "working."

Mr Parham brought his mind, which had been concentrated on conveying the very deepest sympathy of a strong silent man through his little finger, back to the more general issues of the séance.

Mrs Mountain started the gramophone for the fourth or fifth repetition of that French horn solo when Tristan is waiting for Isolde. One saw a dim circle of light and her hand moving the needle. Then the light went out with a click and Wagner resumed.

Mr Mountain was talking to the spinster lady about the best way to get back to Battersea.

"Sssh!" said Sir Titus, as if blowing off steam.

Things were happening. "*Damn!*" said Sir Titus.

"Steady!" said Sir Bussy. "Don't break the circle."

"I was struck by a tin box," said Sir Titus, "or something as hard!"

"No need to move," said Sir Bussy unkindly.

"Struck on the back of the head," said Sir Titus.

"It may have been the tambourine," said Mr Mountain.

"Flas!" said the medium's voice, and something soft, cold and moist struck Mr Parham in the face and fell in his hand.

"Keep the circle please," said old Mrs Mountain.

Certainly this was exciting in a queer, tedious, unpleasant sort of way. After each event there was a wide expectant interval.

"Our friend is coming," said the medium's voice. "Our dear visitant."

The tambourine with a faint jingle floated over the table far out of reach. It drifted towards Sir Titus. "If you touch me again!" threatened Sir Titus, and the tambourine thought better of it and, it would seem, made its way back to the other table.

A light hand rested for a moment on Mr Parham's shoulder. Was it a woman's hand? He turned quietly and was started to find something with a faint bluish luminosity beside him. It was the phosphorescent slate.

"Look!" said Hereward Jackson.

Sir Titus grunted.

A figure was gliding noiselessly and evenly outside the circle. It held the luminous slate and raised and lowered this against its side to show a robed woman's figure with a sort of nun's coif.

"She's come," sighed Mrs Mountain very softly.

It seemed a long time before this visitant spoke.

"Lee-tle children," said a womanly falsetto. "Leetle children."

"Who's the lady?" asked Sir Bussy.

The figure became invisible.

After a little pause the medium answered from his place. "St Catherine."

The name touched a fount of erudition in Mr Parham, "*Which* St Catherine?"

"Just St Catherine."

"But there were *two* St Catherines – or more," said Mr Parham. "Two who had mystical marriages with the Lord. St Catherine of Alexandria, whose symbol is the wheel – the patroness of spinsters generally and the Catherinettes of Paris in particular – and St Catherine of Siena. There's a picture by Memling – perfectly lovely thing. And, yes – there *was* a third one, a Norwegian St Catherine, if I remember rightly. And possibly others. Couldn't she tell us? I would so like to know."

A silence followed this outbreak.

"She's never told us anything of that," said Mrs Mountain.

"I *think* it's St Catherine of Siena," said the spinster lady.

"She is a very sweet lady, anyhow," said Hereward Jackson.

"Can we be told this?" asked Sir Bussy.

The medium's voice replied very softly. "She prefers not to discuss these things. For us she wishes to be just our dear friend, the Lady Catherine. She comes on a mission of mercy."

"Don't press it," said Sir Bussy.

After a tedious interval St Catherine became faintly visible again. She kissed Sir Titus softly on the top of his high forehead, leaving him audibly unreconciled, and then she floated back to the left of Mr Parham.

"I came to tell you," she said, "that the little one is happy – so happy. She plays with flas – lovelier flas than you ever saw. Asphodel. And lovely flas like that. She is with me, under my special care. So she was able to come to you..."

The dim figure faded into utter darkness. "Farewell, my *dear* ones."

"Gaw!" said a familiar voice.

The gramophone ran down with a scratching sound. A deep silence followed, broken for a time only by the indignant breathing of Sir Titus Knowles.

"Wet kisses," he said.

The darkness was impenetrable. Then Mrs Mountain began to fumble with the gramophone, revealing a little glow of light that made the rest of the darkness deeper; a certain amount of scraping and shuffling became audible, and the medium was heard to groan. "I am tired," he complained, "I am terribly tired." Then, to judge by a string of sloppy noises, he seemed to be retracting his ectoplasm.

"That was very interesting," said Sir Bussy suddenly. "All the same — " he went on and then paused — "it isn't what I want. It was very kind of St Catherine, whichever St Catherine she was, to leave Bliss and all that and visit us. And I *liked* her kissing Sir Titus. It showed a nice disposition. He's not a man you'd kiss for pleasure. But... I don't know if any of you have seen that great fat book by Baron Schrenck-Notzing. Sort of like a scientific book. I've been reading that. What he got was something different from this."

His voice paused interrogatively.

"Could we have the light up?" said Mr Mountain.

"In a minute I shall be able to bear it," said Williams, very faint and faded. "Just one more minute."

"Then we shall *see*," said Sir Titus.

"I think we might break the circle now," said Mrs Mountain and rose rustlingly. The hand Mr Parham had been touching slipped out of his reach.

The light seemed blinding at first; the room was bleakly uncomfortable, and everybody looked ghastly. The medium's face was a leaden white, he was leaning back in his chair, in which he was still tied, with his head rolling slackly from side to side as though his neck were broken. Sir Titus set himself to examine his knots forthwith. It reminded Mr Parham of the examination of a casualty. Sir Bussy watched Sir Titus. Mr Mountain and Hereward Jackson stood up and leant over the table. "The sealing wax intact," said Sir Titus. "The knots good and twisted round the chair, just as I left them. *Hullo!*"

"Found something?" asked Hereward Jackson.

"Yes. The thread of cotton between the coat collar and the chair back has been snapped."

"That always gets broken somehow," said Mr Mountain, with scientific detachment.

"But *why?*" asked Sir Titus.

"We needn't bother about that now," said Sir Bussy, and the medium made noises in his throat and opened and closed his eyes.

"Shall we give him water?" asked the spinster lady.

Water was administered.

Sir Bussy was brooding over his fists on the table. "I want more than this." he said and addressed himself to the medium. "You see, Mr Williams, this is a very good show you have put up, but it isn't what I am after. In this sort of thing there are degrees and qualities, as in all sorts of things."

Williams still appeared very dazed. "Were there any phenomena?" he asked of the company.

"Wonderful," said old Mrs Mountain, with reassuring nods of the head, and the spinster lady echoed, "Beautiful. It was St Catherine again."

The lady in black was too moved for words.

Sir Bussy regarded Williams sideways with that unpleasing dropping of his nether lip. "You could do better than this under different conditions," he said in a quasi-confidential manner.

"Test conditions," said Sir Titus.

"This is a friendly atmosphere, of course," said the medium and regarded Sir Bussy with a mixture of adventure and defensiveness in his eyes. He had come awake very rapidly and was now quite alert. The water had done him good.

"I perceive that," said Sir Bussy.

"Under severer conditions the phenomena might be more difficult."

"That too I perceive."

"I'd be willing to participate in an investigation," said Williams in a tone that was almost businesslike.

"After what I've seen and heard and felt tonight," said Sir Titus, "I prophesy only one end to such an investigation – Exposure,"

"How *can* you say such a thing?" cried the spinster lady and turned to Hereward Jackson. "Tell him he is mistaken."

Hereward Jackson had played a markedly unaggressive part that evening. "No doubt he is," he said. "Let us be open-minded. I don't think Mr Williams need shirk an investigation under tests."

"Fair tests," said Williams.

"I'd see they were fair," said Hereward Jackson.

He became thoughtful. "There is such a thing as assisted phenomena," he mused aloud.

"For my part, mind you," said Williams. "I'm altogether passive, whatever happens."

"But," said Mr Mountain in tenoring remonstrance to Sir Bussy, "doesn't this evening satisfy you, sir?"

"This was a very amiable show," said Sir Bussy, "But it left a lot to be desired."

"It did," said Sir Titus.

"You mean to say there was anything not straightforward?" challenged Mr Mountain.

"That *dear* voice!" cried old Mrs Mountain.

"The *beauty* of it!" said the spinster lady.

"If you force me to speak," said Sir Titus, "I accuse this man Williams of impudent imposture."

"That goes too far," said Hereward Jackson; "much too far. That's dogma on the other side."

Mr Parham had stood aloof from the dispute he saw was gathering. He found it ugly and painful. He disbelieved in the phenomena almost as strongly as he disliked the disbelief of Sir Titus. He felt deeply for the little group which had gone on so happily from one revelation to another, invaded now by brawling denial, and brawling accusations, threatened by brawling exposure. Particularly he felt for the lady in mourning. She turned her eyes to him as if in appeal, and they were bright with unshed tears. Chivalry and pity stormed his heart.

"I agree," he said. "I agree with Mr Hereward Jackson. It is possible the medium, consciously or not, *assisted* the phenomena. But the messages were *real*."

Her face lit with gratitude and became an altogether beautiful face. And he did not even know her name!

"And the spirit of my dear one *was* present?" she implored.

Mr Parham met the eye of Sir Titus and met it with hard determination. "Something came to us here from outside," he said; "a message, an intimation, the breath of a soul – call it what you will."

And having said this, the seed of belief was sown in Mr Parham. For never before had he found reason to doubt his own word.

"And you are interested? You want to learn more?" pressed old Mrs Mountain.

Mr Parham went deeper and assented.

Had he heard Sir Bussy say "Gaw," or was that expletive getting on his nerves?

"Now, let's get things a bit clearer," said Williams. He was addressing himself directly to Sir Bussy. "I'm not answerable for what happens on these occasions. I go off. I'm not present, so to speak. I'm a mere instrument. You know more of what happens than I do."

He glanced from Sir Bussy to old Mrs Mountain and then came back to Sir Bussy. There was an air of scared enterprise about him that made Mr Parham think of some rascally valet who plans the desertion of an old and kindly master while still in his employment. It was as plain as daylight that he knew who Sir Bussy was and regarded him as a great opportunity, an opportunity that had to be snatched even at the cost of some inconsistency. His manner admitted an element of imposture in all they had seen that night. And it was plain that Hereward Jackson's convictions moved in accordance with his.

And yet he seemed to believe, and Hereward Jackson seemed to believe, that there was more than trickery in it. Insensibly Mr Parham assimilated the "something in it" point of view. He found himself maintaining it quite ably against Sir Titus.

Williams, after much devious talk, came at last to his point. "If you four gentlemen mean business, and if one could be treated as some of these pampered foreign mediums are treated," he said, "these Eva C's and Eusapia Palladinos and such-like, one might manage to give as good or better than they give. I'm only a passive thing in these affairs, but have I ever had a fair chance of showing what was in me?"

"Gaw," said Sir Bussy. "You shall have your chance."

Williams was evidently almost as frightened as he was grateful at his success. He thought at once of the need of securing a line of retreat if that should prove necessary. He turned to the old lady.

"They'll strip me naked and powder my feet. They'll take flashlight photographs of me with the ectoplasm oozing out of me. They'll very likely kill me. It won't be anything like our good times here. But when they are through with it you'll see they'll have justified me. They'll have justified me and justified all the faith you've shown in me."

CHAPTER FOUR

The Carfex House Séances

Once Sir Bussy had launched himself and his friends upon these metapsychic experiments he pursued the investigation with his customary intemperance. Carnac Williams was only one of several lines of investigation. It is a commonplace of psychic literature that the more a medium concentrates on the ectoplasm and materializations, the less is he or she capable of clairvoyance and the transmission of spirit messages. Carnac Williams was to develop along the former line. Meanwhile Sir Bussy took competent advice and secured the frequent presence of the more interesting clairvoyants available in London.

Carfex House was spacious, and Sir Bussy had a great supply of secretaries and under butlers. Rooms were told off for the materialization work and others for the reception of messages from the great beyond, and alert and attentive helpers learnt the names and business of the experts and showed them to their proper apartments. The materialization quarters were prepared most elaborately by Sir Titus Knowles. He was resolved to make them absolutely spirit tight; to make any ectoplasm that was exuded in them feel as uncomfortable and unwelcome as ectoplasm could.

He and Williams carried on an interminable wrangle about hangings, lighting, the legitimate use of flashlight photography, and the like. Sir Titus even stood out, most unreasonably, against a black velvet cabinet and conceded Williams black tights for the sake of decency with an ill grace. "We aren't going to have any women about," said Sir Titus. Williams showed himself amazingly temperamental and Sir Titus was mulishly obstinate; Sir Bussy, Hereward Jackson, and Mr Parham acted as their final court of appeal and pleased neither party. Hereward Jackson was consistently for Williams.

On the whole Williams got more from them than Sir Titus, chiefly because of Mr Parham's lack of intellectual sympathy with the latter. Constantly the casting vote fell to Mr Parham. With secret delight he heard of – and on several occasions he assisted at – an increasing output of ectoplasm that it entirely defeated Sir Titus to explain. He was forbidden, by the rules and hypothesis that it might conceivably cause the death of his adversary, to leap forward and grab the stuff. It bubbled out of the corners of Williams' mouth, a horrid white creeping fluid, it flowed from his chest, it accumulated upon his knees; and it was withdrawn with a sort of sluggish alacrity. On the ninth occasion this hitherto shapeless matter took on the rude suggestions of hands and a human face, and a snapshot was achieved.

The tests and restrictions imposed upon the trances of the clairvoyants were, from the nature of the case, less rigorous than those directly controlled by Sir Titus, and their results developed rather in advance of the Williams manifestations.

The communications differed widely in quality. One medium professed a Red Indian control and also transmitted messages from a gentleman who had lived in Susa, "many years ago, long before the time of Abraham." It was very difficult to determine where the Red Indian left off and where the ancient from Susa began. Moreover, "bad spirits" got in on the Susa communications, and departed friends of Hereward Jackson sent messages to say that it was "splendid" where they were, and that they were "so happy," and wished everyone could be told about it, but faded out under further interrogation in the most unsatisfactory fashion. At an early stage Sir Bussy decided that he had "enough of that gammon" and this particular practitioner was paid off and retired. There were several such failures. The details varied, but the common factor was a lack of elementary incredibility. Two women mediums held out downstairs, while upstairs in the special room Williams, week by week, thrust his enlarging and developing ectoplasm into the pale and formidable disbelief of Sir Titus.

Of the two women downstairs one was a middle-aged American with no appeal for Mr Parham; the other was a much more interesting and attractive type. She was dusky, with a curiously beautiful oval olive-tinted face and she said she was the young widow of an English merchant in Mauritius. Her name was Nanette Pinchot. She was better educated than the common run of psychic material and had very high recommendations from some of the greatest investigators in Paris and Berlin. She spoke English with a pleasing staccato. Neither she nor the American lady professed to be controlled by the usual ghost, and this was new to all the Carfex House investigators. The American lady had trances of a fit-like nature that threw her slanting-wise across her chair in inelegant attitudes. Mrs Pinchot, when entranced, sat like a pensive cat, with her head inclined forward and her hands folded neatly in her lap. Neither lady had heard of the other. The one lodged with cousins in Highbury; the other stayed in a Kensington hotel. But their line of revelation was the same. Each professed to feel a mighty afflatus from an unknown source which had thrust all commonplace controls aside. There were moments when Mr Parham was reminded of the Hebrew prophets when they said, "the Voice of the Lord came upon me." But this voice was something other than the Voice of the Lord.

Mrs Pinchot gave the fuller messages. The American lady gave descriptive matter rather than positive statements. She would say, "Where am I? I am afraid. I am in a dark place. An arcade. No, not an arcade, a passage. A great huge passage. Pillars and faces on either side, faces carved on the pillars, terrible faces. Faces of Destiny. It is dark and cold and there is a wind blowing. The light is dim. I do not know where the light comes from. It is very dim. The Spirit, which is Will and Power, is coming down the passage like a mighty wind, seeking a way. How great and lonely the passage is! I am so small, so cold, and so afraid. I am smaller. I am driven like a dead leaf before the wind of the great Spirit. Why was I put into this dreadful place? Let me out! *Oh, let me out!*"

Her distress became evident. She writhed and had to be recalled to the things of this world.

By an extraordinary coincidence Mrs Pinchot also spoke of a great passage down which something was coming. But she did not feel herself actually in the passage, nor was she personally afraid. "There is a corridor," she said. "A breeze of expectation blows down it from some unknown source. And Power is coming. It is as if I hear the tramp of iron footfalls drawing near."

Hereward Jackson did not hear these things said. That made it more remarkable that he should bring back a report from Portsmouth. "There is a new Spirit coming into the world," he said. "A man in Portsea has been saying that. He is a medium, and suddenly he has given up saying anything else and taken to warning us of a new time close at hand. It is not the spirit of any departed person. It is a Spirit from Outside seeking to enter the world."

Mr Parham found something rather impressive in these convergent intimations. From the first he had observed Mrs Pinchot closely, and he found it difficult to believe her capable of any kind of fraud, collusion, or mystification. The friendly candour of her normal bearing passed over without a change into her trance condition. He had some opportunities of studying her when she was not under séance conditions; he twice took her out to tea at Rumpelmayer's and afterwards persuaded Sir Bussy to have her down at the Hangar for a weekend. So he was able to hear her talking naturally and easily about art, foreign travel, ideas in general, and even public affairs. She was really cultivated. She had a fine, inquiring, discriminating mind. She had great breadth of view. She evidently found an intelligent pleasure in his conversation. He talked to her as he rarely talked to women, for commonly his attitude to the opposite sex was light and playful or indulgent and protective. But he found she could even understand his anxieties for the world's affairs, his sense of a threatening anarchism and dissolution in the texture of society, and his feeling for the need of a stronger and clearer guidance in our periodic literature. Sometimes she would even anticipate things he was going to say. But when he asked her about the Spirit that was coming into the world she knew nothing of it. Her séance life was quite detached from her daily life. He gave her his books on Richelieu with a friendly inscription and copies of some of his graver articles and addresses. She said they were no ordinary articles.

From the outset she had made it plain that she realized that this new circle she had entered was very different in quality from the usual gathering of the credulous and curious with which a medium has to deal. "People talk of the stupidity of spirit communications," she said at the first meeting. "But does anyone ever consider the vulgar quality of the people to whom these communications have to be made?"

This time, she felt, the grouping was of a different order. She said she liked to have Sir Titus there particularly, for his hard, clear doubt was like walking on a level firm floor. Sir Titus bowed his forehead with an acknowledgment that was not as purely ironical as it might have been. To great men like Sir Bussy, to sympathetic minds like Hereward Jackson, to learning and mental power, spirits and powers might be attracted who would disdain the vague inquiries of the suburban curious.

"And you really believe," said Mr Parham, "these messages that come through you come from the dead?"

"Not a bit of it," said Mrs Pinchot in that sharp definitive way of hers; "I've never believed anything so nonsensical. The dead can do nothing. If these influences are from people who have passed over, they come because these people still live on. But what the living power may be that moves me to speech I do not know. I don't find any proof that all the intimations, or even most of the intimations we receive, come from ghosts – if one may use that old word for once. Even if some certainly do."

"Not disembodied spirits?" said Hereward Jackson.

"Sometimes I think it must be something more, something different and something much more general. Even when the names of departed friends are used. How am I to know? I am the only person in your circle who has never heard my own messages. It may be all delusion. It's quite possibly all delusion. We people with psychic gifts are a queer race. We transmit. What we transmit we do not know. But it's you stabler people who have to explain the things that come through us. We are limited by what people expect. When they expect nothing but vulgar ghosts and silly private messages, what else can we transmit? How can we pass on things they could not begin to understand?"

"True," said Mr Parham, "true."

"When you get greater minds as receivers you will get greater messages."

That too was reasonable.

"But there's something in it very wonderful, something that science knows nothing about."

"Ah! there I agree," said Mr Parham.

In the earlier séances with her there was a sort of "control" in evidence. "I am the messenger of the Advent," he declared.

"A departed spirit?" asked Jackson.

"How can I be departed when I am here?"

"Are there such things as angels, then?" asked Mr Parham. ("Gaw!")

"Messengers. 'Angel' means 'messenger.' Yes, I am a messenger."

"Of someone – or of something – some power which comes?" asked Mr Parham with a new helpfulness in his voice.

"Of someone who seeks a hold upon life, of someone with great power of mastery latent, who seeks to grapple with the world."

"He'd better try upstairs," injected Sir Titus.

"Here, where there are already will and understanding, he finds his helpers."

"But who is this being who comes? Has he been on earth before?"

"A conquering spirit which watches still over the world it has done so much to mould."

"Who is he?"

"Who *was* he?"

"The corridor is long, and he is far away. I am tired. The medium is tired. The effort to speak to you is great because of the Strong Doubter who sits among you. But it is worthwhile. It is only the beginning. Keep on. I can stay but a little while longer now, but I will return to you."

"But what is he coming for? What does he want to do?"

There was no answer. The medium remained for some time in a state of insensibility before she came to. Even then she felt faint and begged to be allowed to lie down for a time before she left Carfex House.

So it was that Mr Parham remembered the answers obtained in the first of the séances with Mrs Pinchot that really took a strong hold of his imagination. The actual sequence of the transmission was perhaps more confused, but this was what stood out in his memory.

It would indeed be a mighty miracle if some new Power did come into human affairs. How much there was to change! A miracle altogether desirable. He was still sceptical of the idea of an actual spirit coming to earth, but it was very pleasant to toy with the idea that something, some actual anticipation of coming things, was being symbolized in these riddles.

The detailed records of all séances, even the most successful ones, are apt to make copious and tedious reading for those who are not engaged in their special study, and it would serve no useful purpose to relate them here. Mr Parham's predilection for Mrs Pinchot helped greatly in the development of that "something-in-it" attitude, which he had first assumed at the Williams séance in Buggins Street. Released from any insistence upon the ghostly element and the survival of the pettier aspects of personalities, the phenomena of the trance state seemed to him to become much more rational and credible. There was something that stirred him profoundly in this suggestion of hovering powers outside our world seeking for some means, a congenial temperament, an understanding mentality, by which they could operate and intervene in its affairs. He imagined entities like the great spirit forms evoked and pictured by Blake and G F Watts; he dreamt at last of mighty shapes.

Who was this great being who loomed up over his receptive imagination in these Carfex House séances? He asked if it was Napoleon the First, and the answer was, "Yes and no"; not Napoleon and more than Napoleon. Hereward Jackson asked if it was Alexander the Great and got exactly the same answer. Mr Parham in the night, or while walking along the street, would find himself talking in imagination to this mysterious and mighty impending spirit. It would seem to stand over him and think with him as in his morning or evening paper he read fresh evidences of the nerveless conduct of the world's affairs and the steady moral deterioration of our people.

His preoccupation with these two clairvoyants led to a certain neglect on his part of the researches of Sir Titus upon Carnac Williams. More and more was he coming to detest the hard and limited materialism of the scientific intelligence. He wanted to think and know as little of these operations as possible. The irritation produced by the normal comments of Sir Titus upon the clairvoyant mediums, and particularly upon Mrs Pinchot and the American lady, was extreme. Sir Titus was no genetleman; at times his phrases were almost intolerably gross, and on several occasions Mr Parham was within an ace of fierce reprisals. He almost said things that would have had the force of blows. The proceedings at these materialization séances were unbearably tedious. It took hours that seemed like æons to get a few ectoplasmic gutterings. The pleasure of seeing how much they baffled Sir Titus waned. On at least three occasions, Mr Parham passed beyond the limits of boredom and fell asleep in his chair, and after that he stayed away for a time.

His interest in Carnac Williams was reawakened after that ninth séance in which a face and hand became discernible. He was at Oxford at the time but he returned to London to hear a very striking account of the tenth apparition from Hereward Jackson. "When at first it became plain," said Hereward Jackson, "it might have been a crumpled diminutive of yourself. Then, as it grew larger, it became more and more like Napoleon."

Instantly Mr Parham connected this with his conception of the great Spirit that Mrs Pinchot had presented as looming over the Carfex House inquiries. And the early resemblance to himself was also oddly exciting. "I must see that," he said. "Certainly I must come and see this materialization stuff again. It isn't fair to Sir Titus for me to keep so much away."

He talked it over with Mrs Pinchot. She showed she was entirely ignorant of what was going on in the room upstairs, and she found the triple coincidence of the Napoleonic allusion very remarkable. For the American lady had also spoken of Buonaparte and Sargon and Genghis Khan in a rambling but disturbing message.

It was like a sound of trumpets from the Unknown, first on this side and then on that.

Once more Mr Parham faced the long silences and boredoms of the tense and noiseless grapple of Sir Titus and Williams. It was after dinner, and he knew that for a couple of hours at least nothing could possibly occur. Hereward Jackson seemed in a happier mood, quietly expectant. Sir Bussy, with a certain impatience that had been increasing at every recent séance, tried to abbreviate or at least accelerate the customary strippings, searchings, markings, and sealings. But his efforts were unavailing.

"Now you have drawn me into it," said Sir Titus in that strident voice of his, "I will not relax one jot or one tittle in these precautions until I have demonstrated forever the farcical fraudulence of all this solemn spooking. I shan't grudge any price I pay for a full and complete exposure. If anyone wants to go, let him go. So long as some witness remains. But I'd rather die than scamp the job at this stage."

"Oh, Gaw!" said Sir Bussy, and Mr Parham felt that at any time now these researches might come to a violent end.

The little man settled into his armchair, pulled thoughtfully at his lower lip for a time and then lapsed, it seemed, into profound meditation.

At last the fussing was over and the vigil began. Silence fell and continued and expanded and wrapped about Mr Parham closer and closer. Very dimly one saw the face of Williams, against the velvet blackness of the recess. He would lie for a long time with his mouth open, and then groan weakly and snore and stir and adopt a new attitude. Each time Mr Parham heard the sharp rustle of Sir Titus Knowles' alertness.

After a time Mr Parham found himself closing his eyes. It was curious. He still saw the pallid brow and cheekbone of Williams when his eyes were closed.

CHAPTER FIVE

The Visitant

After a time Mr Parham's interest in the psychic transparency of the human eyelid gave way to his perception of a very unusual flow of ectoplasm from the medium. It had begun quite normally as a faint self-luminous oozing from the corners of the mouth, but now it was streaming much more rapidly than it had ever done before from his neck and shoulders and arms and presently from the entire front of his vaguely outlined body. It was phosphorescent – at first with a greenish and then with a yellowish-green tint. It came so fast that either by contrast Williams seemed to shrink and shrivel, or else he did actually shrink and shrivel.

It was impossible to decide that; this outflow of matter was so arresting. This Mr Parham felt was worth seeing. He was glad he had come. There was ectoplasm now to choke Sir Titus. Well might Sir Bussy, lost somewhere in the black darkness close at hand whisper "Gaw." The stuff was already animated matter. It did not merely gutter and flow and hang downward, in the spiritless, tallow-like forms it had hitherto assumed. It was different. It had vital force in it. It was not so much slimy as glassy. Its ends lifted and pointed out towards the observers like bulging pseudopodia, like blind animalculæ, like searching fingers, like veiled phantoms.

"*Eh!*" said Sir Titus. "This beats me."

Hereward Jackson was muttering to himself and shivering.

It was strange stuff to watch. Its blunt protrusions touched and flowed into one another. They quivered, hesitated, and advanced. With an astounding rapidity they grew. What were delicate tendrils an instant ago were now long fingers and now blunt lumps. They were transparent, or at least translucent, and one saw streams of whitish and faintly tinted matter flowing within them, as one sees in a microscope the protoplasm of an amoeba streaming about in its body. They grew, they coalesced more and more.

A few seconds or a few moments since, for it was difficult to measure the time this dim process was taking, the forms of these protrusions had been tentacular, fungoid, branchingly obtuse. Now they were coalescing, running together and becoming blunter and more closely involved and more and more one consolidated lumpish labouring aggregation. The coming and going of the swirling currents within grew faster and more interwoven. The colouring became stronger. Streaks of red and purple, exquisite lines of glistening bands of a pale creamy colour became distinguishable. A sort of discipline in these movements was presently apparent.

With a shock it came into Mr Parham's head that he was seeing bones and nerves and blood vessels hurrying to their appointed places in that swimming swirl. But was this possible? Why did he *feel* these were living structures? For they carried an immense conviction to his mind. As he peered and marvelled this internal circulation of the ectoplasm grew dim. A film was extending over it. At first it was perplexing to say why that swirling vesicle should be dimmed, and then came the realization that an opaque skin was forming upon the whole boiling ectoplasmic mass. It became more and more opaque at last as a body. The process so stirred Mr Parham to behold, his own nerves and arteries thrilled with such response, that he felt almost as though he himself was being made.

Shape, a recognizable form, was now imposed upon this growth. At first merely the vague intimation of head and shoulders. Then very rapidly the appearance of a face, like a still slightly translucent mask in the front of the head lump, and then hair, ears, a complete head and shoulders rising as it were out of the chest of the collapsed medium; plainly the upper part of a strange being whose nether limbs were still fluid and dim. A cold handsome face regarded the watchers, with a firm mouth and slightly contemptuous eyes.

And yet it had a strange resemblance to a face that was very familiar indeed to Mr Parham.

"This is beyond me altogether," said Sir Titus.

"I never hoped for anything like this," said Hereward Jackson.

Mr Parham was altogether absorbed in the vision and by the mystery of its likeness. Sir Bussy was no longer equal to "Gaw".

In another moment, as it seemed, or another half hour, the newcomer was completed. He was of medium height, slenderer and taller than Napoleon the First but with something of the same Byronic beauty. He was clothed in a white silken shirt, wide open at the neck and with knee breeches, greyish stockings and shoes. He seemed to shine with a light of his own. He took a step forward, and Williams dropped like an empty sack from his chair and lay forgotten.

"You can turn up the lights," said a firm, clear, sweet, even voice, and stood to see its orders obeyed.

It became evident that Sir Titus had been preparing a surprise. From his chair he bent forward, touched a button on the floor, and the room was brightly lit by a score of electric lamps. As the darkness changed to light one saw his body bent down, and then he brought himself back to a sitting position. His face was ghastly white and awestricken; his vast forehead crumpled by a thousand wrinkles. Never was sceptic so utterly defeated; never was unbeliever so abruptly convinced. The visitant smiled and nodded at his confusion. Hereward Jackson stood beside Sir Titus, paralysed between astonishment and admiration. Sir Bussy also was standing. There was a livelier interest and less detachment in his bearing than Mr Parham had ever seen before.

"For some years I have been seeking my way to this world," said the Visitant, "for this world has great need of me."

Hereward Jackson spoke in the silence and his voice was faint.

"You have come from another world?"

"Mars."

They had nothing to say.

"I come from the Red Planet, the planet of blood and virility," said the Visitant; and then, after a queer still moment that was drenched with interrogation, he delivered a little speech to them.

"I am the Master Spirit who tries and who cleanses the souls of men. I am the spirit of Manhood and Dominion and Order. That is why I have come to you from that sterner planet where I rule. This world is falling into darkness and confusion, into doubt, vain experiments, moral strangeness, slackness, failure of effort, evasion of conflict, plenty without toil, security without vigilance. It has lacked guidance. Voices that might have given it guidance have found no form of utterance. Vague and foolish dreams of universal peace tempt the desires of men and weaken their wills. Life is struggle. Life is effort. I have come to rouse men to their forgotten duties. I have come to bring not peace but a sword. Not for the first time have I crossed the interplanetary gulf. I am the disturber of those waters of life that heal the souls of men. I am the banner of flame. I am the exaltation of history. I breathed in Sargon, in Alexander, in Genghis Khan, in Napoleon. Now I come among you, using you as my mask and servants. This time it is the English who are my chosen people. In their turn. For they are a great and wonderful people still – for all their inexpressiveness. I have come to England, trembling on the brink of decadence, to raise her and save her and lead her back to effort and glory and mastery."

"You have come into the world to *stay?*" Hereward Jackson was profoundly respectful but also profoundly puzzled. "Master! – are you *matter?* Are you earthly matter? Are you flesh and blood?"

"Not as much as I am going to be. But that shall soon be remedied. My honest Woodcock here will see I get some food downstairs and make me free of his house. Meat – sound meat in plenty. At present I'm still depending in part upon that fellow's nasty ectoplasm. I'm half a phantom still."

He glanced ungratefully at Carnac Williams, who, having contributed his best, lay flat as an empty sack now upon the shaded floor of the cabinet. No one went to his assistance.

Hereward Jackson stooped forward peering. "*Is he dead?*" he asked.

"Phew! the channels one must use!" said the Master Spirit with manifest aversion. "Don't trouble about *him*. Leave him, poor Sludge. He can lie. But you I have need of. You will be my first colleagues. Woodcock, my Crassus, the commissariat?"

"There's food downstairs," said Sir Bussy, slowly and grudgingly, but evidently unable to disobey. "There'll be one or two menservants up still. We can find you meat."

"We'll go down. Wine, have you? Red wine? Then we can talk while I eat and drink and put real substance into this still very sketchy body of mine. All night we'll have to talk and plan the things we have to do. You three and I. You brought me, you invoked me, and here I am. No good scowling and doubting now, Sir Titus; your days of blatant denial are past. So soon as I am equal to it you shall feel my pulse. Which door goes down? Oh! that's a cupboard, is it?"

Hereward Jackson went across to the door upon the passage and opened it. The passage seemed larger and more brightly lit than Mr Parham remembered it. Everything indeed seemed larger. And that light contained rays of an intense and exalting hopefulness. The two other men followed the Master Spirit as he went. They were dumb-founded. They were astounded and docile.

But someone was missing! For some moments this shortage perplexed the mind of Mr Parham. He counted Sir Bussy, One, Sir Titus, Two, and Hereward Jackson, Three. But there had been another. Of course! – Himself! Where was he?

His mind spun round giddily. He seemed to be losing touch with everything. Was he present at all?

And then he perceived that imperceptibly and incomprehensibly, the Master Spirit had incorporated him. He realized

128

that an immense power of will had taken possession of him, that he lived in a new vigour, that he was still himself and yet something enormously more powerful, that his mind was full and clear and certain as it had never been before. Mutely these others had accepted this stupendous and yet unobtrusive coalescence.

"We must talk," said a voice that was his own voice made glorious, and a fine white hand came out from him, shaking its fingers, and motioned the others on.

And they obeyed! Marvelling and reluctant, perhaps, but they obeyed.

BOOK THREE

THE STRONG HAND AT LAST

CHAPTER ONE

An Arm Outstretched

The evangel of the Lord Paramount of England was swift and direct.

Clad thinly in the incorporated identity of Mr Parham, the Senior Tutor of St Simon's, publicist and historian, sustained at the outset by the wealth of this strangely subdued Sir Bussy which he commandeered without scruple, waited upon in a state of awe stricken devotion by Hereward Jackson, and attended hygienically by the cowed and convinced Sir Titus Knowles, the Master Spirit, without haste and without delay, imposed his personality upon the national imagination. Without delay and yet without apparent haste, he set about the task for which he had become incarnate.

With unerring judgment he chose and summoned his supporters to his side and arranged what in the case of any inferior type would have been called a vulgar publicity campaign. That is the first necessary phase in any sort of human leadership. To begin with, one must be known. Vulgarization is the road to empire. By that the most fine-minded of men must come to power, if they would have power. The careers of Cæsar and

Napoleon opened with a bold operation of the contemporary means of publicity. They could open in no other way.

The country was weary of parliamentary government, weary of a conservatism which did not reduce the taxes upon property and enterprise to a minimum, weary of a liberalism that it could not trust to maintain overwhelming but inexpensive armaments, weary of the unintelligible bickerings of liberalism and labour, weary of the growing spectre of unemployment, weary of popular education, religious discussion, and business uncertainty, disappointed by peace and dismayed at the thought of war, neurasthenic and thoroughly irritable and distressed. The papers it read attacked the government and would not support the opposition. Politics could not escape from personalities, and none of the personalities succeeded in being more than actively undignified or industriously dull. Everybody nagged everybody. Trade was bad, the new talking movies a clanging disappointment, county cricket more and more tedious, and the influenza hung about maddeningly. Whenever one tried to do anything one found one had a cold. Criticism and literature fostered discord with whatever was old and would not countenance hope for anything new. Aimless scepticism was the "thing." Nobody seemed to know where to go or what to do, and the birth rate and death rate, falling together, witnessed together to the general indecisiveness. The weather was moody and treacherous. The general election had pleased nobody. It had taken power out of the hands of a loyal if dull conservative majority, faithful to the honoured traditions of an expanding empire, and transferred it to the control of a vague and sentimental idealism in which nobody believed. The country was ripe for some great change.

It was at a mass gathering of the Amalgamated Patriotic Societies in the Albert Hall, convened not very hopefully to protest against any pampering of the unemployed by their fellows on the government benches, that the Lord Paramount, still thinly personating the vanished Mr Parham, rose, like a beneficent star upon the British horizon. When he stood up to speak he was an unknown man except to the elect few to whom he had already revealed himself. When at last, amidst an unparalleled storm of enthusiasm, he resumed his seat, he was already and irrevocably leader of a national renascence. The residue of the agenda was washed away and forgotten in the wild storm of enthusiasm that beat upon the platform.

Yet his début was made with the very minimum of artificiality. His voice rang clear and true into the remotest circles of that great place; the handsome pallor of his face, lit ever and again by an extraordinarily winning smile, focussed every eye. His bearing was inaggressive, and yet his whole being radiated an extraordinary magnetism. His gestures were restrained but expressive; the chief of them the throwing out of a beautifully formed hand. "Who is this man," whispered a thousand lips, "that we have never known of him before?"

His speech was entirely devoid of rhetorical gymnastics. His style can be best described as one of colossal simplicity. He touched the familiar and obvious to a new life. His discourse carried along platitudes as hosts carry time-honoured banners and one familiar phrase followed another, like exiled leaders refreshed and renewed returning to their people. With a few closely knit phrases he gathered together the gist of the previous speakers. Some of them had been perhaps a trifle querulous, over-explicit, or lengthy, and it was marvellous how he plucked

135

the burning heart from the honest and yet plaintive copiousness that had preceded him and held it out, a throbbing and beating indignation. It was true, he conceded, that our working classes, under the poisonous infection of foreign agitators, deteriorated daily; it was true that art and literature had become the vehicles of a mysterious malaria, true that science was mischievous and miasmatic and that the very pulpit and altar were touched by doubt. It was true that our young people had lost all sense of modesty in the poisoned chalice of pleasure and that our growing hosts of unemployed seemed to lack even the will to invent anything to do. Nevertheless...

For a moment his golden voice held its great audience in the immense expectation of that overarching word. Then, very gently and clearly and sweetly, it told of what Britain had been to the world and what she still might be, this little island, this jewel in the forehead of the world, this precious jewel, this crowned imperial jewel, set in the stormy frosted silver of the seas. For, after all, these workers of ours – properly safeguarded – were still the best in the world, and their sons and daughters heirs of the mightiest tradition that had ever been hewn from the crucibles of time. (No time to correct that; it had to go. The meaning was plain.) Superficially our land might seem to have given way to a certain lassitude. That made it all the more urgent that we should thrust all masks and misconceptions aside now, and stand forth again in this age of the world's direst need, the mighty race, the race of leaders and adventurers that we were and had always been. *But...*

Again a moment of expectation; every face in that quintessential assembly intent.

Was all our pride and hope to be dashed and laid aside to subserve the manœuvres of a handful of garrulous politicians and their parasites and dupes? Was Britain to be forever gagged by its infatuation with elected persons and the national voice of our great people belied by the tediums and dishonesties of a parliamentary institution that had long outlived its use? Through years of impatience the passionate negative had been engendering itself in our indignant hearts. Let us borrow a phrase from an unexpected quarter. The poor rebels on the outer fringe of the Socialist party, that fringe the Socialist party was so anxious to deny, the Bolsheviki, the Communistky, the Cooks and Maxtons, and so forth, used a phrase that went far beyond their courage. That phrase was Direct Action. Not for such as they were, was the realization of so tremendous a suggestion. For direct action could be a great and glorious thing. It could be the drawing of the sword of righteousness. It could be the launching of the thunderbolt. The time had come, the hour was striking, for honest men and true women and all that was real and vital in our national life to think of Direct Action, to prepare for Direct Action; to discipline themselves for the hour of Direct Action, when they would hold and maintain, strike and spare not.

For some moments the Master Spirit was like a strong swimmer in a tumultuous sea of applause. As the tumult fell to attention again he sketched out his line of action very briefly and so came to his peroration. "I ask you to return to the essential, the substantial things of life," he said. "Here I stand for plain and simple things – for King and Country, for Religion and Property, for Order and Discipline, for the Peasant on the Land and for all Men at their Work and Duty, for the Rightness of the

Right, the Sacredness of Sacred Things and all the Fundamental Institutions of Mankind."

He remained standing. The voice died away. For some moments there was a great stillness and then a sound like "Ah!"– a long universal "Ah!" and then a thunder of expression that rose and rose. English audiences they say are hard to move, but this one was on fire. Everyone stood. Everyone sought the relief of gesticulation. All the great hall seemed to be pressing and pouring down towards its Master made manifest. Everywhere were shining eyes and extended hands. "Tell us what to do," cried a hundred voices. "Show us what to do. Lead us!" Fresh people seemed to be flowing into the place as those who had been there throughout pressed down the gangways. How they responded! Surely of all gifts of power that God gives his creatures that of oratory has the swiftest reward! The Lord Paramount faced his conquered audience, and within, restored to the religious confidence of an earlier time, he thanked his God.

It was impossible to leave things at that point; some immediate action was needed. "What are we to tell them to do?" pressed the chairman.

"Form a league," said the Master simply.

Hands were held up to command silence. The chairman's thin voice could be heard reiterating the suggestion. "Yes, form a league," thundered the multitude. "What are we to call the league?"

"League of Duty," suggested Hereward Jackson, jammed close to the Master.

"The Duty Paramount League," said the Master, his voice cutting through the uproar like the sweep of a sword. The multitude vibrated upon that.

A little speechifying followed, heard eagerly but impatiently. The League, someone said, was to be the Fascisti of Britain. There were loud cries of "British Fascisti" and "The English Duce" (variously pronounced). Young Englishmen, hitherto slack and aimless, stood up and saluted Fascist fashion and took on something of the stiff, stern dignity of Roman *camerieri* as they did so.

"And who is he?" cried a penetrating voice. "What is his name? He is our leader. Our Deuce! We will follow him."

"Doochy!" someone corrected...

Cries and confusion, and then out of it all the words, "Duty Paramount! The Master Paramount! Paramount!" growing to a great shout, a vast vocal upheaval.

"Hands up for adhesions," bawled a tall, intensely excited man at the Master Spirit's elbow, and the whole multitude was a ripe cornfield of hands. It was an astounding gathering; young men and old men, beautiful women, tall girls like flames and excited elderly persons of every size and shape, all fused in one stupendous enthusiasm, and many of them waving sticks and umbrellas. Never had there been a religious revival to compare with it. And every eye in all that swaying mass was fixed on the serene determination of the Master Spirit's face.

Flashes of blinding lavender-tinted light showed that press cameras were in action.

"Turn this place into a headquarters. Enrol them," said the Master Spirit.

He felt a tug at his sleeve. It was the first of a number of queer little backward tugs he was to feel even in the first exaltation of his ascent. "We've only got the place until midnight," said a thin, unnecessary, officious-mannered little man.

"Disregard that," said the Master Spirit and prepared to leave the auditorium.

"They'll turn us out," the little man insisted.

"Turn *that* out! *Never!*" said the Master Spirit, waving a hand to the following he had created, the stormy forces he had evoked, and scorched the doubter with his blazing eyes. But still the creature insisted.

"Well, they'll cut off the lights."

"Seize the switches! And tell the organist not to play the National Anthem until he is told to. Tell him to play some stirring music as the enrolment goes on."

The timid man shrunk away, and others more resolute obeyed the Master's behests. "Turn us out" indeed! The organist after a brief parley arranged to play "O God Our Help in Ages Past," with variations, wandering occasionally into "Onward, Christian Soldiers" and "Rule Britania," until a suitable relief could be found for him, and to such magnificent music it was that the League of Duty Paramount was born.

The enrolment continued until dawn. Thousands of names were taken. They poured past the little tables endlessly. Their eyes blazed, their noses resembled the first Duke of Wellington's, their chins protruded more and more. It was amazing that the Albert Hall could have held so many earnest and vigorous people...

The Master's task for that evening was done. He had fought his first fight on the road to power. Reverential hands guided him down steps of faded baize. He found himself in a little anteroom, and Hereward Jackson was offering him a glass of water. The chairman of the meeting stood out at the centre of a select circle of devotees. Mrs Pinchot, dark and mutely worshipping, had managed somehow to get into this inner grouping. Her eyes were full of understanding. "Too late for the morning papers," said the chairman, "but we shall see that the evening press gets everything full and good. A wonderful speech, sir! Do you mind a few photographers from the picture papers taking shots at you?"

"Let them," said the Master Spirit.

He considered. "I am to be seen at Carfex House. I shall make that my headquarters. Let them come to me there."

For a moment that rare smile of his dazzled the chairman, touched Mrs Pinchot like a glancing sunbeam, and he had gone.

"Not tired, sir?" asked Hereward Jackson anxiously in the car.

"It is not for me to be tired," said the Master Spirit.

"I have an excellent tonic I can give you at Carfex House," said Sir Titus.

"Chemicals when I must," said the Master, with that characteristic gesture of his hand.

Yet he was sensible of fatigue and oddly enough of just one faint twinge of anxiety. There was one little speck upon the splendour of this triumph. These two men were manifestly faithful, and Jackson was full of emotion at the immense success of the meeting, but – there ought to have been a third man in the car.

"By the by," said the Master Spirit, leaning back restfully in the big Rolls-Royce and closing his eyes with an affectation of complete indifference. "Where is Sir Bussy Woodcock?"

Jackson thought. "He went away. He went quite early. He got up suddenly and went out."

"Did he say anything?"

"Something – it always sounds like 'Gaw.' "

The Master Spirit opened his eyes. "He must be sent for – if he is not at Carfex House. I shall want him at hand."

But Sir Bussy was not at Carfex House. He had not gone home. The place, however, was entirely at the disposal of the Master Spirit and his retinue. The servants had everything in readiness for them, and the major domo offered to telephone to Marmion House to restore communications with Sir Bussy. But if there was a reply it did not get through to the Master Spirit, and next morning Sir Bussy was still missing. He did not reappear until late the next afternoon and then he drifted into his own property, the most detached and observant person in what was rapidly becoming a busy and militant hive. The organization of the staff of the Master Spirit and the apportionment of rooms to the secretaries he engaged, had gone on rapidly in the absence of the legal owner of the house. Among the secretaries, most energetic and capable of helpers, was little Mrs Pinchot, the medium. Others were chosen from among the little Oxford group of "Parham's Young Men."

Next morning after a séance with a number of photographers, the Master Spirit motored to Harrow School, where as a result of headlong arrangements he was able to address the boys in the morning. His address was substantially the same as that he had given at the Albert Hall, and the enthusiasm of the generous youngsters, led by the more military masters, was a very glorious experience. While he lunched with the head, the gallant lads, neglecting all thought of food, bolted off to put on their cadet uniforms, and an informal parade of the corps was held to bid him farewell, with shouts of "Duty Paramount!" and "We are ready!"

There was little classroom work for the rest of that day at Harrow.

A strong contingent of reporters was present, and next morning saw the demonstration fully reported and pictured in all the daily papers. So his message came through to that greater outer world, the general public, and awakened an immediate response.

The following afternoon saw him repeating his triumph on the playing fields of Eton.

The time was ripe, and men had been waiting for him. In a few weeks the whole Empire knew of the Duty Paramount movement and the coming of the Master Paramount (the formal title of Lord Paramount came later) to lead England back into the paths she had forsaken. The main newspaper groups supported him from the outset; Lord Bothermey became his devoted standard bearer, and all the resources of modern journalism were exerted in his favour. He was urged in leading articles that would have been fulsome had they referred to any mere mortal leader, to conduct his manifest mission of control and suppression fearlessly and speedily. His popularity with the army, navy, and flying corps, and particularly with the very old and very young officers in these services, was instantaneous and complete. Literature cast off the triviality and scepticism that had overtaken it and flamed to his support. Mr Bloodred Hipkin, the Laureate of Empire, burst into his swan song at his coming and Mr Berandine Shore, overjoyed at the fall of the entire detestable race of politicians, inundated the press with open letters to proclaim him even greater than Mussolini. He was cheered for twenty minutes at the Stock Exchange. The feminine electorate was conquered *en masse* by the Byronic beauty of his profile, the elegance of his gestures, and the extraordinary charm of his smile.

England fell into his hands like a ripe fruit. It was clear that the executive and legislative functions were his for the taking.

CHAPTER TWO

The Coup d'Etat

The Master Spirit was incapable of hesitation. In uniforms of a Cromwellian cut, designed after the most careful consideration of the proper wear for expelling legislative assemblies and made under pressure at remarkable speed, the chiefs of the Duty Paramount movement and a special bodyguard armed with revolvers and swords, marched under his leadership to Westminster at the head of a great popular demonstration. The Houses of Parliament were surrounded. The Police offered a half-hearted resistance, for the Metropolitan Police Commissioner was himself a strong man and could understand what was happening to the world. An attempt, essentially formal, was made to treat this historical march upon Westminster as ordinary traffic and divert it towards Chelsea; this failing, the police, in accordance with a prearranged scheme, evacuated the building, paraded in good order in Parliament Square, and marched off in Indian file, leaving the League in possession. For some minutes Miss Ellen Wilkerson offered a formidable resistance in one of the corridors, but reinforcements arrived, and she was overpowered. The "Talking Shop" had fallen.

The House of Commons was in session and did not seem to know how to get out of it. The Master Spirit, supported by the staff he had gathered about him – except Sir Bussy, who was again unaccountably missing – entered by the Strangers' entrance and came through the division lobby on to the floor of the House. At the significant brown band across the green carpet he stopped short.

The atmosphere of the place was tensely emotional as this tall and slender and yet most portentous figure, supported by the devoted lieutenants his magic had inspired, stood facing the Speaker and his two bewigged satellites. Someone had set the division bells ringing, and the House was crowded, the Labour party clustered thickly to his left, Commander Benworthy bulky and outstanding. There was little talk or noise. The great majority of the members present were silently agape. Some were indignant but many upon the right were manifestly sympathetic. Above, the attendants were attempting, but not very successfully, to clear the Strangers' and Distinguished Strangers' Galleries. The reporters stared or scribbled convulsively and there was a luminous abundance of ladies in their particular gallery.

Methodical and precise as ever, the tapes in the dining- and smoking-rooms had announced, "Dictator enters House with armed force. Business in suspense," and had then ceased their useful function. From behind the Speaker's chair a couple of score of the bodyguard, with swords drawn, had spread out to the left and right and stood now at the salute.

It would have needed a soul entirely devoid of imagination to ignore the profound historical significance of this occasion, and the Master was of imagination all compact. His stern popular. There was a good deal of bumping against liberals who were doing exactly the same thing at a slightly different angle. Mr St George went out stoutly, and as if inadvertently, his hands behind his back. It was as if he had been called away by some private concern and had failed to observe what was going on. His daughter who was also a member followed him briskly. Sir Simon John and Mr Harold Samuel remained whispering together and taking notes until the advancing shadows of physical expulsion were close at hand. Their gestures made it clear to everyone that they considered the Lord Paramount was acting illegally and that they were greatly pleased to score that point against him.

Many of the conservatives were frankly sympathetic with the Lord Paramount. Mr Baldwin was not in the house, but Sir Austin Chamberland stood talking, smiling and looking on, at the side of Lady Asper, who exulted brightly and clapped her pretty hands when Waxton was tackled and overpowered. She seemed eager that more labour members should join in the fray and get similar treatment, and disappointed when they did not do so. Mr Emery, the great fiscal imperialist, stood on a seat the better to watch proceedings and smiled broadly at the whole affair, making movements of benediction. He knew already that he was marked for the Lord Paramount's Council. The Lord Paramount, intent on such particulars, realized suddenly that he was being cheered from the opposition benches. He drew himself up to his full height and bowed gravely.

"*Who goes home?*" a voice cried; and the cry was echoed in the corridors without. It was the time-honoured cry of parliamentary dissolution, that has closed the drama of five hundred parliaments.

determination was mellowed but not weakened by a certain element of awe at his own immense achievement. To this House, if not to this particular chamber, Charles the First had come in pursuit of the tragic destiny that was to bring him to Whitehall; and after him, to better effect had come Cromwell, the great precursor of the present event. Here, through a thousand scenes of storm and conflict, the mighty fabric of the greatest empire the world had ever seen had been welded and reshaped. Here had spoken such mighty rulers and gladiators as Walpole and Pelham, Pitt and Burke, Peel and Palmerston, Gladstone and Disraeli. And now this once so potent assembly had waxed vulgar, senile, labourist, garrulous and ineffective, and the day of rejuvenescence, the restoration of the Phoenix, was at hand. The eyes of the Master Spirit, grave and a little sorrowful, were lifted as if for guidance to the fretted roof and then fell thoughtfully upon the mace, "that bauble," which lay athwart the table before him. He seemed to muse for a moment upon the mighty task he had undertaken, before he addressed himself to the wigged and robed figure at the head of the assembly.

"Mr Speaker," he said, "I must ask you to leave the chair." He turned half-face to the government benches. "Gentlemen, the Ministers of the Crown, I would advise you to yield your portfolios without demur to my secretaries. For the good of His Majesty's realm and the needs of our mighty Empire I must for a time take these things over from you. When England has found her soul again, when her health has been restored, then all her ancient liberties of speech and counsel will return to her again."

For a perceptible interval everyone present might have been a waxwork image, so still and intent did they all stand. It might have been some great historical tableau set out at Madame

Tussaud's. It seemed already history, and for all the length of that pause it was as if the Lord Paramount were rather witnessing what he had done than actually doing it. It became flattened but bright like a coloured picture in a child's book of history...

The action of the piece was resumed by a little significant detail. Two bodyguards came forward and placed themselves at either elbow of the Speaker.

"I protest in the name of the Commons of England," said the Speaker, standing and holding his robes ready to descend.

"Your protest is duly noted," said the Master Spirit, and turning slowly, ordered and motioned his guards to clear the House.

They did their duty without haste or violence.

On the left hand, herding thickly, was this new labour government, this association of vague idealists and socialist adventurers and its supporters. Mr Ramsy McDougal stood against the table, as ever a little apart from his colleagues, an image of unreadiness. Mr Parham had only seen him on one or two occasions before, and looking at him now through the Lord Paramount's eyes, he seemed more gaunt and angular than ever, more like a lonely wind-stripped tree upon some blasted health, more haggard and inaccurate in his questionable handsomeness. He was evidently looking about him for support. His eyes wandered appealingly to the reporters' gallery, to the opposition benches, to the ladies' gallery and to the roof that presumably veiled his God from him, and then they came back to the knots and masses of his own followers. It was clear above the general murmur that he was speaking. He made noises like a cow barking or like a dog which moos. The Lord Paramount heard himself

denounced as "the spirit of unrighteousness." Then there was a appeal to "fair play." Finally something about going to "raise th fiery cross." As two of the League guards approached him, guided by the Lord Paramount's signal, his gestures which indicated a rallying place elsewhere became more emphatic. For a moment he posed tall and commanding, arm lifted, finger pointing heavenward, before he folded himself up and retired.

Behind him Sir Osbert Moses had seemed to be pleading in vain with a sheepish crowd of government supporters for some collective act of protest. Mr Coope, the extremist, was plainly an advocate for violence, but managed nothing. For the most part these labour people seemed as usual only anxious to find out what was considered the right thing to do and to do it as precipitately as possible. The attendants gave them no help, but the League guards herded them like sheep. But Mr Philip Snowfield, very pale and angry, remained in his place, uttering what appeared to be inaudible imprecations. As the guards approached him he moved away from them towards the exit but still turned at intervals to say what were visibly disagreeable things and to thump the floor with his stick. "Mark my words," he could be heard hissing, "you fellows will be sorry for this foolery." Commander Benworthy hovered huge and protective above him. The only actual scuffle was with that left-wing desperado, Waxton, who was dealt with in accordance with the peculiar ju-jutsu of the Lord Paramount's guards. He was carried out face downwards, his hair dragging on the floor.

The other occupants of the government benches decided not to share his fate and remained vertical and unhandled in their slow retreat. Most of them sought a certain dignity of pose, and folded arms, a sideways carriage, and a certain scornfulness were

The Lord Paramount found himself in the handsome passage that leads from the Commons to the Lords. A solitary figure sat there, sobbing quietly. It looked up and revealed the face of that Lord Cato, who was formerly Sir Wilfrid Jameson Jicks. "*I* ought to have done it," he whispered. "*I* ought to have done it months ago." Then his natural generosity reasserted itself and, dashing away a tear, he stood up and held out his hand frankly and brotherly to the Lord Paramount.

"You must help *me* now, for England's sake," said the Lord Paramount.

determination was mellowed but not weakened by a certain element of awe at his own immense achievement. To this House, if not to this particular chamber, Charles the First had come in pursuit of the tragic destiny that was to bring him to Whitehall; and after him, to better effect had come Cromwell, the great precursor of the present event. Here, through a thousand scenes of storm and conflict, the mighty fabric of the greatest empire the world had ever seen had been welded and reshaped. Here had spoken such mighty rulers and gladiators as Walpole and Pelham, Pitt and Burke, Peel and Palmerston, Gladstone and Disraeli. And now this once so potent assembly had waxed vulgar, senile, labourist, garrulous and ineffective, and the day of rejuvenescence, the restoration of the Phoenix, was at hand. The eyes of the Master Spirit, grave and a little sorrowful, were lifted as if for guidance to the fretted roof and then fell thoughtfully upon the mace, "that bauble," which lay athwart the table before him. He seemed to muse for a moment upon the mighty task he had undertaken, before he addressed himself to the wigged and robed figure at the head of the assembly.

"Mr Speaker," he said, "I must ask you to leave the chair." He turned half-face to the government benches. "Gentlemen, the Ministers of the Crown, I would advise you to yield your portfolios without demur to my secretaries. For the good of His Majesty's realm and the needs of our mighty Empire I must for a time take these things over from you. When England has found her soul again, when her health has been restored, then all her ancient liberties of speech and counsel will return to her again."

For a perceptible interval everyone present might have been a waxwork image, so still and intent did they all stand. It might have been some great historical tableau set out at Madame

Tussaud's. It seemed already history, and for all the length of that pause it was as if the Lord Paramount were rather witnessing what he had done than actually doing it. It became flattened but bright like a coloured picture in a child's book of history...

The action of the piece was resumed by a little significant detail. Two bodyguards came forward and placed themselves at either elbow of the Speaker.

"I protest in the name of the Commons of England," said the Speaker, standing and holding his robes ready to descend.

"Your protest is duly noted," said the Master Spirit, and turning slowly, ordered and motioned his guards to clear the House.

They did their duty without haste or violence.

On the left hand, herding thickly, was this new labour government, this association of vague idealists and socialist adventurers and its supporters. Mr Ramsy McDougal stood against the table, as ever a little apart from his colleagues, an image of unreadiness. Mr Parham had only seen him on one or two occasions before, and looking at him now through the Lord Paramount's eyes, he seemed more gaunt and angular than ever, more like a lonely wind-stripped tree upon some blasted health, more haggard and inaccurate in his questionable handsomeness. He was evidently looking about him for support. His eyes wandered appealingly to the reporters' gallery, to the opposition benches, to the ladies' gallery and to the roof that presumably veiled his God from him, and then they came back to the knots and masses of his own followers. It was clear above the general murmur that he was speaking. He made noises like a cow barking or like a dog which moos. The Lord Paramount heard himself denounced as "the spirit of unrighteousness." Then there was an appeal to "fair play." Finally something about going to "raise the fiery cross." As two of the League guards approached him, guided by the Lord Paramount's signal, his gestures which indicated a rallying place elsewhere became more emphatic. For a moment he posed tall and commanding, arm lifted, finger pointing heavenward, before he folded himself up and retired.

Behind him Sir Osbert Moses had seemed to be pleading in vain with a sheepish crowd of government supporters for some collective act of protest. Mr Coope, the extremist, was plainly an advocate for violence, but managed nothing. For the most part these labour people seemed as usual only anxious to find out what was considered the right thing to do and to do it as precipitately as possible. The attendants gave them no help, but the League guards herded them like sheep. But Mr Philip Snowfield, very pale and angry, remained in his place, uttering what appeared to be inaudible imprecations. As the guards approached him he moved away from them towards the exit but still turned at intervals to say what were visibly disagreeable things and to thump the floor with his stick. "Mark my words," he could be heard hissing, "you fellows will be sorry for this foolery." Commander Benworthy hovered huge and protective above him. The only actual scuffle was with that left-wing desperado, Waxton, who was dealt with in accordance with the peculiar ju-jutsu of the Lord Paramount's guards. He was carried out face downwards, his hair dragging on the floor.

The other occupants of the government benches decided not to share his fate and remained vertical and unhandled in their slow retreat. Most of them sought a certain dignity of pose, and folded arms, a sideways carriage, and a certain scornfulness were popular. There was a good deal of bumping against liberals who were doing exactly the same thing at a slightly different angle. Mr St George went out stoutly, and as if inadvertently, his hands behind his back. It was as if he had been called away by some private concern and had failed to observe what was going on. His daughter who was also a member followed him briskly. Sir Simon John and Mr Harold Samuel remained whispering together and taking notes until the advancing shadows of physical expulsion were close at hand. Their gestures made it clear to everyone that they considered the Lord Paramount was acting illegally and that they were greatly pleased to score that point against him.

Many of the conservatives were frankly sympathetic with the Lord Paramount. Mr Baldmin was not in the house, but Sir Austin Chamberland stood talking, smiling and looking on, at the side of Lady Asper, who exulted brightly and clapped her pretty hands when Waxton was tackled and overpowered. She seemed eager that more labour members should join in the fray and get similar treatment, and disappointed when they did not do so. Mr Emery, the great fiscal imperialist, stood on a seat the better to watch proceedings and smiled broadly at the whole affair, making movements of benediction. He knew already that he was marked for the Lord Paramount's Council. The Lord Paramount, intent on such particulars, realized suddenly that he was being cheered from the opposition benches. He drew himself up to his full height and bowed gravely.

"Who goes home?" a voice cried; and the cry was echoed in the corridors without. It was the time-honoured cry of parliamentary dissolution, that has closed the drama of five hundred parliaments.

The Lord Paramount found himself in the handsome passage that leads from the Commons to the Lords. A solitary figure sat there, sobbing quietly. It looked up and revealed the face of that Lord Cato, who was formerly Sir Wilfrid Jameson Jicks. "*I* ought to have done it," he whispered. "*I* ought to have done it months ago." Then his natural generosity reasserted itself and, dashing away a tear, he stood up and held out his hand frankly and brotherly to the Lord Paramount.

"You must help *me* now, for England's sake," said the Lord Paramount.

CHAPTER THREE

How London Took the News

The state of London outside the House of Commons on that memorable May evening was one of gaping astonishment. As the twilight deepened to night and the illuminated advertisements grew bright, the late editions of the evening papers gave the first intimations of the coup d'état, and an increasing driftage of people towards Westminster began. The police, still functioning normally outside Palace Yard, were increased as the crowds, entirely unaggressive and orderly crowds, thickened. Some of the rougher elements from Pimlico and Chelsea showed a mild riotousness, but they were kept well in hand. The guards were under arms in Wellington Barracks, and the normal protection of Buckingham Palace was increased, but there was no need of intervention to protect the monarchy. No one in authority attempted to invoke the military against the Master Paramount, and it is open to question whether the officers, and particularly the junior officers, would have consented to act in such a case. Since the days of the Curragh mutiny there has always been an implicit limit to the powers of the politicians over the army. As the expelled Members of Parliament came out by the various exits into the streets, they had receptions dependent upon their notoriety and popularity. Generally the crowd showed nothing but an amused sympathy for their débâcle. Their names were shouted after them when they were recognized, usually with the addition of "Good old"—so and so. Women members were addressed affectionately by their Christian names when these were known.

Many of them got away unobserved. The idea that they were the people's agents and representatives had faded out of English life. They were simply people who had "got into Parliament" and now were being turned out of it. When later on the Master Paramount and the chiefs of the Duty Paramount League emerged, they were received, not so much with enthusiasm as with an observant acquiescence. Few failed to mark the great distinction of the Master's presence. The staffs of the new rulers repaired to Downing Street to accelerate the departure of the private establishments of the dismissed ministers and to prepare for the installation of the heads of the provisional government in the official residences. Until a very late hour that night an affectionate crowd besieged Buckingham Palace "to see," as they put it, "that the King was all right." At intervals members of the Royal Family appeared to reassure the people and were received with loyal cries and the better-known verses of the National Anthem. There was no demand for speeches and no interchange of views. It was a *rapprochement* too deep for words.

Next day the remarkable news in the morning papers filled London with crowds of visitors from the suburbs and provincial towns. They came up to see what was going on, wandered about for the day, and went home again. All day long, large crowds stagnated about the Houses of Parliament. A multitude of hawkers, selling buns, winkles, oranges, and suchlike provender, did a flourishing trade. Attempts at oratory were suppressed by the police, both there and in Trafalgar Square.

So the new régime took possession. The Crown, as became a constitutional monarchy, accepted the new state of affairs without comment or any gesture of disapproval. A special levee and a garden party to entertain the League of Duty Paramount were arranged at Buckingham Palace, and the Lord Paramount was photographed, for worldwide publicity, tall and erect, in an attitude of firm but entirely respectful resolution, at his monarch's right hand. He was wearing the livery of a Cabinet Minister, the Garter, in which order a timely vacancy had occurred, and the plaque of the Order of Merit. His white and beautifully chiselled face was very grave and still.

CHAPTER FOUR

The Grand Council in Session

With a tact and sagacity as great as his courage, the Lord Paramount gathered about him a number of counsellors who were in effect his ministers. He consulted and directed them, but they had no collective power; their only collective function was cooperation upon the schemes he outlined for their guidance. Occasionally in council they would offer suggestions which were received with attention, considered and commented upon by the Lord Paramount. Sometimes, but rarely, their suggestions would be allowed to sway the course of the national policy. But on the whole he preferred that they should come to him privately and individually with their proposals, rather than interrupt the proceedings of the Council meetings.

The Council included all that was best among the leaders of English life. The mighty barons of the popular press were there, and prominently Lord Bothermey. The chief military, naval and air experts were intermittently represented. Coal and steel magnates were well in evidence, particularly those most closely associated with armament firms, and one or two rather evasive personalities of the Sir Bussy Woodcock type attended by command. Sir Bussy might or might not be there; he continued to be difficult to locate. He seemed to become present suddenly and then to become conspicuously absent. The Governor of the Bank of England was present ex officio, though the Lord Paramount found he smiled far too much and said far too little, and there were several leading representatives of the Big Five, who also proved to be markedly silent men with a far-away facial habit. Labour was represented at the Lord Paramount's invitation, by Mr J H Humbus, and women by the Countess of Crum and Craythorpe. Lord Cato was of course a member, and, for some reason that the Lord Paramount never had very clear in his mind, Mr Brimstone Burchell seemed always to be coming in or going out or talking in much too audible undertones to someone while the Council was in session. No one had asked him; he just came. It was difficult to find an appropriate moment to say something about it. On the whole he seemed to be well disposed and eager to take entire charge of army, navy, air force, munitions, finance, or any other leading function which might be entrusted to him. In addition to these already prominent members a number of vigorous personalities hitherto unknown to British public life, either chosen from among "Mr Parham's Young Men," scions of noble families, or connected with the militant side of the Duty Paramount League, took a silently active part in the proceedings. Alfred Mumby, Colonel Fitz Martin, Ronald Carberry, Sir Horatio Wrex, and the young Duke of Norham, were among the chief of these. Mrs Pinchot, the only reporter present, sat in a little low chair at the Lord Paramount's right hand and recorded all that happened in shorthand in a gilt-edged notebook. Hereward Jackson, the faithful disciple, also hovered helpfully close to him.

The procedure was very simple and straightforward. The Council would assemble or be collected according to the alacrity of the individual members, and the Lord Paramount would enter quite informally, waving a hand to this man and greeting that, and so make his way to the head of the table. There he would stand; Hereward Jackson would say "Ssh!" and everyone standing or sitting or leaning against the wall would cease to gossip and turn to listen. Explicitly and simply the Lord Paramount would put his views to them. It was very like a college lecturer coming in and talking to a batch of intelligent and sympathetic students. He would explain his policy, say why this had to be done or that, and indicate who it was should undertake whatever task opened before them. An hour or even more might be spent in this way. Then he would drop into his seat, and there would be questions, mostly of an elucidatory nature, a few comments, a suggestion or so, and, with a smile and a friendly word of dismissal, everything was over, and the Council went about its business, each man to do what he knew to be his duty. So simple a task was government now that the follies of party, the presumption and manoeuvres of elected people, the confusion and dishonesties inseparable from the democratic method had been swept aside.

The third meeting of the Council was the most important of the earlier series, for then it was that the Lord Paramount gave these heads of the national life a résumé of the policy he proposed to pursue.

Let them consider at first, he said, the position and the manifest dangers and destinies of this dear England of ours and its Empire to which they were all devoted. He would ask them to regard the world as a whole, not to think of it in a parochial spirit, but broadly and sanely, looking beyond the immediate tomorrow. Directly they did so they would begin to realize the existence and development of a great world struggle, which was determined by geography and by history, which was indeed in the very nature of things. The lines of that struggle shaped themselves, rationally, logically, inevitably. Everything else in the world should be subordinated to that.

Something almost confidential crept into his manner, and the Council became very silent and attentive. He indicated regions upon the green baize table before him by sweeping gestures of his hands and arms, and his voice sank.

"Here," said the Lord Paramount, "in the very centre of the Old World, illimitably vast, potentially more powerful than most of the rest of the world put together – " he paused dramatically – " is *Russia*. It really does not matter in the least whether she is Czarist or Bolshevik. She is the final danger – the overwhelming enemy. Grow she must. She has space. She has immense resources. She strikes at us, through Turkey as always, through Afghanistan as always, and now through China. Instinctively she does that – necessarily. I do not blame her. But preserve ourselves we must. What will Germany do? Cleave to the East? Cleave to the West? Who can tell? A student nation, a secondary people, a disputed territory. We win her if we can, but I do not count on her. The policy imposed upon the rest of the world is plain. We must circumvent Russia; we must encircle this threat of the Great Plains before it overwhelms us. As we encircled the lesser threat of the Hohenzollerns. In time. On the West, here, we outflank her with our ally France and Poland her pupil; on the East with our ally Japan. We reach at her through India. We strive to point the spearhead of Afghanistan against her. We hold Gibraltar on her account; we watch Constantinople on her account. America is drawn in with us, necessarily our ally, willy-nilly, because she cannot let Russia strike through China to the sea. There you have the situation of the world. Broadly and boldly seen. Fraught with immense danger - yes. Tragic - if you will. But fraught also with limitless possibilities of devotion and courage."

The Lord Paramount paused, and a murumr of admiration went round the gathering. Mr Brimstone Burchell's head nodded like a Chinese automation's to express his approval. The statement was so perfectly lucid, so direct and compact. Yet it was identically the same speech that Mr Parham had delivered to Sir Bussy, Mr Hamp, Camelford, and the young American only a month or so previously, at the dinner table of the former! How different now was its reception when it came from the lips of the Lord Paramount speaking to understanding minds! No carping criticism, or attempts to disregard and ignore, no preposterous alternatives of world organization and the like follies, no intimation of any such alternatives. If Sir Bussy had whispered his habitual monosyllable it was done inaudibly.

"And that being our general situation," the Lord Paramount continued, "which is the most becoming thing for a Great Nation to do? To face its Destiny of leadership and championship, open-eyed and resolute, or to wait, lost in petty disputes, blinded by small considerations, until the inevitable antagonist, grown strong and self-conscious, its vast realms organized and productive, China assimilated and India sympathetic and mutinous against its established rulers, strikes at the sceptre in its negligent hands — maybe strikes the sceptre clean out of its negligent hands? Is it necessary to ask that question of the

Council of the British peoples? And knowing your answer to be what it must be, then plainly the time for Duty and Action is now. I exhort you to weigh with me the preparations and the strategy that have to be the guiding form of our national policy from this time forth. The time to rally western Europe is now. The time to call plainly to America to take up her part in this gigantic struggle is now."

This time the little man sitting at the table was clearly heard. His "Gaw!" was deep and distinct.

"Sir Bussy," said the Lord Paramount in a penetrating aside, "for six long years you have said that word 'Gaw' at me, and I have borne with you. Say it no more."

He did not even pause for an answer, but went on at once to sketch the determinations before the Council.

"It is my intention," he said, "so soon as home affairs are regularized, to make an informal tour of Europe. Here, between these four walls, I can speak freely of an adventure we all have at heart, the gallant efforts of Prince Otto von Barheim to overthrow the uncongenial republican régime that now disfigures, misrepresents, and humiliates the loyal and valiant German people. It is a lukewarm thing, half radical and Bolshevist and half patriotic, and Germany is minded to spew it out. I have had communications from a very trustworthy source, and I can say with confidence that that adventure is on the high road to success. Prince Otto, like myself, has a profound understanding of the philosophy of history, and like myself he recalls a great nation to its destiny. The good sword of Germany may soon be waiting in its scabbard for our signal.

"Yes! I know what you think at this moment, but, believe me, it will be with the consent of France. Nevermore will Britain move without France. M. Parème shall be consulted and I will see to that. The situation would be delicate had we still a parliamentary régime. Happily no questions in the House now can disturb our negotiations. Snowfield is gagged and Benworthy silenced. Trust France. She is fully aware that now it is we alone who stand between her and a Geman-Italian combination. We reconcile. The French mind is realistic, logical and patriotic. The other European nations may need Dictators, but in France, the Republic is Dictator; the army and the nation are one, and, guaranteed security, suitably compensated in Africa and Nearer Asia, France will be ready to take her proper place in the defence of the West against its final danger. The age-long feud of the Rhineland draws to an end. The peace of Charlemagne returns. Even the speeches of M. Parème lose their belligerent note. Such little matters as the language question in Alsace and various repayments and guarantees find their level of unimportance. We have been living too much in the counting house. Europe draws together under pressure from the East and from the West. These things I propose to confirm by personal interviews with the men I shall find in charge of the European nations. Then to our course of action: first a renewal, a confirmation and intensification of the blockade of Russia – by all Europe, by the United Strong Men of Europe; secondly a vigorous joint intervention to restore the predominance of European ideas and European finance in China; thirdly a direct challenge to Russian propaganda in India and Persia, a propaganda in reality political – social and economic now only in phrase and pretension. If we mean to encircle this mighty threat to all we hold dear, then the time for encirclement is here and now. And so, when at last the Day comes it will not be the Slav aggressive we shall have facing us, but the Slav anticipated and at bay."

The Lord Paramount paused and did his best to ignore the one flaw upon that perfect gathering. Sir Bussy, looking exceedingly small and wicked and drumming softly on the table with his stumpy fingers, spoke, addressing, as it were, the blank universe. "And how is America going to take this sort of stuff?"

"She will be with us."

"She may have other ideas."

"She *has* to be with us," said the Lord Paramount with a rising intonation, and a murmur of approval came from the corner in which Lord Cato was standing. His face was very pink, and his little eyes were round and bright. His bearing had the unsubdued aggressiveness of an unsmacked child's. He had always regarded America as impertinent and in need of a good snubbing and, if need be, of further chastening. He could not believe that a nation so new could really consist of grown-up people.

"The Americans," Sir Bussy informed the world, "don't learn history in English public schools."

No one regarded him.

"I have begun by sketching the frame of circumstance about our national life," the Lord Paramount resumed, "because the small troubles of internal politics – and relatively they are very small – fall into place directly we recognize the fact that we are a militant people, that our empire is a mighty camp of training for the achievement of our enduring leadership. To this great struggle all our history is a crescendo. When you tell me that we have a million unemployed I rejoice to think we have that much man power free at once for the great adventure. Before 1914 our industrial system had a margin, a necessary margin of unemployment of about five to nine per cent. Now that margin has increased to eleven or twelve percent – I will not trouble about the exact figures. A large element of these unemployed come, out of the coal-mining industry, which was abnormally inflated after the war. But our gross production has not diminished. Note that! What we are witnessing is a worldwide process, in which industry produces as much as ever, or more, but has so increased its efficiency that it calls for fewer hands. Clearly this so-called unemployment is really a release of energy. These people, in many cases young men, must be taken in hand and trained for other ends. The women can go into munitions. If only on account of unemployment, our great Empire needs to take a gallant and aggressive line. What we have saved we must spend. We must not bury our talent in out-of-work sloth. I am no Individualist, I am no Socialist; these are phrases left over by the Nineteenth Century, and little meaning remains in them now. But I say, of him who does not work for his country, neither shall he eat in it, and that he who will not work generously must be made to work hard; and I say also that wealth that is not active and productive for our imperial ends needs to be called upon to justify itself. Wantoning in pleasure cities, lavish entertainments in huge hotels, jazz expenditure, must cease. A special tax on champagne... Yes a tax on champagne. It is poison for soul and body. No more nightclubs for London. A censorship of suggestive plays and books. Criticism by honest police officials – worthy, direct-minded men. Golf only for hygienic ends. Race meetings without special trains. Even the shooting and hunting restrained. Service! Everywhere Service. Duty Paramount. In High and Low alike. These things have been said already upon the slighter stage of Italy; it is for us to say them now, imperially, in tones of thunder, to the very ends of the earth."

It seemed that he had done. In the appreciative silence that ensued, the noise of an elderly and edentate gentleman, talking through a thick moustache, became evident. The speaker had been at the back of the cluster to the right of the Lord Paramount, but now he came forward in a state of agitated resolution, and grasping with his right hand the back of the chair in which Sir Bussy was sitting, crossing his legs and leaning forward at an almost perilous angle, he gesticulated in an oratorical manner with his left. The noise he made rose and fell. Word was not separated from word, but now and then a cough snapped off a length of it. It was a sort of ectoplasmic speech. Very like ectoplasm. Ectoplasm? Ectoplasm?

(For a moment the mind of the Lord Paramount was blurred.)

This venerable figure was Lord Bylass of Brayne. At intervals it was possible to distinguish the submerged forms of such words and phrases as "tariff"..."adequate protection"..."safeguarding" ..."dumping"..."insensate foreign competition"..."colonial preference"..."an empire sufficient unto itself"..."capable, sir, of absorbing every willing worker in the country."

For three or four minutes the Lord Paramount endured this interruption with patient dignity, and then he held up a hand to signify that he had heard sufficient for a reply.

"A state is a militant organization, and a militant organization that is healthy and complete must be militant through and through," he began, with that illuminating directness which had made him the leader and master of all these men. "Tariffs, Lord Bylass, are now the normal everyday method of that same conflict for existence between states which is the substance of all history and which finds its highest, noblest expression in war. By means of tariffs, Lord Bylass, we protect our economic life from confusion with the economic life of other states, we ensure the integrity of our resources against the day of trial, we sustain our allies and attack the social balance and well being of our enemies and competitors. Here in this council, free from eavesdroppers, we can ignore the pretence that tariffs are designed for the enrichment or security of the common citizen and that they, by themselves, can do anything to absorb unemployed workers. Forgive me, Lord Bylass, if I seem to contradict your arguments while accepting your conclusions. Tariffs do not enrich a country. They cannot do, they never have done, anything of the sort. That is a deception, and I think a harmful deception, that the squalid necessities of that system of elective government we have so happily set aside have forced upon politicians. We can drop it here and now. Tariffs, like every other form of struggle, involve and require sacrifices. If they create employment in one trade by excluding or handicapping the foreign product, then manifestly they must destroy it in another which has hitherto exported goods in payment, direct or indirect, for the newly protected commodity. A tariff is a method of substituting an inconvenient production for a convenient one. In order to cause greater inconvenience elsewhere. The case for protection rests on grounds higher and nobler than considerations of material advantage or disadvantage. We must have tariffs and pay for tariffs, just as we must have armies and navies and pay for them. Why? Because they are the continuing intimation of our national integrity. Our guns and bombs explode only during the war phase, but a tariff sustains a perpetual friction and menace; it injures while we sleep. And I repeat, for it is the very essence of our faith, it is the cardinal belief of our League of Duty Paramount that a sovereign state, which boasts a history and unfurls a flag, must remain either a militant state through and through, pressing its rivals as hard as it can in every possible way, during peace time and war time alike, or it must become a decadent and useless absurdity fit only to be swept into the cosmopolitan dustbin."

The ringing voice ceased. Lord Bylass, who had resumed his perpendicular attitude during the reply of the Lord Paramount, said something either in the nature of approval, disapproval, extension, or qualification of what had gone before, and after perhaps a dozen minor questions had been raised and compactly disposed of the Council settled down to the apportionment of the mighty tasks in hand. First one and then another would sketch his conception of cooperation, and often the Lord Paramount would say no more than "Do it" or "Wait" or "Raise that again in a week's time" or "Not like that." A few of the members for whom there seemed to be no immediate call withdrew to an ante-room to talk together over the tea, sherry, and lemonade served there. Some of the more restless spirits departed altogether. Among these was Sir Bussy Woodcock.

The mind of the Lord Paramount seemed to go after him and watch him and yet it knew what he would do.

He was to be seen standing pensive on the doorstep of No. 10, Downing Street, that doorstep which has been trodden by every famous man in British affairs for a couple of centuries, and looking with his mouth askew at the dense inexpressive crowd which blocked the opening into Whitehall. The police had formed a cordon, and except for the chauffeurs of the waiting automobiles there were only a few pressmen, press photographers and obvious plain-clothes men standing about in the street itself. But beyond was that mysterious still congestion of the English people, almost cow-like in its collective regard, giving no intimations of its feelings, if indeed it had any feelings, towards this gallant new rule which had relieved it of any lingering illusions about self-government. It was an almost completely silent crowd, save for the yapping of the vendors of the Lord Paramount's photographs. The afternoon was warm and overcast with grey clouds that seemed like everything else to be awaiting orders. The very policemen were lost in passive expectation. Everybody was accepting the Lord Paramount inertly. Sir Bussy remained quite still for nearly a minute. "*Gaw,*" he whispered at last and turned slowly towards the little gate to his right that led down the steps to the Horse Guards Parade.

With his customary foresight he had sent his car round there, where the crowd was inconsiderable.

As he vanished through the gate a plain-clothes policeman with an affectation of nonchalance that would not have deceived a baby, detached himself from his fellows and strolled after him. *By order!*

In another twenty minutes the session was over and the Council was actively dispersing.

Lanes were made in the crowd by the departing automobiles. Its more advantageously situated ranks were privileged to see, afar off, the Lord Paramount himself, accompanied by his little dark woman secretary and a tall, slender, devoted-looking man who was carrying a huge portfolio, cross swiftly from No. 10 to the Foreign Office and vanish under its archway.

Towards seven the Lord Paramount reappeared and went in the big new Rolls-Royce he had purchased on behalf of the nation, to the War Office, and there he remained until long after midnight.

CHAPTER FIVE

The Lord Paramount Studies his Weapons

There were moments even in the opening phase of this great adventure of the Lord Paramount when it was difficult for him to believe himself true, but his sense of duty to those he was lifting out of their ten-year post-war lethargy made him conceal these instants – for they were no more than instants – of weakness from everyone about him, even from the faithful and sustaining Mrs Pinchot and the indefatigable Hereward Jackson. His ordinary state of mind was one of profound, of almost exultant admiration for his own new vigour of purpose and action. He knew that his ascendancy meant a march towards war, war on a vaster and handsomer scale than had ever yet illuminated the page of history. This might have dismayed a lesser soul. But he knew himself the successor of Napoleon and Cæsar and Alexander and Sargon, adequate to the task before him. And he knew what history demands of great nations. His mission was to make history and to make it larger and heavier with a greater displacement of the fluidities of life than it had ever been made before.

As he made it he wrote it in his mind. He saw his own record, the story of his war, towering up at the end of the great series of autobiographic war histories from Thucydides to Colonel Lawrence and Winston Churchill. *Parham De Bello Asiatico.* That he would do in the golden days of rest, after the victory. It was pleasant to anticipate those crowning literary hours amidst the stresses of present things. He would find himself making character sketches of himself and telling in the third person of his acts and decisions in the recognized style of such records.

It was queer at times how strongly his anticipations of this record imposed themselves upon his mind. There were phases and moments when he did not so much seem to be doing and experiencing things as relating them to himself.

It was manifest that among the most urgent of his duties was the rapid acquisition of a broad and exact knowledge of the equipment and possibilities of the armed forces of the Empire. Of these he had now to be the directive head, the supreme commander. On him would fall the ultimate responsibility in the day of battle. Other men might advise him, but it was he who must control, and who can control without adequate knowledge? Lucky for him that his mind was as swift as an eagle and that he could grasp the import of a scheme while lesser intelligences still struggled with its preliminary details.

He sought among ex-war ministers, sea lords, and high permanent officials in the combatant departments, for informants and experts with whom he could work. It was profoundly important to know and take the measure of all such men. And they had to know him, they had to experience his personal magnetism and be quick to understand and ready to obey him. At first there was some difficulty in getting the right tone. In all the fighting services there is an habitual distrust of politicians, an ingrained disposition to humbug and hoodwink interfering civilians, and this tradition of reserve was sufficiently strong to retard their first surrender to the Lord Paramount's charm and energy, for some time.

Moreover, there were many restraints and reservations between different sections of the services that were hard to overcome. Most of these men betrayed not only the enthusiasm but the narrowness of the specialist's concentrated mind. Air experts ridiculed battleships; naval men showed a quiet contempt for the air; gas was a sore subject with nearly everybody; gunners considered everything else subsidiary to well-directed gunfire, and the tank people despised sea, air, gunfire, and chemical warfare in nearly equal proportions. "We go through," was their refrain. There were even men who held that the spearhead of warfare was propaganda and that the end to which all other operations must be directed was the production of a certain state of mind (variously defined and described) in the enemy government and population. The Empire was, in fact, partially prepared for every conceivable sort of warfare with every conceivable and many inconceivable antagonists, and apart from a common contempt for pacificists as "damned fools" and for cosmopolitans as dreamers and scoundrels, its defenders did not as yet possess an idea in common to ensure their co-operation when the moment of conflict came.

Such were the fruits of our all too copious modern inventiveness and our all too destructive criticism of simple political issues. Such were the consequences of a disputatious parliamentary system and the lack of any single dominating will. The navy was experimenting with big submarines and little submarines, with submarines that carried aircraft inside them and submarines that could come out on land and even climb cliffs, with aircraft carriers and smoke screens, and new types of cruiser; the gunners were experimenting; the army was having a delightful time with tanks, little tanks and big tanks, hideous and ridiculous and frightful and stupendous tanks, tanks that were convertible at a pinch into barges, and tanks that would suddenly expand wings and make long flying hops, and tanks that became field kitchens and bathrooms; the air force killed its two young men or more a week with patient regularity, elaborating incredible stunts; Gas Warfare was experimenting; each was going its own way irrespective of the others, each was doing its best to crab the others. The Lord Paramount went hither and thither, inspecting contrivances that their promoters declared to be marvellous and meeting a series of oldish young and youngish old men, soured by the fermentation of extravagant hopes.

Sir Bussy, an unwilling consultant upon many of these expeditions, found a phrase for them so lacking in dignity that for a time it troubled the Lord Paramount's mind.

"Like a lot of damned schoolboys," said Sir Bussy, "mucking about with toy guns and chemical sets in an attic. Each one on his own – just as disconnected as he can be. With unlimited pocket money. What do they think they are up to? What do they think it is for – all this damned militarism? They don't know. They lost connection long ago, and there they are. They'll just set the place on fire. What else do you expect of them?"

The Lord Paramount made no reply, but his swift mind tackled the challenge. He was capable of learning even from an enemy.

"Lost connection," that was the illuminating phrase.

Disconnected – that was the word. Because they had had no one and no great idea to marshal them in order and unify their efforts. They were the scattered parts of a great war machine which had quietly disarticulated itself after 1918 and followed its divergent traditions and instincts, and it was for him to assemble them into co-operation again. After that remark of Sir Bussy's he knew exactly what to say to these forgotten and unhonoured experts. He knew the one thing of which they stood in need: Connection. To everyone he spoke of the nature of the campaign ahead and of the particular part to be played in it.

That was the magic touch for which they had been waiting. It was wonderful how these sorely neglected men brightened at his words. He made them see – Russia; he projected the minds of the airmen towards mighty raids amidst the mountains of central Asia and over the dark plains of eastern Europe; he lit the eyes of the special undersens services with the words "a relentless blockade"; he asked the mechanized soldiers how they would go over steppes and reminded them darkly of the prophetic fact that the first writing on the pioneer tank had been in Russian. To the naval men he spoke also of another task. "While we do our work in the Old World, you are the sure shield between us and the follies of the New."

Yes, that meant America, but the word 'America' was never said. America which might do anything, which might even go "modern" and break with history – even her own brief and limited history. The fewer years she was given to think before the crisis came, the better for the traditions of our old world.

Many of these brave, ingenious men to whom the Lord Paramount came were sick at heart with hope deferred. Year by year they had invented, contrived, and organized, and still the peace held. There were breezes, but these died away. These workers in the obscurity read pacificist articles in the newspapers;

they heard continually of a League of Nations that was to make a futility of all the dear lethal inventions they had given the best of their years to perfect. A clamour for economics, the bitter ingratitude of retrenchment, threatened them. He brought new life and hope to their despondent souls.

From amidst the miscellany of experts and officials the figure of a certain General Gerson emerged gradually to a sort of pre-eminence. He emerged by a kind of innate necessity. He seemed to know more than the others and to have a more exhaustive knowledge. He had a genius for comprehensive war plans. There was something quintessential about him, as though he concentrated all that Mr Parham had ever read, seen, thought, or felt about soldiers. Undeniably he had force. He was the man to whom it became more and more natural to turn in any doubtful matter. He was presently almost officially the Lord Paramount's right hand in military things. It was not that the Lord Paramount chose him so much as that he arrived. He became the embodiment of the material side of power. He was the sword – or shall we say the hand grenade? – to the Lord Paramount's guiding brain and will. He was his necessary complement. He translated imperial vision into practical reality.

He was not exactly a prepossessing person. His solid worth had to be discovered without extraneous aid. He was sturdily build, short and rather thick set, with exceptionally long, large, and hairy hands. His head was small and bomb-shaped and covered with a wiry fuzz. His nose was short but not insignificant, a concentrated, wilful nose. His mouth was large, vituperative in form when open, and accustomed to shut with emphasis. Generally he kept it shut. His bristling moustache was a concession to military tradition rather than an ornament, and his yellow skin was blue spotted as the result of an accident with some new explosive powder. One eye, because of that same accident, was of glass; it maintained an expression of implacable will, while its fellow, alert and bright brown, gathered information. His eyebrows were the fierce little brothers of his moustache. He wore uniform whenever he could, for he despised "mufti men," but also he despised the splendours of full uniform. He liked to be a little soiled. He liked common and rather dirty food eaten standing, with the fingers instead of forks, and he resorted to harsh and violent exercises to keep fit.

His fitness was amazing, a fierce fitness. "In this world," he said, "the fittest survive." But he despised the mawkish games of feebler men. In the country, when he could, he cut down trees with great swiftness and animosity; or he pursued and threw over astonished and over-domesticated cows, rodeo-fashion. In towns, he would climb swiftly up the backs of high houses and down again, or box, or work an electric drill and excavate and repave back yards. The electric drill bucked up the neighbours tremendously and created a hostile audience that was of use in checking any tendency to slack off. On such occasions he dressed lightly and exposed and ventilated an impressive breadth of hairy chest.

The Lord Paramount was more and more compelled by the logic of his own undertakings to respect and defer to this heroic associate as time went on, but he would not have looked like him for the lordship of a dozen worlds.

From the first the advice of General Gerson had something of the dictatorial.

"You ought to do so and so," he would say and add compactly, "they expect it of you." And the Lord Paramount would realize that that was so.

It was, for example, borne in upon him through something in the bearing and tone of General Gerson that it behoved him to display a certain temerity in his attitude to the various new, ingenious, and frightful things that were being accumulated to ensure the peace of the Empire. It was not in the nature of the Lord Paramount to shrink from personal danger, but he might have been disposed to husband his time and nervous energy in regard to those things, if it had not been for Gerson's influence. Gerson was hard. And a ruler who rules Gerson must be hard also. A certain hardness is a necessary part of greatness. Good to be reminded of that. At times he found himself sustaining his own determination by talking to himself in quite the old Parham fashion. "I owe it to myself," he said. "I owe it to the world."

So he looped the loop over London, holding tight and keeping his face still and calm. He wore strange and dreadful-looking gas masks and went into chambers of vaporous abomination, where instant death would have been the result of a pin prick to his nozzle. It was a pity his intrepid face was so disguised, for it would have been well for weaker-spirited men to mark its observant calm. Rather reluctantly he had to see a considerable number of cats, sheep, and dogs demoralized and killed by poison gas, the precious secret of General Gerson's department, that Gas L of which Camelford had spoken, for which no antidote was known. It seemed to hurt damnably in the two or three minutes before the final collapse. Unless all forms of animal expression are a lie, it was death by intolerable torture. "I owe it," he repeated, for there was mercy in his nature.

"This gas we do not use," he said firmly, "except as an ultimate resort."

"War," said Gerson, sighing contentedly as the last victim ceased to writhe, "war *is* an ultimate resort."

The Lord Paramount made no answer because he felt he might be sick. He seemed to have Mr Parham's stomach, and very often in those feats of hardihood he had occasion to feel sick. He spent some chilly and clammy hours at the bottom of the Solent, and he raced at twenty miles an hour in a leaping, bumping tank across the rough of Liss Forest, and both occasions tested him out. He wore *boules quiés* and fired immense chest-flattening guns by touching a button, and he was wetted to the skin and made sickest of all by tearing down the Channel against a stiff south-wester at forty miles an hour in a new mystery boat that was three parts giant torpedo.

"It was the lot of Nelson too," he said, coming ashore greenly triumphant but empty to the depths of his being. "His heart kept in the right place even if his stomach betrayed him..."

CHAPTER SIX

The Logic of War

Several times did the Lord Paramount return to the topic of poison gas with Gerson. He did not want it to be used, but at the same time the logic of war made him anxious to be sure of an effective supply. Camelford's threat of holding it up haunted him with a very tiresome persistence. And Gerson had been a poison gas expert.

The Lord Paramount wanted war to be magnificent. Wars are the red letters that illuminate the page of history. The resolute tramp of infantry, the inspiring jingle and clatter of cavalry, the mounting thunder of the guns; that was the music to which history had gone since history was worthy of being called history, and he wished that the old tunes could still be played and history still march to them. Some of these new machines and new methods, he perceived, had the hardness and intolerance of a scientific thesis; they despiritualized warfare, they made it indiscriminate; almost they abolished heroism in favour of ingenuity and persistence, these scientific virtues. At the climax men would be just carried forward willy-nilly. He would gladly have subscribed to any common understanding to eliminate the aeroplane, the submarine, and all gas from civilized hostilities, as bacteria and explosive bullets have already been eliminated. But Gerson would have none of these exclusions. "War is war," said he, "and what kills and breaks the spirit best is what you have to use."

"But the bombing of towns! Poison gas on civilians. Poison gas almost haphazard."

"What right have they to be civilians?" said Gerson.

"Probably shirking a levy or something. In the next war there won't be any civilians. Gas dosen't have a fair deal. Everyone's against it. Ask me, I should say it improves fighting. Robs them of the idea there's something safe behind them. How's the old nigger song go? Bombs –

'Kicking up ahind and afore
And a yaller gas aspreading out ahind old Joe'
Turns 'em back to it."

"Practically – at Geneva we have undertaken not to use gas."

"Query – the 'practically.' 'Fit comes to that, we've renounced the use of war – by the Kellogg Pact and such-like flummery. Doesn't prevent every Power in Europe, and Washington too, keeping its Poison Gas Department up to strength and working overtime. No – sir. For propaganda purposes you may begin a war gentlemanly and elegant, but wait till the game warms up! Then you gouge. Then you bite off noses. And the gas comes in – trust me."

"Yes," said the Lord Paramount, yielding. "Yes. It's true. To impose a decision one must be stern."

He composed himself for some moments as an image of implacable sternness.

The expression in the eye of General Gerson was no doubt reluctant respect.

"And now for the most probable campaigns," began the Lord Paramount, and stirred the maps that lay upon the table before them. "First – Russia."

"Things might very well begin there," said Gerson.

For a time they discussed the possibilities arising out of a clash with Moscow. "In that event," said Gerson, "if nothing occurs in nearer Europe, we would have to run a sort of second-rate war. As we did in Palestine with Allenby. For a time, anyhow. The new things are for closer populations. We can't send a lot of ultra-modern stuff out there. Aeroplanes with machine guns – in sufficient abundance, of course – ought to settle anything that we're likely to have against us in India or Central Asia. Central Asia has always fallen back on nomadism hitherto, cavalry swarms, Parthians, Huns, Mongols, and so on. But that game's up, against aeroplanes and machine guns. The wing will beat the horse. New chapter of history. And the Afghan game of sitting among rocks and sniping at you goes the same way. The bird comes down on him. Every sort of what I might call barbaric and savage warfare is over now – twenty years out of date. We've got 'em. Russia in Asia would be a comparatively easy war. But we can't count on restricting it to Asia."

"I hope to do so."

"Hope, yes – I said, 'count on it.' And besides, there's Petersburg – what they *will* call Leningrad – and a little raid from that as a base to Moscow, just to settle things. We may be forced to do that. We might fight in Central Asia for ten years and settle nothing... And who knows? If things get difficult with us – our friends in Berlin... Or even nearer... You never know."

He scrutinized the Lord Paramount.

183

"It isn't safe," he said, making it plainer, "to lean over Europe and fight Russia."

"I do not think it will be like that," said the Lord Paramount.

"No. But it might be."

Gerson left that doubt to rankle.

"I don't care what agreements you make," he said, "not to use this or that. States that can keep such agreements aren't really at war at all. It's just sport, s'long as you have rules. War don't begin until law ends. It isn't necessary if any sort of agreement can be made and enforced. All this agreeing not to use gas." Gerson smiled and showed his black teeth and pointed his witticism – "well, it's gas and nothing else. The decisive factor in any first-class war now has to be gas delivered from the air. Work it out – it's as plain as daylight. It's the only way to decision. All modern war from now on will be a fight to be able to drop gas in quantity on the most crowded, sensitive nervous centre of the enemy. Then and then only will the other side give in. They *have* to give in. You go on gassing till they do... What other idea of war can there be now?"

It was hard stuff but the man was right. The thoughtful face of the Lord Paramount grew resolute.

"I admit the logic of it." The white hand clenched.

"I believe the Germans have the most powerful explosives in the world," said Gerson. "If we left it at that they'd be on top. They're still the ingenious devils they always were. The Republic didn't alter much – and now that's over for good, thank God. 'Ware their chemists, say I! All the same we, as it happens, just now, and God knows for how long, have absolutely the lead in poison gas. Ab-solutely. It happens so."

"I know," said the Lord Paramount. "Gas L."

He was secretly pleased to see Gerson's amazement. "But — who *told* you of that?"

The white hand waved the question aside. "I know, my dear Gerson," smiled the Lord Paramount, "I happen to know. Works at Cayme, eh?"

"Well, there you are! If we had a war in Europe now we could astonish the world... Do you know *all* about Gas L?"

"I don't," said the Lord Paramount. "Tell me."

"*Well,*" said Gerson, "well," and leant forward over his clenched fists on the table in a pose that was somehow suggestive of a cat with its forefeet tucked under it. He stuck his head on one side.

He gave information reluctantly and confusedly. He was not accustomed to give information to anyone. He was not accustomed to give anything to anyone. But gradually before the mind of the Lord Paramount the singularity of Gas L became plain.

This was the gas Camelford had spoken of at that dinner at Sir Bussy's which still haunted his mind. This was the unknown gas that needed the rare earths and basic substances that it seemed only Cayme in Cornwall could supply. Even at the time, that gas had touched Mr Parham's imagination and set him speculating. "Don't the scientific men, the real scientific men know about it?" he asked. "The devil of all this scientific warfare is that science keeps to secrets, and there's always someone, in some other country, hard on your track. Look how we tackled the German gas on the western front. In a week or so."

"You're right, precisely," said Gerson, "and that is just why I'd like to get to business with Gas L before very long. Before it's blown upon. Before they've set men to think it out. It's true

Cayme *may* be the only source of the stuff, and in that case the British monopoly is assured. But are we safe?"

The Lord Paramount nodded. But he wanted more particulars.

The real poison it seemed was not Gas L, but Gas L combined with nearly a hundred times its volume of air. It was very compressible. You let a little sizzle out from its reservoir, it vaporized, expanded, and began to combine. "It hurts. You remember those cats in the experimental chamber," said Gerson. It didn't decompose for weeks. It drifted about and it was still distressful when it was diluted to the merest trace. All the London area could be devastated with a score of tons. And there was no anti-gas known. For all the other known war gases there were anti-gases. But Gas L you had to counter with an impervious mask, adherent at its edges, keeping your air respirable with a combined oxygen maker and carbon dioxide absorber slung under the arm. You had, in fact, to put your men in a sort of sub-aerial diver's helmet that it needed training to adjust. "Think of the moral effect of it," said Gerson. "Paris or Berlin, a dead city, dead from men to rats, and nobody daring to go in and clean it up. After such a sample the world would howl for peace at any price whatever."

The Lord Paramount saw it for a moment as in a vision. The Place de la Concorde – still. Paris without a sound. Stiff bodies crumpled by the last agony...

He came back to Gerson with an effort.

"Plainly Cayme is the key position of our defences," he said. His mind searched among the possibilities of the situation. "Why shouldn't we nationlize it right away?"

"Why not?" said Gerson and seemed to chew unpleasant things. He finished his chewing. "I will tell you why not.

"*We,*" he said, "know how to make Gas L. We know that. But we don't know how to prepare those basal substances – which are peculiar. And we don't know how to separate those rare earths. That *they* know; they've got secret processes at Cayme. It's a question of linked processes. Probably no single man knows all of them properly. Unless it's Camelford. (Camelford again!) If we seize Cayme, if we make any trouble about Cayme, then, for one thing, we call the attention of foreign experts to what is going on. See?"

The Master Spirit and the Master General eyed each other comprehendingly.

"What exactly – *is* Cayme?"

"Cayme in Lyonesse," began Gerson.

"Lyonesse?" said the Lord Paramount softly. His mind went back to his youth, his ardent poetic but still classical and seemly youth, when Tennyson was still admired and the lost land of King Arthur cast a glamour on the Cornish coast. For a moment or so he could have imagined he was dreaming, so strong was the flavour of unreality the magic name threw over the story. Then distant Lyonesse and Avalon sleeping under the sunset gave place to the blotched and formidable visage of Gerson again.

"It's the new works the Star and Rocket Research Combine have made. It's a sort of joint subsidiary. Romer Steinhart & Co. Camelford. Some American capital. But Woodcock's the moving spirit on the business side. He's become a sort of alter ego of Camelford. Camelford's just taken hold of him and got him. He's a devil of a buyer and cornerer. They're up to something big together. God knows what goes on there! But it isn't Gas L.

They're up to something of their own. Some revolution in dyes or films or artificial this, that, or the other. That's what *they* want the stuff for. Cheap films in schools or some such foolery. Think of it! Wasting our gas for the sake of kids in schools! They dole us out the material for our own gas, just as they think proper. At any price they like. And make a favour of it."

The mind of the Lord Paramount returned to the point that had held it up some moments before.

"Lyonesse? But *why* Lyonesse?"

"You don't know? I admit it's been done very quietly. They don't want to advertise it. Two or three square miles of ground brought up out of the sea, down by the village of Cayme and out towards Land's End. The stuff is out there. The works are supposed to be at Cayme, but really they're out beyond low water mark, that was. And there's some old poem or legend or something..."

"So it really is Lyonesse!"

"That's what they call it."

"They've built up a place from the sea bottom?"

"No! They've raised the sea bottom and built a place on it. Something between a gas works and a battleship."

"But how – ! Raised the sea bottom?"

"God knows how they did it. There it is. Raised. Mineral veins and all. And while we're at peace we can't raid 'em, we can't search 'em, we can't seize 'em. We can't get at them. That's the one flaw in our military situation. The weak point is the merchant at home. I always said it would be. People say the workers will give trouble. Workers, damn them! never give trouble unless someone eggs them on. They're all as patriotic as I am, really. They're human. They hate foreigners until their minds get spoilt. Strike at the eggers-on, say I, and the workers are yours for the drilling. But there's no national love or loyalty between businessmen and soldiering. Not the big businessmen. I mean the big worldwide traders. Of course, we've got so-called nationalist motorcar men and nationalist brands of this and that, but even the men with a straight Union Jack on car or can will hold us up if possible. Still, at the worst, they can be bought. There's something to be said for an army with an all-British equipment out and out. Battles won on Empire food and all that. But it isn't that sort of chap I mean. I mean the men who handle the broad products. This new sort. These new Big Civilians. Who think of the industry before they think of the flag. Who're getting outrageous ideas. It was a *bit* like this once or twice in the Great War: they objected to waste, but whatever is going on now is ever so much bigger. What is going on now is fundamental. These people are cornering Victory. That's what it comes to. Making a corner in Victory. Much they care for the Empire! I'm under no illusions. If the Empire wants Victory next time, the Empire has got to pay for it, and there's times when I think that it won't get it even if it pays. Suppose they hold it up *anyhow!*"

The Lord Paramount was thinking profoundly. The fine and regular teeth nibbled at the knuckles of the shapely hand. He had an idea. Meanwhile with the undertow of his mind he followed Gerson.

"There was a time," said Gerson, "when the man of science knew his place in the world. He kept his place just as the engineer on a battleship kept his place. You had to keep a sharp eye on finance always – finance being so largely Jews and international in spirit – but their women like titles and show and they're sort of silly with the women. And at bottom a Jew is always afraid of a soldier. But your man of science you could trust outright. You could – once. All you had to do with him was to slap him into uniform, give him temporary rank for the duration, and he got so fierce and patriotic he'd kill his mother to please you. And the businessmen too. They *loved* a belt and sword. They'd crawl for a bit of ribbon. The old sort of businessman who went into shop or workshop at fourteen. Natural born patriots. They'd give the army anything it asked for. Once. Not now. All that has changed. This damned modern education, these new ideas, creep about everywhere. They're a sort of poison gas of the mind. They sap discipline. The young men of science, the clever ones, are all going Bolshy or worse. You'd be astonished. You can't count on them. It's extraordinary. And the businessmen and the bankers are rotten with pacificism. They get it out of the air. They get it from America. God knows how they get it! 'Does war *pay?*' they ask. Does war pay? Pretty question that! We get along now simply because the rich men are afraid of the Communists and the Communists won't have any truck with a richman. The poor pacificist keeps the rich pacificist in order for us. But will that last? If ever that quarrel eases off and they look around them, you'll have the United States of Everywhere, and fleets and armies will be on the scrap heap and sojers in the casual ward. Look at the situation! About this gas. Here we are, with the master gas of the world! Here we are, as we are. England's opportunity if ever there was opportunity. Go right out now and we win. And before we can take a firm line with anyone we have to ask ourselves: 'shall we get our guns in time? Are we safe for high explosive? And in particular – will Mr Camelford and Sir Bussy Woodcock please to kindly let us have our gas?' Gurr! When I think of it!"

Even great military experts must not be allowed to talk forever. The Lord Paramount sighed and drew himself up in a manner that conveyed the conference was at an end. He tapped the table between them and nodded and spoke reassuringly.

"When the time comes, *mon général*," he said, "you shall have your gas."

(And then again that momentary pang of doubt.)

CHAPTER SEVEN

Sir Bussy Is Recalcitrant

As soon as the Lord Paramount returned to London Sir Bussy was sent for.

It was a curious encounter. These two men had had scarcely a word together in private since that marvellous evening of the Advent when the Master Spirit had come and taken Mr Parham to himself. Yet all the time the little man had been hovering in a very curious and persistent manner in the background of the Lord Paramount's perceptions.

There was little of the tactful Parham now in the calm firm mastery with which the Lord Paramount spoke, and it was as if Sir Bussy had shrunken from his former sullen dominance to the likeness of a wary and resentful schoolboy under reproof.

The Lord Paramount was seated at his desk, lordly and serene. He was as large again as Mr Parham. Compared with Sir Bussy he was enormous. "I want a word with you, Woodcock," he said.

The new tone.

Sir Bussy grunted faintly. No chair had been placed for him. He considered the situation, dragged one across the room, and

193

sat down. What a little fellow he was! "Well?" he said ungraciously.

"I think of making you responsible for the military supplies of the Empire and particularly of non-ferrous metals, explosives, and – gas."

Straight to the point. Sir Bussy had nothing ready by way of reply. How *wordless*! A white finger pointed to him; a clear eye regarded him. "Have you any objection?"

"Large order," said Sir Bussy.

He attempted no excuse.

"It's a responsible position," the Master's voice pursued him. "No doubt."

"I say 'responsible.' "

"I seemed to hear you say it."

The same Sir Bussy as ever.

" 'Responsible' means that if these things are not forthcoming in limitless abundance on the day of need, it is *you* will answer for it."

"Wha'd' you *want* with gas?" Sir Bussy asked abruptly and unexpectedly.

"It is of vital importance."

The quick mind of the Lord Paramount leapt at once at the revealing discovery that Sir Bussy thought instantly of gas.

"But it isn't historical," said Sir Bussy. "It isn't in tradition."

"What has that to do with it?"

"Isn't all this stuff – carrying on history?"

"This stuff?"

"The military organization of the Empire, national and imperial ascendancy, flags, armies, frontiers, love of the Empire, devotion, sacrifice, and having a damned good go at Russia."

"Manifestly."

"What else *could* it be?" Sir Bussy reflected. "Lemme see, where were we?"

It was evident that he had been thinking profoundly by the things he had next to say.

"Well," he began, developing his premeditated argument, "then why not play your traditional game with the traditional pieces? Why drag in modern science? Use historical armies and fleets for historical destinies and leave gas and tanks and submarines out of it. If you must still play about with flags and frontiers, go back to Brown Bess and foot slogging and ten-pounder field guns and leave these modern things alone. Chemistry doesn't belong to your world. It isn't for you. It's *new*. It's out-size."

For a moment the Lord Paramount was baffled. Sir Bussy was still Sir Bussy the unexpected. Then a beautiful word came like an angel of light to the rescue. The Lord Paramount pronounced it like a charm. "Continuity," he said and leant back to observe its effect.

The intellecutual elements of Mr Parham that he had absorbed into his constitution suddenly asserted themselves. The Lord Paramount departed from his customary use of pithy and direct speech and argued a point.

"You are mentally underdeveloped, Woodcock," he went on — when he should not have gone on. "You are a very good fellow, but you are uneducated. Your historical imagination is that of a child of five. You have no sense of continuity whatever. All things progress by stages — *evolve* — if we must use that word. You do not understand that. It is you who are old-fashioned with your ideas of revolutions and strange new beginnings and progress

195

that never looks back. Your brain accepts that sort of stuff because nature abhors a vacuum. Let me tell you a little secret, Sir Bussy. As one who knows something of history. There never has been a revolution in all history. There have been so-called revolutions; that is all – times when the clock struck – violent and confused periods; mere froth upon the great stream of events – Yes. Begin anew – No. It is the past that rules; it is the past that points us on to our assured Destinies."

"No way out, in fact?" said Sir Bussy.

"None."

"Evolve or nothing?"

"That's the law of it."

"No fresh starts?"

"Continuity."

"So the railway train had to evolve, I suppose, bit by bit, slipping its end carriages and expanding out its footboards, until it became an aeroplane, and the mainmast of the sailing ship hollowed out into a funnel and squatted close until the cook's galley became the furnace room and his kettle became a boiler. Always continuity. Eh? No gaps. No fresh start. Why, damn it! a child of five knows that it's only by fresh starts man can keep alive!"

The Lord Paramount stared at his adversary, regretting now that he had stooped to argue with this obstinate and obscure mentality.

"I tell you these Powers and Policies of yours are worn out and done for," Sir Bussy went on. "It's a dream you're in. A damned old dream. It wouldn't matter if you weren't sleepwalking and wandering into dangerous places. Gas and high explosives don't belong to your game. Brains don't grow at

Aldershot, the soil's too sandy. They dry up there. These experts of yours, these mongrels, these soldiers who dabble in chemistry and engineering, and these engineers and chemists who dabble in soldiering, will let you down when the crash comes... Soldiering's a profession of incompetents and impostors, jobbing about with engineering firms and second-rate chemical combines... You won't get the stuff you want, and even if you get it, your experts won't be able to use it. Or they'll use it all wrong..."

The Lord Paramount decided that there must be no more argument,

"That is for me to decide," he said. "Your role is to facilitate supplies in every possible way."

"And suppose I don't choose to."

"There is such a thing as treason even in peace time, Sir Bussy."

"Treason!" said Sir Bussy. "What! and axes on Tower Hill? Put the cards down. I'll see you."

It was the first open opposition the Lord Paramount had encountered since his triumphant accession to power, and he found himself strangely perturbed. There was a tremulous quiver in his nerves, and he felt the need for self-control. Sir Bussy stood for much more than himself. An impulse to order his arrest had to be restrained. If anything of that sort was to be done it must be done as undramatically as possible. Behind him were such men as Camelford – incalculable factors.

The Lord Paramount turned his eyes to the window and regarded the fine lines of the corner of the United Services' Museum for a moment or so. How he hated Sir Bussy! Still not looking at his recalcitrant visitor he touched a little bell on his desk.

"I have given you fair warning," he said. "You can go."

Sir Bussy vanished instantly, leaving the faint flavour of a "Gaw" behind him.

Chapter Eight

A Little Tour of Europe

For some time after Sir Bussy had left him the Lord Paramount remained staring out of his window in Whitehall, in a state of some perplexity.

He was like a reader who has lost his place in a story and omitted to turn down the page.

He had forgotten himself.

He had argued.

He had forgotten himself, and some subtle magic in the queerly formidable little creature, Sir Bussy, had called the suppressed and assimilated Mr Parham. Something, at any rate, of Mr Parham. For a moment or so it had been almost as though he were Mr Parham. Instead of just telling Sir Bussy of his task and his danger he had disputed, had listened to what the fellow had to say and for some moments allowed it to weigh in his mind. Indeed, it still weighed in his mind.

Lords Paramount should not do things in this fashion. They know. They know altogether. They are decisive at once. Otherwise what right had they to assume a lordship over their fellows? At any cost their prestige for instant rightness must be upheld. It had been a queer incident, and it must not recur. The

199

memory of one of the late Mr Parham's dinner-table arguments, of that late Mr Parham with whom his own being was so mysteriously linked, had taken on a monstrous disproportion. He must recover scale.

He turned sharply. Hereward Jackson had entered the room noiselessly and then coughed.

There was something extraordinarily reassuring about Hereward Jackson. He was a born believer; he radiated faith; his mental deference, his entirely unquestioning loyalty was like a perpetual tonic to the Master. And a perpetual example to everyone else about him.

"All is ready," he said. "You can lunch in the air with a flask and a tin of sandwiches, and the new Dictator in Berlin will be awaiting you about three."

For the Lord Paramount had arranged to make a brief circuit of Europe, to marshal the strong men of the Continent about a common policy. They, too, masters indeed in their own houses, were still manifestly in need of a leader to unite them for a common control of the chaotic forces of this age. That leader the Lord Paramount proposed to be, a dictator among the dictators, master of masters, the leader of the new Crusade that would reunite Christendom.

He made the circuit in open military aeroplanes. Before his incorporation with the Lord Paramount Mr Parham had had no experience of flying except for one or two fine-weather crossings in the big Paris-London omnibuses. Now, muffled to the eyes, with the sweet fresh air whipping his cheeks and chin and the tip of his nose, mounting, beating the air, swooping like a bird, he realized for the first time what a delight and glory flying may be. Accompanied by companion planes carrying his secretarial staff, and escorted by a number of fighting planes, which ever and again would loop the loop or fall headlong like dead leaves and recover miraculously within fifty feet of the ground, fly turning over screw-like, pattern in squares and long wedges, chase each other in interlacing circles, and perform a score of similar feats for his diversion, the squadrons of the Lord Paramount swept over the pleasant land of Kent and the Channel, coasted by Dunkirk and athwart mouth after mouth and green delta after green delta of the Rhine, and so, leaving the sleeping law courts of the Hague to the left, turned eastward over the plains to Berlin. Berlin was his first objective, for in strict accordance with his forecast to the Council of the Empire the smouldering and resentful nationalism of Germany had broken out, and the Dictator Von Barheim was now effectual master of Germany. He had to be talked to a little, and assurances had to be won from him. Then to Paris to revive the spirit of Locarno. Afterwards Rome. And then, before the week was out, a scythe-like moving of the outer edge, King Paramitri, Count Paroli, Paraminski, and then a spectacular flight at a great height to Madrid and Parimo de Rivera. For Parimo was still at Madrid it seemed. All kindred-spirited men. All patriot master spirits, devoted to the honoured traditions of mankind; to flag and fatherland, to faith and family.

At every European capital the aeroplanes rose like swarms of autumnal starlings to greet the great conservator. Once he was within twenty feet of a collision, but his airman displayed astonishing quickness and skill. A youthful and too ardent Italian got out of control and nose-dived into the crowd on the Pincio at Rome, and there was a slight ground accident which burnt out two bombers at Warsaw, but no other misadventures.

The exhilaration of circling over one great capital after another, over its parks, towers, bridges, and bristling buildings, its encirling hills and clustering suburbs, and the banking and curving about to come down in a swift, clean rush was immense. What ancient conqueror ever made such a hawk's swoop into an allied city? Then followed the bumping rush up to the aerodrome, and then it was the proudly impassive marble face relaxed for the smiling descent from the machine, the greetings, the cameras, the applause.

The vigour of the Lord Paramount's personality, which had been a little impaired in his wrangle with Sir Bussy, was entirely restored by this European tour. His interview in Berlin was pure dominance. There had been street fighting, and the south-east region of the city was said to be in a mess with bombs and machine guns; there was still a little shooting audible in that direction, but Unter den Linden was packed with a patriotic crowd in a state of exalted delight at this immediate personal recognition of the new régime by the master mind of Britain. Everywhere the old imperial flag had reappeared.

The room in which these two dictators met was furnished with Prussian severity; everything was very simple, very necessary, and very, very big and heavy. Intimate relics of Frederick the Great occupied a position of honour in a glass case. The snuffbox would have carried through a long campaign, and there was room for luggage in the boots. Both men wore military uniforms. Von Barheim aped the still venerated figure of Bismarck and was none the more flexible in mind or manner for the compression of a tight cuirass; the Lord Paramount wore the simple yet effective service dress of a British general. The cap with its gilt-edged peak, the red bank with its richly simple adornments, the well-tailored uniform suited his tall figure extremely.

For a time it was a little difficult to get Von Barheim away from the question of war responsibility. He came back to it again and again, and he betrayed a regrettable resentment on account of the post-war policy of France. He harped upon the Rhine. When will Europe forget that ancient dispute? When will Europe look forward? Well it is to be traditional, historical, national, and loyal, but one should not be too rigidly and restrictedly traditional, historical, national, and loyal. If only one could give Europe English eyes! – to see the world. The Lord Paramount perceived that willy-nilly he must play the schoolmaster. "May I put my conceptions of the world situation to you?" he asked.

Germany's man of iron nodded a joyless consent.

"Here," said the Lord Paramount with a sweeping gesture of his hand over the table, "in the very centre of the Old World, illimitably vast, potentially more powerful than all the rest of the world put together – " he made a momentary pause – "is Russia. Consider Russia."

"Their ally in 1914," said Von Barheim.

"But not now."

"Which is just why they ought to be reasonable and not make themselves intolerable to us."

"They have Poland at their beck and call."

"*Poland!*"

The Lord Paramount said no more about Poland. He came back to the unalterable certain greatness of Russia in the future and so proceeded to unfold the standard British conception of world policy in the light of that fact, using almost the same phrases as those he had employed in the recent council, making indeed only one or two modifications, dictated by consideration for the patriotic feelings of Von Barheim. "What part will Germany play in this?" he asked. "Germany, the heart of Europe, the central nation? If she is not the forefront of Westernism against Asia she becomes the forefront of Russia against Europe."

"She can be her own forefront," said Von Barheim, but the Lord Paramount disregarded that.

He felt he was winning and enlarging Von Barheim. The lucidity of Mr Parham and the magnetism of the Lord Paramount made indeed an irresistible combination. Strange to think how badly that comprehensive exposition had been received when first it had been given to mortal ears at Sir Bussy's table. Slowly but surely this sturdy German mind was turned away from its sombre preoccupations as the new conceptions opened out before it. Von Barheim seemed to breathe a fresher air.

The Lord Paramount came to his climax. "If I could go from here to Paris with some definite proposal," he said and laid a firm white hand on Von Barheim's arm, "if I could restore the Frank to his eastern kindred in friendship and co-operation, I feel I should not have lived in vain."

"Danzig," said Von Barheim compactly. Then added: "And the other points I have explained to you."

"And why not Danzig? Between the Polish border and the Pacific there is room for compensation."

"If it is *that* sort of proposal," said Von Barheim and turned about to face his visitor squarely. "I did not understand at first... If we can re-arm freely. A big honest enterprise."

They had come to business.

204

Von Barheim clapped his hands in Oriental fashion, and a secretary instantly appeared. "Get a map of the world," he said. "Bring a big atlas."

And before eleven next morning the Lord Paramount was in Paris closeted with M. Parème. M. Parème wore the frock coat without which all French statesmanship is invalid, and the Lord Paramount had assumed a dark lounge suit of the most perfect cut.

M Parème was sceptical, realist, swift, and epigrammatic. His manner was more hostile than his matter. For Frenchmen all bargaining is a sort of quarrelling. One side must give in. And this was bargaining of the most elaborate sort. Slowly the Lord Paramount unfolded his vast designs. Slowly and with much resistance M. Parème assimilated those designs. But always with safeguarding conditions.

"Germany goes eastward to the north," said Monsieur Parème. "Good. In the country to the north of Moscow there ought to be excellent scope for German energy – particularly in the winter. Later compensations may come in South America. Again good. France does not touch America. She did all she wished to do over there in the Mexican expedition. We are to go southward and eastward, following out our traditional destinies in Syria and North Africa. Again – good. But it is clearly understood that in the final settlement there is nothing in this arrangement to exclude France from additional – indemnifications in Central Asia or North China?"

Leaving a number of issues open in this region, M. Parème turned suddenly to other possibilities. Suppose the Lord Paramount's proposals collapsed. Such things had been known to occur. Suppose that at the eleventh hour Germany did not abide by this bargain but were to attack France in alliance with Italy, would Britain bind herself to come in on the side of her ancient ally? He was very insistent that Britain held to that. These negotiations must not be supposed to set that older understanding aside. On the other hand, if Italy were to attack France while Germany, through a counter-revolution or any other cause, failed to support Italy so that Italy was left alone vis-à-vis to France, then France would be free to deal with Italy and her boundaries and her African possessions without any interference from Great Britain. That was understood? It was to be a simple duel in that case, and all Great Britain would do would be to keep the ring. And in case of the joint defeat of France and Great Britain the latter Power would of course undertake to repay to France all of whatever indemnity she might have to pay in addition to such penalities as were directly imposed upon herself, and regardless of any economic difficulties in which she might find herself?

The Lord Paramount's confidence in victory made him very yielding upon such issues.

Their talk became less difficult when it turned to America.

"And across the Atlantic," asked M. Parème, "our friends the Prohibitionists seem to want to prohibit war."

"They won't intervene," said the Lord Paramount as one who knows absolutely.

"Can you even begin to understand the mental operations of America?" said M. Parème.

"If they *did* choose to interfere," said M. Parème, "they have an overwhelming fleet, and France has a considerable coast line. Would Great Britain undertake in that case to retain at least two thirds of her naval forces in European waters south and west of the British Channel, so as to defend the French coast?"...

At last the Lord Paramount had his understanding plain. France would assist and also France would share. The German ambassador, in spite of the very grave doubts of M. Parème, was called in for an informal confirmation. Then, without haste and without delay, the Lord Paramount returned to his aeroplane, and the British squadrons, with an escort of French aces, streamed, stunting gaily, up the sky. The whole sky was a pattern of aeroplanes. It was very beautiful. It had the splendour of newness, the splendour of order, the thrill of convergent power.

"Rome," said the Lord Paramount.

It was in quite a different key that he met the mighty Paramuzzi, pattern of all the militant great men of the age, a genius almost too stupendous for Italy. "This is a man," said Mr Parham at their meeting. "*Ecce Homo,*" said Paramuzzi.

It was necessary now, in the most grandiose manner possible, to offer Italy the fourth place in and the fourth share of the spoils of this mighty adventure of Western Europe against the East. She had, moreover, to be a little disillusioned about her future in North Africa. Her attention had to be deflected to Greece, the Balkans, and (a brain wave of the Lord Paramount's) the Crimea.

The understanding was achieved.

At Rome things were done in the classical style – or perhaps if one may employ a slight contradiction in terms, the neo-classic style. The white colonnades of the Victor Emmanuel monument formed a becoming background to the scene. The Lord Paramount wore a British Court costume with the Garter and Order of Merit under a cloak of his own design. Paramuzzi met the occasion in black velvet and silver with a hat adorned with a number of expectionally large ostrich plumes. They met in the focus of a great semi-circle of cameras.

"Hail, Cæsar Britannicus!"

"Hail, Cisalpine Cæsar!"

There was some tremendous saluting by serried Fascisti. They were patterned across the Piazza Venetia. Never was saluting carried to higher levels than in Italy under Paramuzzi. They did marvellous things with their hands, their chests, their legs and knees, their chins and noses. They brought down their hands with a slap so unanimous and simultaneous that it was as if the sky had cracked.

"Hail, Cæsar Britannicus!" and then the Fascist cry. London cannot do things in this style.

When the two great men were alone there was a moment of intense spiritual communion. Paramuzzi thrust his face with intense dilated eyes close to the Byronic visage of his visitor. He thrust a tightly clenched fist even nearer: *"Power!"* he said. *"Power!"* The other fist came to help in a sort of wrenching gesture.

"Exactly," said the Lord Paramount, backing a little with Anglo-Saxon restraint and then bowing stiffly.

Paramuzzi englobed a planet with extended hands. His eyes devoured the Englishman.

"The world," he said. "And what we are! Virility! The forces of life!"

"Yes," said the Lord Paramount. "Yes."

"I love life," said Paramuzzi, "I love life with an exorbitant passion. And death and danger, the red essence of life. Discipline, yes – but death and danger. I delight in untamed horses. Attempts at assassination amuse me."

And then, with a lapse into great tenderness: "And music. Our Italian Scarlatti... *And love!* Sincere, passionate, headlong love! The love of disciples and devotees! Realized."

"For me," said the Lord Paramount succinctly, "my duty."

He perceived he had scored a point. Paramuzzi would have liked to have said that.

To the Nordic mind of the Lord Paramount this encounter had a slight flavour of extravagance, and a certain anxiety invaded his mind as to the outcome of their negotiations; but when it came to business Paramuzzi proved to be a very reasonable man. He was lavish with his assurances and quite ready to accept the fourth share as if it were the first. It was evident the Italian people would receive it as the first and triumph. For there was glamour about this Paramuzzi. He could bring all the glory of Rome out of his sleeve; he could make an old hat look like empire, and a swarming and swelling population of illiterates adequate security for limitless loans...

The King of the House of Savoy was something of an anticlimax...

In such fashion it was that the Lord Paramount wove his net of understandings and gathered his allies together for his Asiatic war, the great effort of Europe against Asia. Europe versus Asia. He felt like Herodotus preaching the unity of Christendom; he felt like King Philip of Macedonia preparing the campaigns that Alexandar led. He felt like Cæsar marching southward. Like Peter the Hermit. Like John the Baptist. Like – But indeed all history welled up in him. He believed all the promises he extorted. He perceived indeed that these promises were made with a certain resistance, with implicit reservations, but for a time he was able to carry on and disregard the faint flavour of unreality this gave his great combination. He was convinced that if only he held his course his own will was powerful enough to carry the European mind with him.

His squadrons throbbed over Europe, and above him was the blue sky – and above the blue that God of Nations who surely rules there, though so many pseudo-intellectual men have forgotten it. The Lord Paramount, in an ecstasy of self-confidence, waved his white hand aloft.

The God of Nations grew real again as the Lord Paramount recreated him. The God of Battles came back reassured and sat down again upon the Great White Throne.

"*My* God," said the Lord Paramount.

Whatever obsessions with local feuds might cloud the minds of his kindred dictators, whatever sub-policies and minor issues (from a world point of view) might be complicating their thoughts, surely there was nothing so comprehensive and fundamental and profoundly and essentially true as his own statement of British policy. After all, he owed something to the vanished Parham's intelligence. It was unjust not to admit something brilliant about poor old Parham. The Parham that had been. The man had had penetration even if he had had no power. He had been too modest and inaggressive, but he had had penetration. The more often his admirable summation of the international situation was repeated the more clear and beautiful it seemed.

"The lines of the next world struggle shape themselves," said the Lord Paramount to Paramuzzi, "rationally, logically, inevitably. Need I explain the situation to your Latin lucidity? Here– " and he made a sweeping gesture in the air before them, for now he could do it without a table – "here, illimitably vast, potentially more powerful than most of the world put together, is Russia…"

Et cetera.

And so to the aeroplane again, droning loudly over the mountain crests, a god of destiny, a being history would never forget.

Europe became like a large-scale map spread out beneath him. It was as if he sat in Mr Parham's study at St Simon's and had lapsed into daydreams with his atlas on his knee. How often had Mr Parham passed an evening in that very fashion! And so soaring over Europe, he could for a time forget almost altogether his dispute with Camelford and Sir Bussy; the paradoxical puzzle of the gas supply he could ignore almost completely, and those queer impish doubts which scuttled about in the shadows of his glory.

CHAPTER NINE

War with Russia

The results of the Lord Paramount's meteoric circlings in the European heavens would no doubt have become apparent in any event, very soon. But their development was forced on with a very maximum of swiftness by a series of incidents in Persia, Turkestan, Afghanistan, and along the northwest frontier of India.

For such a crisis the mind of the Lord Paramount was fully prepared. He could draw a map of Central Asia from memory and tell you the distance between all the chief strategic points. Fact was only assisting his plans. For a century it had been evident to every sound student of history, under the Soviet rule just as plainly as under the Czar, that the whole welfare and happiness of Russia depended upon access to the sea. From the days of Peter the Great to those of the enlightened and penetrating Zinovieff, the tutors of Russian intelligence had insisted upon the same idea. Dostoievsky had given it the quality of a mystical destiny. It was inconceivable to them that Russia could prosper, flourish, and be happy without owning territories that would give her a broad, uninterrupted, exclusive outlet upon the Pacific, the Indian Ocean, and the Mediterranean.

The school of British thought that had produced Mr Parham was entirely of that opinion, and for an industrious century the statecraft of Britain had schemed, negotiated, and fought with the utmost devotion for the strangulation of Russia. The vast areas of Russia in Europe and Asia could not be productive and prosperous without serious injury to the people in Great Britain. That was axiomatic. If Russia established herself upon the sea, Britain would be irrevocably injured. That there might be a way of trading the products and needs of that great territory in an entirely satisfactory manner without the conquest, assimilation, or stringent suppression of Turks, Persians, Armenians, Baluchis, Indians, Manchus, Chinese, and whoever else intervened, was equally preposterous to the realistic minds of Russia. It was one of those great questions of ascendancy out of which the shapes of history are woven.

Steadfastly, automatically, these two great political systems had worked out the logical consequences of their antagonism. The railway in Central Asia had been and remained primarily, a weapon in this war. The Russians pushed up their strategic railways from Askabad and Merv and Bokhara; the British replied with corresponding lines. Teheran and Kabul festered with abominable Russian spies and propagandists, scoundrels of the deepest dye, and with the active and high-minded agents Britain employed against them.

With the coming of the aeroplane the tension had tightened exceedingly. Over Meshed and Herat buzzed the Russians and the British, like wasps who might at any time sting.

This was the situation with which the Lord Paramount had to deal. He meant to force a decision now while the new régime in Russia was still weak and comparatively unprepared. Although

214

the anti-British propaganda of the Russians was extraordinarily effective – "anti-imperialist" they called it – there was every reason to believe that their military discipline, munitions, and transport preparations in Uskub and Turkomania were still far below the Czarist level.

The crisis was precipitated by an opportune British aviator who nose-dived in flames into the bazaar at Kushk and killed and cooked several people as well as himself. A violent anti-British riot ensued. Bolshevik propaganda had trained these people for such excesses. A British flag was discovered and duly insulted, and shots were fired at two colleagues of the fallen airman who circled low to ascertain his fate.

The news, in an illuminated form, was at once communicated to the press of the world, and the Lord Paramount dictated a spirited communication to Moscow that followed the best precedents of Lord Curzon.

The Russian reply was impolite. It declared that British aeroplanes had no business over the Turkoman Soviet republic. It reiterated charges of sustained hostility and malignity against the British government since the fall of the Kerensky régime. It enlarged upon the pacific intentions and acts of Soviet Russia and the constant provocation to which it had been subjected. It refused point-blank to make any apology or offer any compensation.

The Lord Paramount communicated this ungracious and insolent reply to the Powers, with an appeal for their sympathy. He announced at the same time that as a consequence of this culminating offence a state of war now existed between the United Soviet Republics and the British Empire. Neutral Powers would observe the customary restraints towards belligerents.

Herat and Kandahar were promptly occupied by Russian and British troops respectively, as precautionary measures, and a powerful British air force, supporting a raid of friendly Kurds, took and sacked Meshed. Herat was bombed by the British simultaneously with the far less effective bombing of Kandahar by the Russians. Although only high explosives and incendiary bombs were used in both cases, the Afghan population of these two towns, oblivious to the gigantic urgencies of the situation, displayed the liveliest resentment against Britain. This was manifestly unfair. This was clearly the result an unscrupulous propaganda. They might perhaps be allowed a certain resentment for Herat, but it was Soviet bombs which burst in Kandahar.

The Lord Paramount had succeeded in doing what even Mr Brimstone Burchell had failed to do. He had got his war with Russia – and Afghanistan thrown in.

The day following the declaration of hostilities, the British and Japanese, acting in strict accordance with a secret agreement already concluded through the foresight of the Lord Paramount, proclaimed the Chinese Kuomintang as an ally of Russia, published documents alleged to have been stolen by trustworthy agents from Russian and Chinese representatives in proof of this statement, and announced the blockade of China. The Japanese also landed very considerable forces to protect the strategic points in the railway system of eastern China from anything that might threaten them.

The British people, always a little slow at the uptake, took a day or so to realize that another World War was beginning. At first the hostilities seemed to be all Asia way, and merely spectacular for the common man. The music halls were laughing rather cynically at this return to war, but in quite a patriotic and anti-Bolshevik key. It was a joke against peace talk, which has always been rather boring talk to the brighter sort of people. The Lord Protector considered it advisable to create a press control bureau to make it perfectly clear to the public what was to be thought and felt about the conflict. True, there was none of the swift patriotic response that had made England the envy of the world in 1914, but unemployment was rife, and the recruiting figures were sufficiently satisfactory to preclude an immediate resort to conscription. Anti-Russian propaganda could be developed gradually, and enthusiasm could be fanned as it was required.

He issued a general order to commanding officers everywhere: "A cheerful activity is to be maintained. Everyone on the move briskly. Every flag flying and every band busy. This is to be a bright and hopeful war. A refreshing war."

The instant fall in the numbers of the unemployed was featured conspicuously in all the papers.

CHAPTER TEN

America Objects

B
ut now, after these confident beginnings, came a pause for thought. So far he had been doing his best to leave America out of the reckoning. He had counted on a certain excitement and discontent over there. His concerted action with Japan, and particularly the revelation of a secret understanding with Tokio, was, he knew, bound to produce irritation. But he was now to realize the extreme sensitiveness of American opinion, not only to any appearance of interference with American shipping, but also to any tampering with American interests in China and eastern Siberia. And he was to realize reluctantly how alien to British ideas American thought has become.

He was suddenly and strenuously visited by the new American ambassador. Abruptly on the heel of a telephone message at one o'clock in the morning the American ambassador came.

Through some conspiracy of accidents the Lord Paramount had not yet met the American ambassador. Mr Rufus Chanson had been in France, where his wife had been undergoing an operation. Now he had come back post-haste, and a communication from Washington had brought him headlong to the Lord Paramount in the small hours.

His appearance recalled at once a certain Mr Hamp, a banker whom Mr Parham had met at that memorable dinner at Sir Bussy's. He had the same rather greyish complexion, the same spectacles; he stooped in the same way, and he spoke with the same deliberation. If he had not been Mr Rufus Chanson, he would certainly have been Mr Hamp.

He was received in the War Office room that had now become the Lord Paramount's home. He was ushered in almost furtively by an under secretary. Mrs Pinchot, with whom the Lord Paramount had been relaxing his mind, sat in one corner throughout the interview watching her master with dark adoring eyes.

"My lord!" said Mr Chanson, advancing without a greeting. "What does this mean? What does it all mean? I've hardly kept touch. I got papers on board the boat, and my secretary met me at Dover. I'm thunder-struck. What have you been doing? Why have I got this?" He waved an open document in his hand.

The Lord Paramount was surprised by his visitor's extreme agitation, but remained calm. "Mr Chanson, I believe," he said and offered his hand and motioned to a chair. "May I ask what is the matter?"

"Don't say you've been deliberately interfering with American shipping at Tientsin," implored Mr Chanson. "After all that has passed. Don't say you've seized five ships. Don't say that it's by your orders the *Beauty of Narragansett* was fired on and sunk with seven men. As things are, if that is so – God knows what our people won't do!"

"There is a blockade."

The American appealed to heaven. "*Why* in the name of Holiness, is there a blockade?"

"There has been some incident," the Lord Paramount admitted. He turned to Mrs Pinchot, who rustled with her papers. Her little clear voice confirmed, "*Beauty of Narragansett* refused to obey signals and sunk. Number of drowned not stated."

"My God!" said Mr Chanson. "Will you British people never understand that in the American people you're dealing with the most excitable people on God's earth? Why did you let it happen? You're asking for it."

"I don't understand," said the Lord Paramount calmly.

"Oh, God! He doesn't understand! The most sensitive, the most childish, the most intelligent and resolute of nations! And he outrages their one darling idea, the Freedom of the Seas, and he sinks one of their ships and seven of their citizens as though they were so many Hindoos!"

The Lord Paramount regarded the scolding, familiar-mannered figure and contrasted it with any possible European diplomatist. Surely the Americans were the strangest of all strangers. And yet so close to us. It was exactly like being scolded by a brother or an intimate schoolfellow, all seemliness forgotten.

"We gave notice of our intention. We were within our rights."

"I'm not here to argue points. What are we going to do about it? Couldn't you have given way just on that particular thing? I can't help myself, I have to give you this dispatch."

He didn't offer to give it. He seemed indeed to cling to it.

"Listen to me, my Lord Paramount," he said. "The President is a man of Peace; He's God's own man of Peace; but remember also he's the spokesman of the American people and he has to speak as their representative. This dispatch, sir, is going to the newspapers as we talk. It can't be held. Here it is. You may think it hectoring, but half the folks over there will say it isn't hectoring enough. The Freedom of the Seas! They're mad for it. Even the Middle West, which hasn't an idea what it means, is mad for it. Seizures! And sinking us! Never did I think, when I came to St James's, I should have to deal with such a situation as this... Everything so pleasant. The court. The kindly friends. And now this fierceness... My wife, sir, over there has taken to her bed again. All the good Paris did her – undone!"

He put the paper on the table and wrung his liberated hands. He subsided into distressful mutterings.

The Lord Paramount took the dispatch and read it swiftly. His face grew pale and stern as he read. Dismay and indignation mingled in his mind. "Hectoring" was certainly the word for it. It made the historical Venezuela message seem a love letter. These Americans had never been adepts at understatement. Britain had to discontinue the blockade "forthwith" – a needless word – restore certain seized ships, compensate...

When he had finished reading he turned back a page, in order to gain time before he spoke. He was thinking very rapidly how the country would take this, how Canada would take it, how the Empire and the world would be affected. He was already very anxious about his proposed allies in Europe, for none had shown a decent promptitude in carrying out the terms of the understandings he had made with them. Germany, Poland, Yugoslavia, Italy had done nothing against Russia, had not even closed a frontier, and France, though she had partly mobilized, had made no clear intimation of her intentions and done nothing further in the way of cooperation. All of them seemed to be waiting – for some further cue. What was going to happen to these hesitating associates when they heard of this quarrel with America?

"My dear sir," he said. "My dear sir. In Britain we have always been willing to recognize the peculiar difficulties of American diplomacy. But this dispatch – !"

"Yeh!" said the American ambassador. "But don't think it's just talking."

"It goes too far. We know how urgent the exigencies of party politics can be over there. But the embarrassment – ! It is almost a habit with American statesmen to disregard every difficulty with which we may be struggling on this side... I will try to take this patiently, this string of insults. But – The President must have written it at fever heat."

"Can't you say that the shooting was a mistake? Hot-headed subordinates and all that?"

For a moment the Lord Paramount thought, and then, with a start and a glance at Mrs Pinchot he exclaimed, "Good heavens! Go back on a man who obeys orders!"

"You'll hold to it, it was by order?"

"A general order – yes."

The American shrugged his shoulders and despaired visibly.

"I must consider the situation," said the Lord Paramount. "Your President has put me in a very terrible position. I have come into public affairs to restore honour to human life. I have vowed myself to a high-spirited England. I have come to carry out great policies that will save all that is precious in Western civilization. I do not think that this public of yours in America dreams of the immense issues of this struggle that is now beginning. Nor your President. And while I gather together the forces of this great

223

Empire for a world conflict, suddenly this petty affair is seized upon to distress, to complicate – I don't know – possibly to humiliate… What good, I ask you can this hectoring do? What end can it serve?"

"Yeh!" the American ambassador intervened. "But what I want you to understand, sir, is, that this message isn't simply hectoring with an eye to the next election, and it isn't just to be set aside as tail-twisting the British lion. You'll get things all wrong if you try to see it like that. The American people are a childish people, perhaps, but they're large. They see things big. They have some broad ideas. Perhaps suddenly they'll grow up into something very fine. Even now they have a kind of rightness. And, rightly or wrongly, they have got this idea of the Freedom of the Seas as strongly now as they have the Monroe idea; they've got it and the President has got it; and if there isn't something done to put this in order, and if your people go seizing or shooting at any more of our ships, well – I'm not threatening you. I'm talking in sorrow and dismay – you'll get an ultimatum."

"My *dear* sir!" said the Lord Paramount, still resisting the unpleasant idea. "But an ultimatum means – "

"What I'm telling you. It means war, sir. It means something nobody on either side of the Atlantic has ever had the courage to figure out…"

CHAPTER ELEVEN

Disloyalty

For the truly great, dark days are inevitable. Purple is the imperial colour. All great lives are tragedies. Across the splendour of the Lord Paramount's ascendancy there began now to fall the shadows of approaching disaster. His mood changed with the mood of his adventure. America had misunderstood him, had almost wilfully refused to respect the depth and power of his tremendous purpose. He had not realized how widely she had diverged from the British conception of history and a European outlook upon world affairs. And suddenly all his giant schemes were straining to the breaking point. The incident of the *Beauty of Narragansett* and the note from the American President was the turning point of his career.

He had known this adventure with human affairs was heroic and vast; he had not realized its extreme and dangerous intricacy. He felt suddenly that he was struggling with a puzzle. It was as if he had been engaged in an argument and had been trapped and involved and confused. His mind was curiously haunted by that dispute of Mr Parham's with Camelford and Hamp and Sir Bussy. They seemed always in the back of his picture now, welcoming any setback, declaring his values false and his concepts obsolete, and foreshadowing some vague and monstrous new order of things in which he had no part. That vague and monstrous new order of things was at the same time the remotest, least distinct, and most disconcerting element in all this side-show of unpleasant apprehensions.

He had believed himself the chosen head of the united British peoples. Under the stress of the presidential note he was to discover how extremely un-British British peoples could be. That realization of the supreme significance of the Empire, of which Seeley and Kipling had been the prophets, had reached only a limited section of the population. And the intensity with which that section had realized it had perhaps a little restricted its general realization. Had imperial patriotism come too late? Had it yet to penetrate outwardly and *down?* Had it failed to grip, or had it lost its grip on the colonial imagination?

Not only the masses at home, but the Dominions had drifted out of touch with and respect for, or perhaps had never really been in touch with, the starry pre-eminence of Oxford and Cambridge thought, with army and navy and ruling-class habits and traditions, with the guarded intimacies of London and all that makes our Britain what is today. These larger, vaguer multitudes were following America in a widening estrangement from the essential conceptions of British history and British national conduct. For some years the keen mind of Mr Parham had sensed this possible ebb of the imperial idea. It had troubled his sleep. Failing it, what was there before us but disintegration? Now the heroic intelligence of the Lord Paramount was suffused by those anxieties of Mr Parham. Could it be that he might have to play a losing game? Might it be that after all his destiny was not victory but the lurid splendour of a last stand for ideas too noble for this faltering world?

When he had seized power the London crowd had seemed oafishly tolerant of this change of régime. It had not applauded, but it had not resisted. Evidently it did not care a rap for Parliament. But, on the other hand, had there been enthusiasm for the dictatorship? Now it became apparent that whatever enthusiasm there might be was shot and tainted by the gravest discontent. As he drove down Whitehall in his big blue car with Mrs Pinchot and Hereward Jackson to take the air in Richmond Park for his one precious hour of waking rest in the day, he discovered an endless string of sandwich men plodding slowly up the street.

"Leave Russia alone," in red, was the leading inscription. This when we were actually at war with Russia. That at least was open treason. Other boards more wordy said: "Leave China alone. We have enough to worry about without grabbing China." A third series declared: "We don't want War with America." That was the culminating point of the protest. These men were plodding up the street unhindered. Not a patriot was in action. No one had even thought of beating them about their heads. And yet sandwich men are particularly easy to beat about their heads. The police had done nothing.

What on earth did the people want? National dishonour? He could not disdain these sandwich boards. He was taken too much by surprise. He looked. He turned his head about. He gave himself away. People must have observed his movements, and it was necessary to do something promptly. The car pulled up. "Get out," he said to Hereward Jackson, "go back and have this stopped. Find out who supplied the money."

He went on his way past the Houses of Parliament, locked up and, as it seemed to him that day, silently and unfairly reproachful. He was moody with Mrs Pinchot in Richmond Park. "They are stirring up my own people against me," he said suddenly out of a great silence. Some interesting work was being done in the park with military telpherage, but his mind was preoccupied, and his questions lacked their usual penetrating liveliness.

Presently he found himself phrasing the curt sentences of a Decree of public security. That is what things had come to. There would have to be a brief opening, detailing the position of danger in which the Empire was placed. Then would follow the announcement of new and severe laws against unpatriotic publications, unpatriotic agitation, and the slightest suggestion of resistance to the civil and military authorities. The punishments would have to be stern. Real plain treason in war time calls for death. Military men obliged to kill were to be released from all personal responsibility if their acts were done in good faith. Attacks on the current régime were to involve the death penalty – by shooting. In any case. An Empire that is worth having is worth shooting for.

When he returned, stern and preoccupied, to his desk at the War Office, ready to dictate this Decree, he found Hereward Jackson with a medley of fresh and still more disconcerting news. The sandwich men of Whitehall were only the first intimations of a great storm of protest against what speakers were pleased to call the provocation of America.

All over the country meetings, processions, and a variety of other demonstrations were disseminating a confused but powerful objection to the Lord Paramount's policy. The opposition to his action against Russia was second only in vigour to the remonstrances against the American clash. "Right or wrong," said one prominent Labour leader at Leicester, "we won't fight either Russia or America. We don't believe in this fighting. We don't believe it is necessary. We were humbugged last time – but never again." And these abominable sentences, this complete repudiation of national spirit, were cheered!

"One must shoot," muttered the Lord Paramount; "one must not hesitate to shoot. That would be the turning point," and he called on Mrs Pinchot to take down his first draft of the Decree.

"We must have this broadcast forthwith," he said. "This rot must be arrested, these voices must be silenced, or we go to pieces. Read the Decree over to me..."

With the publication of the American blockade message throughout the Empire, all the multiplying evidences of hesitation, disintegration, and positive disloyalty underwent an abrupt and alarming magnification. The Dominions, it became evident, were as disposed as the masses at home toward a dishonourable pacificism. They were as blind to the proper development of the imperial adventure. The Canadian Prime Minister sent the Lord Paramount a direct communication to warn him that in no case could Britain count on Canadian participation in a war with the United States. Moreover, British armed forces in Canadian territory and Canadian waters would have to be immobilized as a precautionary measure if the tension of situation increased further. He was making all the necessary preparations for this step.

A few hours later protests nearly as disconcerting came in from South Africa and Australia. In Dublin there were vast separatist republican meetings, and there was a filibustory raid of uncertain significance against Ulster. At the same time a string of cipher telegrams made it plain that the insurrectionary movement in India was developing very gravely. A systematic attack upon the railway systems behind the North-West Frontier was evidently going on; the bombing of bridges and the tearing up of the tracks at important centres was being carried out far more extensively than anyone could have foreseen. The trouble was taking a religious turn in the Punjab. A new leader, following, it would seem, rather upon the precedent of Nanak, the founder of the Sikhs, had appeared out of the blue and was preaching a sort of syncretic communist theology, intended to unite Moslem and Hindu, communist and nationalist, in a common faith and a common patriotism. He was actively militant. His disciples were to be fighters, and their happiest possible end was death in battle.

Amidst the confusion one cheering aspect was the steady loyalty of the Indian princes. They had formed a sort of voluntary Council of India of their own, which was already co-operating actively with the imperial authorities in the suppression of disorder and the defence of the frontier. Their readiness to take over responsibilities was indisputable.

Such events, the Lord Paramount argued, should have raised the whole of Britain in a unison of patriotic energy. All social conflicts should have been forgotten. A torrent of patriot recruits should be pouring into the army from every position in life. They would have done so in 1914. What had happened since to the spirit and outlook of our people?

Well, the Decree of Public Security must challenge them. Its clear insistence on unquestioning loyalty would put the issue plainly. They would have to search their hearts and decide.

A further series of anxieties was caused by the ambiguous behaviour of his promised allies in Europe. Some of them were taking action in accordance with the plain undertakings of their strong men. France and Italy had mobilized, but on their common frontier. Von Barheim, on the telephone, pleaded that he was embarrassed by a republican and antipatriotic revolt in Saxony. Turkey had also mobilized, and there was complex nationalist trouble in Egypt.

The Lord Paramount became more and more aware of the extreme swiftness with which things happen to responsible statesmen as the war phase comes round. The American situation had developed from a featureless uneventfulness to an acute clash in four days. Hour after hour, fresh aspects of the riddle of Empire elaborated themselves. He had drawn together all the threads of Empire into his own hands. There were moments when he felt an intolerable envy of Paramuzzi with his straightforward penisula and his comparatively simple problem.

CHAPTER TWELVE

The Servitude of the Mighty

As the situation became more complicated and the urgent dangers crowded closer and closer upon the Lord Paramount, this realization of the atmosphere of haste in which the great decisions of our modern world are made grew more and more vivid and dominant in his vision of the role he had to play.

"I found my task too easy at the beginning," he said to Mrs Pinchot. "Plainly there has to be a struggle, an intricate struggle. I had counted on national and imperial solidarity. I find I have to create it. I had counted on trusty allies, and I find I must take precautions against them. I thought I should be sustained by patriotic science and patriotic finance and patriotic business enterprise, and I find men without souls that evade my inspiration. I fight against forces of dissolution more powerful than I ever dreamt could be launched against the established order of human life. Only our army, our navy, the church, and the old conservative classes stand out amidst this universal decay. They keep their form; they still embody imperial purpose. On these at least I can rely. But see what falls upon me."

"My demi-God!" breathed Mrs Pinchot, but lest it should be a source of embarrassment to both of them he affected not to hear. He became magnificently practical.

"I must organize my life so that not a moment of time nor an ounce of energy goes to waste. Here I shall install myself for good. Here I must trust you to control my staff and arrange my hours. Here you must make me as much of a home as I can have, as well as an office. Your intelligence I know I can count upon, as I count upon your loyalty. Gradually we will select a staff from the civil service to act as a filter for news and for responsibility. We will apportion each man his task. At present we have still to assemble that machine. Economy of force, efficiency of action…"

Very rapidly these ideas bore fruit, and the Lord Paramount's life began to be ordered so as to squeeze the utmost work out of his marvellous brain in his gigantic struggle to keep the Empire and the world upon the rails of established tradition.

Sir Titus Knowles, formerly so antagonistic, had now become the rude but subjugated servant of the Master's revealed greatness. To him was entrusted the task of keeping the Lord Paramount fit. He dieted and when necessary he drugged this precious body. He pursued its chemical variations in all their manifestations with sedulous watchfulness. He prescribed its phases of rest and its intervals of sleep.

Sir Titus had found his place in life.

All day and all night, at every half hour, a simple meal, a. cutlet, or a roast fowl would be prepared. Had the moment come to eat? If not, the meal was dismissed and the next in succession was brought into readiness for service. So too the Lord Paramount's couch or his bed was always there for repose or slumber.

War and diplomacy have been compared to the game of chess, but it is chess with a board of uncertain shape and extent and with pieces with unlimited powers of spontaneous movement. At any moment astounding adjustments of view must be possible, if this game is to be carried to a triumphant conclusion. In his own room he had a comparatively clear table, from which all papers not immediately under consideration were banished. Usually it bore only a water bottle and glass and a silver bowl in which every day Mrs Pinchot arranged a fresh mass of simple but beautiful flowers. She and she alone shared this workroom with him, silent and watchful, the only being whose continual close proximity did not interfere with the mighty workings of his mind. Thence he moved to and fro between the large apartment in which General Gerson and Field-Marshal Capper had tables covered with maps, and a series of other apartments containing books and files for reference, in which expert secretaries waited, ready to leap to their feet and answer the slightest inquiry. Beyond and out of hearing were typists and other copyists. Further were an outer circle of messengers, waiting rooms for visitors, and the like.

Sir Titus arranged that the Lord Paramount should take exercise in artificially oxygenated chambers, clad in a restricted but becoming costume reminiscent of a Spartan athelete. There also he rode horseless saddles that bucked and reared in the most hygienic fashion, or he rowed in imaginary boat races with dials recording his speed, or he punched leather balls, or cycled on stationary bicycles, or smacked golf balls at targets that registered the force and distance of his drive – always in a manner, Sir Titus arranged, to exhilarate him and sustain his self-confidence. And once a day he would drive out with Mrs

Pinchot through the sullen and yet stimulating atmosphere of the capital.

A simple life it was in essence that the Lord Paramount led during this phase, a life of industrious servitude for the sake of all the noblest traditions of mankind.

Book Four

The Second World War

CHAPTER ONE

The Big Guns Go Off

The Lord Paramount was able to give exactly fifty-three minutes of thought altogether to the threatened Canadian defection before he made a decision. There was one sustained stretch of rather under thirty minutes, before he got up on the morning after he had learnt of this breach on the imperial front; the other twenty-three-odd minutes were in scraps, two or three at a time. There were also some minutes of overlap with the kindred questions of Australia and South Africa. His decision was to take a spirited line both with Canada and the United States.

The truth is that in this matter and every matter with which he dealt he did not think things out in the least. Men of action do not think things out. They cannot. Events are too nimble for them. They may pause at times and seem to think, but all they do in fact is to register the effective sum of such ideas as they had accumulated before they became men of action. Like most Englishmen of his type and culture, the Lord Paramount had long allowed a certain resentment against American success to fester in his mind. He had long restrained a craving to behave with spirit towards America. Just to show America. In a crisis this was bound to find release.

He resolved to make an immense display of naval force and throw the battle fleet and indeed all the naval forces available across the Atlantic to Halifax, unannounced. It was to be like a queen's move in chess, a move right across the board, bold and dangerous, to create a new situation. Suddenly this awe-inspiring array, with unknown orders and unrevealed intentions, would loom up from nothingness upon the coast of Nova Scotia. This rendezvous was to be approached from a north-easterly direction so as to avoid the liner routes and create an effect of complete surprise. It was to be a blow at the nervous equilibrium of the American continent.

A powerful squadron would enter the Gulf of St Lawrence and detach an array of small craft to steam up to Ottawa, while the main fleet, with its multitudinous swarming screen of destroyers, torpedo craft and aeroplanes was to spread out in a great curve eastward from Cape Sable, a mighty naval crescent within striking distance of New York. When these manœuvres were completed the outgoing and incoming liners to New York, Boston, and Halifax need never be out of sight of a British warship or so, cruising ready for action, for nearly a thousand miles. The battleships and battle cruisers were to be instructed to make themselves conspicuous and to hold up and impress shipping. The moral effect on both Canada and the United States could not fail to be immense. More than half the American fleet, the Lord Paramount understood, was in the Pacific based on San Francisco, vis-à-vis to Japan; many ships were reported in dock, and the preponderance of British strength therefore would be obvious to the crudest intelligence.

Meanwhile the exchange of views with Washington was to be protracted in every possible way until the display of force could be made.

It took, he found, just forty-two minutes more of the Lord Paramount's time to launch the cardinal orders for this stupendous gesture. Once more the unthinking urgency with which the crowning decisions in history must be made impressed itself upon his mind. The acts of history, he realized, are but the abrupt and hazardous confirmation of the vague balance of preceding thought.

A multitude of other matters were pressing upon his attention. All the while he was full of unanswered criticisms of the thing he was doing. But there was no time at all to weigh the possibilities of failure in this attempt to browbeat the New World. It seemed the plain and only way of meeting and checking the development of the American threat and so bringing the ambiguous hesitations of the European Powers to an end. He dismissed some lurking doubts and transferred his attentions to the advantages and difficulties of accepting a loan of Japanese troops for service in India. That was the next most urgent thing before him. Bengal was manifestly rotten with non-co-operation and local insurrectionary movements; a systematic wrecking campaign was doing much to disorder railway communications, and the Russo-Afghan offensive was developing an unexpected strength. He realized that he had not been properly informed about the state of affairs in India.

It was impossible to carry out the orders of the Lord Paramount as swiftly as he had hoped. The Admiralty seemed to have had ideas of its own about the wisdom of entirely denuding the British coasts, and with many ships a certain unpreparedness necessitated delays. The Admiralty has long been a power within a power in the Empire, and the Lord Paramount realized this as a thing he had known and forgotten.

It was three days before the Grand Fleet was fairly under way across the Atlantic. It included the *Rodney,* the *Royal Sovereign,* and three other ships of that class, the *Barham, Warspite, Malaya,* and two other battleships, the *Hood* and *Renown* and another battle cruiser and the aircraft carriers, *Heroic, Courageous,* and *Glorious.* A screen of destroyers and scouting light cruisers had preceded it and covered its left wing.

The first division of the minor flotilla coming up from Plymouth had started twelve hours ahead of the capital ships. These latter converged from north and south of the British Isles to a chosen rendezvous south of Cape Farewell.

The American navy, he learnt in the course of another day, was already in movement; it was unexpectedly prompt and in unexpected strength. The Lord Paramount was presently informed that a force of unknown composition, but which was stated to include the *Colorado,* the *West Virginia,* and at least ten other battleships, was assembling between the Azores and the Gulf of Mexico and steaming northward as if to intercept the British fleet before it reached the Canadian coast. This was a much more powerful assembly of ships than he had supposed possible when first he decided on his queen's move. But that move was now past recall.

Something of the chessboard quality hung over the North Atlantic for the next three days. The hostile fleets were in wireless communication within thirty-six hours of the Lord Paramount's decision, and on a chart of the Atlantic in an outer room flagged pins and memoranda kept him substantially aware of the state of the game.

Neither government was anxious to excite public feeling by too explicit information of these portentous manœuvres. Neither, as a matter of fact, admitted any official cognizance of these naval movements for three days. Nothing was communicated to the Press, and all inquiries were stifled. The American President seemed to have been engaged in preparing some sort of declaration or manifesto that would be almost but not quite an ultimatum. Steadily these great forces approached each other, and still the two governments assumed that some eleventh-hour miracle would avert a collision.

A little after midnight on May 9th the fringes of the fleet were within sight of each other's flares and searchlights. Both forces were steaming slowly and using searchlights freely. Movement had to be discreet. There was an unusual quantity of ice coming south this year and a growing tendency to fog as Newfoundland was approached. Small banks of fog caused perplexing disappearances and reappearances. The night was still and a little overcast, the sea almost calm, and the flickering reflections on the clouds to the south were the first visible intimation the British had of the closeness of the Americans. Wireless communication was going on between the admirals, but there were no other exchanges between the two fleets, though the air was full of the cipher reports and orders of each side.

Each fleet was showing lights; peace conditions were still assumed, and survivors from the battle describe that night scene as curiously and impressively unwarlike. One heard the throbbing of engines, the swish and swirl of the waters about the ships, and the rhythmic fluctuations in the whir of the aeroplanes above, but little else. There was hardly any talk, the witnesses agree. A sort of awe, a sense of the close company of Fate upon that westward course kept men silent. They stood still on the decks and watched the pallid searchlights wander to and fro, to pick out and question this or that destroyer or cruiser, or to scrutinize some quietly drifting streak of fog. Some illuminated ship would stand out under a searchlight beam, white and distinct, and then, save for a light or so, drop back into the darkness. Then eyes would go southward to the distant flickerings of the American fleet, still out of sight below the horizon.

Like all naval encounters, the history of these fatal hours before the Battle of the North Atlantic remains inextricably confused. Here again the time factor is so short that it is almost impossible to establish a correct sequence of events. What did such and such commander know when he gave this or that order? Was this or that message ever received? It is clear that the American fleet was still assembling and coming round in a great curve as it did so to the south of the British forces. These latter were now steaming south-westward towards Halifax. The American Admiral, Semple, was coming into parallelism with the British course. He agreed by wireless not to cross a definite line before sunrise; the two fleets would steam side by side until daylight with at least five miles of water between them. Then he took upon himself to inform Sir Hector Greig, the British commander-in-chief, of the general nature of his instructions.

"My instructions," said his message, "are to patrol the North Atlantic and to take whatever steps are necessary to prevent any possibility of hostile action against Canada or the United States of America in North American waters."

Sir Hector replied: "My instructions are to patrol the seas between Great Britain and Canada, to base myself upon Halifax and send light craft up the St Lawrence River."

Each referred the situation back to his own government. The Lord Paramount was awakened at dawn and sat in his white silk pyjamas, drinking a cup of tea and contemplating the situation.

"Nothing must actually happen," he said. "Greig must not fire a shot unless he is fired at. He had better keep on his present course... The Americans seem to be hesitating..."

It was still night at Washington, and the American President had never gone to bed.

"Are the British in great force?" he asked.

Nobody knew the strength of the British.

"This cheap Mussolini at Westminster is putting us up some! I don't see why we should climb down. How the devil is *either* party to climb down? Is there no way out?"

"Is there no way out?" asked the Lord Paramount, neglecting his tea.

"Battleships are made for battles, I suppose," said someone at Washington.

"Aw – don't talk that stuff!" said the President. His intonation strangely enough was exactly what a scholarly imperialist would expect it to be. "We made 'em because we had the Goddamned experts on our hands. Wish to hell we hadn't come in on this."

An ingenious person at Washington was suggesting that if the American fleet wheeled about to the south and turned eastward towards Great Britain, Greig would either have to follow with all his forces, split his fleet, or leave England exposed.

"That will just repeat the situation off Ireland," said the President.

245

Until it was too late some hitch in his mind prevented him from realizing that every hour of delay opened a score of chances for peace. A sleepless night had left him fagged and unendurably impatient. "We can't have the two fleets steaming to and fro across the Atlantic and not firing a gun. Ludicrous. No. When we built a fleet we meant it to be a fleet. And here it is being a fleet – and a fleet it's got to be – and behave accordingly. We've got to have the situation settled out here now. We've got to end this agony. Semple must keep on. How long can they keep on parallel before anything happens?"

A brisk young secretary went to inquire.

Meanwhile the Lord Paramount had got into a warm dressing gown and was sketching out the first draft of a brilliant memorandum to the President. It was to be conciliatory in tone, but it was to be firm in substance. It was to take up the whole unsettled question of the freedom of the seas in a fresh and masterful manner. The room was flooded with sunlight, and in a patch of that clear gay brightness on his table were some fresh lilies of the valley, put there by the forethought of Mrs Pinchot. She had been sent for to put the memorandum in order as soon as his pencil notes were ready.

Almost simultaneously messengers of disaster came to both these men.

The brisk young secretary returned to the President.

"Well," said the President, "how long can we carry on before we see 'em?"

"Sir," said the brisk young secretary, with such emotion in his voice that the President looked up and stared at him.

"Ugh!" said the President and clutched his hands as if he prayed, for he guessed what that white-faced young man had to tell.

"The *Colorado*," said the young man. "Blown out of the water. We've sunk a great battleship..."

It was Hereward Jackson broke the news to the Lord Paramount.

His face, too, lit with a sort of funereal excitement, told its message.

"Battle!" he gasped. "We've lost the *Rodney*..."

For some moments the consciousness of the Lord Paramount struggled against this realization. "I am dreaming," he said.

But if so the dream would not break, and the tale of the disaster began to unfold before him, irreversibly and mercilessly, as if it were history already written. News continued to come from the fleet, but there was no further sign that the direction and inquiries he continued to send out were ever received and decoded.

The grey dawn over the dark Atlantic waters had discovered the two fleets within full view of each other and with a lane of vacant water perhaps three miles broad between them. The intention of the two admirals had been to have a five-mile lane, but either there had been some error in reckoning on one side or the other, or else there had been encroachment by the minor craft. Ahead, under the skirts of the flying night were strata of fog which veiled the sea to the west. Each admiral, though still hopeful of peace, had spent every moment since the fleets became aware of one another in urgent preparation for action. The battleships on either side were steaming line ahead with rather more than sufficient space to manoeuvre between them.

The *Colorado* was heading the American line followed by the *Maryland* and *West Virginia*; then, a little nearer the British, the *Idaho, Mississippi*, and *New Mexico* followed, and after them the *California* and at least seven other battleships. These three groups were all prepared to wheel round into a battle formation of three columns. In each case the battle cruisers were following the battleships; the *Hood* was the tail ship of the British, and the aircraft ships were steaming under cover of the battleships on the outer side. Beyond them were light-cruiser squadrons. The two main lines of warships were perhaps a little more than five miles apart. Nearer in were the flotillas of destroyers and special torpedo craft held like hounds on a leash and ready at an instant's signal to swing round, rush across the intervening space, and destroy or perish. Submarines were present on the outer verge of the fleets awaiting instructions. The British seem also to have had special mine layers in reserve for their contemplated operations on the American coast. The aeroplane carriers were tensely ready to launch their air squadrons and made a second line behind the screen of battleships and battle cruisers.

As the light increased, the opaque bank of fog ahead began to break up into fluffy masses and reveal something blue and huge beyond. Shapes appeared hunched like the backs of monstrous beasts, at first dark blue, and then with shining streaks that presently began to glitter. A line of icebergs, tailing one after the other in receding symmetry, lay athwart the course of the British fleet and not four miles from the head of that great column. They emerged from the fog garment like a third Armada, crossing the British path and hostile to the British. It was as if the spirit of the Arctic had intervened on the American side. They made the advancing leviathans look like little ships. To the British battle fleet they were suddenly as plain and menacing as a line of cliffs, but it is doubtful whether Admiral Semple ever knew of their existence.

Perhaps Greig should have informed Semple of this unexpected obstacle. Perhaps there should have been a discussion. It is so easy to sit in a study and weigh possibilities and probabilities and emerge with the clearest demonstration of the right thing he ought to have done. What he actually did was to issue a general order to the fleet to change direction two points to the south. He probably never realized that these huge ice masses were almost invisible to the American fleet and that his change of direction was certain to be misunderstood. It must have seemed perfectly reasonable to him that the Americans should make a corresponding swerve. So far it had been for him to choose the direction. To the American admiral, on the other hand, quite unaware of the ice ahead, this manœuvre could have borne only one interpretation. The British, he thought, were swinging round to fight.

Perhaps he too should have attempted a further parley. What he did was to fire a shot from one of his six-pounders across the bows of the *Rodney*. Then he paused as if interrogatively.

Just one small intense flash of light, pricking through the cold tones of the dawn, the little hesitating puff of dense whirling smoke just beginning to unfold, the thud of the gun – and then that pause. It was as if a little thing had occurred and nothing else had altered.

Each admiral must have been torn most abominably between the desire to arrest a conflict and the urgent necessity of issuing final orders for attack. It is good to have the best of arguments, but if battle is to ensue it is of supreme importance to strike the first blow. No one now will ever know if at this stage there was any further attempt on the part of either admiral to say anything, one to the other.

All the survivors speak of that pause, but no one seems able to say whether it lasted for seconds or minutes. For some appreciable length of time, at any rate, these two arrays of gigantic war machines converged upon each other without another shot. For the most part the doomed thousands of their crews must have been in a mood of grim horror at the stupendous thing they were doing.

Who knows? There may have been an exaltation. The very guns seemed to sniff the situation incredulously with their lifted snouts. With a whir the first aeroplanes took the air and rose to swoop. Then the *Maryland* let fly at the two most advanced of the British destroyers with all her available smaller guns and simultaneously in a rippling fringe of flashes both lines exploded in such an outbreak of thudding and crashing gunfire as this planet had never witnessed before.

The inevitable had arrived. America and Britain had prepared for this event for ten long years; had declared it could never happen and had prepared for it incessantly. The sporting and competitive instincts of the race had been inflamed in every possible way to develop a perverted and shuddering impulse to this conflict. Yet there may have been an element of amazement still, even in the last moments of Greig and Semple. Imagination fails before those last moments, whether it was rending, cutting, or crushing metal, jetting steam or swirling water that seized and smashed and stamped or scalded the life out of their final astonishment.

The *Colorado* had caught the convergent force of the *Rodney* and *Royal Sovereign*; she was hit by their simultaneous salvoes; her armour must have been penetrated at some vital spot, and she vanished in a sheet of flame that roared up to heaven and changed into a vast pillar of smoke. The *Rodney*, her chief antagonist, shared her ill luck. The sixteen-inch guns of the *Colorado* and *Maryland* had ripped her behind, something had happened to her steering gear; without any loss of speed she swept round in a curve, and the *Royal Sovereign*, plastered and apparently blinded by the second salvoes of the *Maryland*, struck her amidships with a stupendous crash. An air torpedo, some witnesses declare, completed her disaster. But that is doubtful. The American aircraft certainly got into action very smartly, but not so quickly as all that. The *Rodney*, say eye-witnesses, seemed to sit down into the water and then to tilt up, stern down, her futile gun turrets towering high over the *Royal Sovereign*, and her men falling from her decks in a shower as she turned over and plunged into the deeps just clear of the latter ship.

A huge upheaval of steaming water lifted the *Royal Sovereign* by the bows and thrust her aside as though she were a child's toy. Her upreared bows revealed the injuries she had received in the collision. As she pitched and rolled over the ebullitions of the lost *Rodney*, the *Maryland* pounded her for the second time. Her bruised and battered gunners were undaunted. Almost immediately she replied with all her eight big guns, and continued to fight until suddenly she rolled over to follow the flagship to the abyss. Down the British line the *Warspite* was also in flames and the *Hood*, very badly ripped and torn by a concentration from the *Arizona, Oklahoma,* and *Nevada,* had had a series of explosions. The *Idaho* also was already on fire.

So this monstrous battle began. Aften the first contact all appearance of an orderly control disappeared. To get into battle formation the main squadrons had to swing round so as to penetrate the enemy force, and so even this primary movement was never completed. Further combined tactical operations there were none. The rapid cessation of command is a necessary feature of modern marine fighting. The most ingenious facilities for adjusted movement become useless after the first impact. Controls are shot away, signaling becomes an absurdity, and the fight enters upon its main, its scrimmage phase, in which weight tells and anything may happen. The two lines of battleships, already broken into three main bunches, were now clashing into each other and using every gun, each ship seeking such targets as offered and doing its best by timely zigzagging to evade the torpedo attacks that came dashing out of the smoke and confusion. The minor craft fought their individual fights amidst the battleships, seeking opportunities to launch their torpedoes, and soon a swarm of aeroplanes released from the carriers were whirring headlong through the smoke and flames. The temperament and tradition of both navies disposed them for attack and in-fighting, and no record of shirking or surrender clouds the instance magnificence of that tragic opening.

Never before had the frightful power of modern guns been released at such close quarters. These big ships were fighting now at distances of two miles or less; some were in actual contact. Every shell told. For the first time in the twentieth century battleships were rammed. The *Royal Oak* ran down the *Tennessee*, the two ships meeting almost head on but with the advantage for the *Royal Oak*, and the *Valiant* was caught amidships by the *New Mexico* which herself, as she prepared to back out of her victim, was rammed broadside on by the *Malaya*. All these three latter ships remained interlocked and rotating, fighting with their smaller armaments until they sank, and a desperate attempt to board the *New Mexico* was made from both British battleships. "Fire your guns as often as possible at the nearest enemy" had become the only effective order. "Let go your torpedo at the biggest enemy target."

The battle resolved itself slowly into a series of interlocked and yet separate adventures. Smoke, the smoke of the burning ships and of various smoke screens that had been released by hard-pressed units, darkened the sky and blocked out regions of black fog. A continuous roar of crashing explosions, wild eruptions of steam and water, flashes of incandescence and rushes of livid flame made a deafening obscurity through which the lesser craft felt their way blindly to destroy or be destroyed. As the sun rose in the heavens and a golden day shot its shafts into the smoke and flames the long line of the first battle was torn to huge warring fragments from which smoke and steam poured up to the zenith. The battleships and battle cruisers still in action had separated into groups; the *Queen Elizabeth*, the *Barham*, and the *Warspite,* which had got its fires under control, fought, for example, an isolated action with the *Pennsylavnia* and the *Mississippi* round the still burning and sinking *Idaho*. The three British ships had pushed right through the American line, taking their antagonist with them as they did so, and this circling conflict drifted far to the south of the original encounter before its gunfire died away and the battered and broken combatants followed each other to the depths. The huge American aircraft carrier, the *Saratoga*, was involved in this solemn and monstrous dance of death; her decks were swept by a hurricane of fire, and she could no longer give any aid to her aeroplanes, but she made such remarkably good use of her eight-inch guns that she alone survived this conflict. She was one of the few big ships still afloat in the afternoon, and she had then nearly a thousand rescued men aboad of her. Most of the airmen, after discharging their torpedoes, circled high above the battle until their fuel gave out, and then they came down and were drowned. One or two got on to the icebergs. The *West Virginia*, thrusting to the west of the *Royal Sovereign* group, struck one of these icebergs and sank later. The *Revenge* and *Resolution,* frightfully damaged but still keeping afloat, found themselves towards midday cut off from the main fight by ice and were unable to re-engage.

After the first shock of the encounter between the giant ships the role of the destroyer flotillas became more and more important. They fought often in a black and suffocating fog and had to come to the closest quarters to tell friends from enemies. They carried on fierce battles among themselves and lost no chance of putting in a torpedo at any larger ship that came their way.

The torpedoes of the aircraft showed themselves particularly effective against the light cruisers. They were able to get above the darknesses of the battle and locate and identify the upper works of their quarries. They would swoop down out of the daylight unexpectedly, and no anti-aircraft guns were able to do anything against them. The *Nevada*, it is said, was sunk by a British submarine, but there is no other evidence of submarine successes in the fight. It is equally probable that she was destroyed by a floating mine – for, incredible as it seems, some floating mines were released by a British mine carrier.

No one watched that vast fight as a whole; no one noted how the simultaneous crashes of the first clash, that continuing fury of sound, weakened to a more spasmodic uproar. Here and there would be some stupendous welling up of smoke or steam, some blaze of flame, and then the fog would grow thin and drift aside. Imperceptibly the energy of the conflict ebbed. Guns were still firing, but now like the afterthoughts of a quarrel and like belated repartees. The reddish yellow veils of smoke thinned out and were torn apart. Wide spaces of slowly heaving sea littered with rocking débris were revealed. Ever and again some dark distorted bulk would vanish and leave a dirty eddy dotted with struggling sailors, that flattened out to a rotating oily smudge upon the water.

By three in the afternoon the battle was generally over. By half-past three a sort of truce had established itself, a truce of exhaustion. The American flag was still flying over a handful of battered shipping to the south-west, and the British remnant was in two groups, separated by that fatal line of icebergs. These great frozen masses drifted slowly across the area of the battle, glassy and iridescent in the brilliant daylight, with streams of water pouring down their flanks. On one of them were two grounded aeroplanes and at the water line they had for fenders a fringe of dead or dying men in life belts, fragments of boats and such like battle flotsam. This huge cold intervention was indubitably welcome to the now exhausted combatants. Neither side felt justified in renewing the conflict once it had broken off. There is no record who fired the last shot nor when it was fired.

And so the Battle of the North Atlantic came to its impotent conclusion. It had not been a battle in any decisive sense, but a collision, a stupendous and stupendously destructive cannonade.

Fifty-two thousand men, selected and highly trained human beings in the prime of life, had been drowned, boiled to death, blown to pieces, crushed, smashed like flies under a hammer, or otherwise killed, and metallurgical and engineering products to the value of perhaps five hundred million pounds sterling and representing the toil and effort of millions of workers had been sent to the bottom of the sea. Two British battleships and three American were all in the way of capital ships that emerged afloat, and the losses of light cruisers and minor craft had been in equal or greater proportion. But, at any rate, they had done what they were made to do. The utmost human ingenuity had been devoted to making them the most perfect instruments conceivable for smashing and destroying, and they had achieved their destiny.

At last the wireless signals from home could penetrate to the minds of the weary and sickened combatants. They found themselves under orders to cease-fire and make for the nearest base.

That was in fact what they were doing. The *Revenge* and the *Resolution* accompanied by the cruisers *Emerald* and *Enterprise* and a miscellaneous flotilla, all greatly damaged and in some cases sinking, were limping on their way to Halifax. The airplane carrier *Courageous,* with a retinue of seaplanes and an escort of seven destroyers had turned about to the Clyde. To the south the American survivors, in unknown force, were also obeying urgent wireless instructions to withdraw. Acting under directions from their respective admiralties, a number of the still fairly seaworthy craft, including the *Saratoga,* the *Effingham,* the *Frobisher,* the *Pensacola,* and the *Memphis,* all flying white flags above their colours, were engaged in salvage work among the flotsam of the battle. There was no cooperation in this work between the British and Americans. And no conflict. They went about their business almost sluggishly, in a mood of melancholy fatigue. Emotion was drained out of them. For a time chivalry and patriotism were equally extinct. There are tales of men weeping miserably and mechanically, but no other records of feeling. There were many small craft in a sinking condition to be assisted, and a certain number of boats and disabled seaplanes. There were men clinging to the abundant wreckage, and numbers of exhausted men and corpses still afloat.

The surviving admirals, captains, and commanders, as message after message was decoded, realized more and more plainly that there had been a great mistake. The battle had been fought in error, and they were to lose no time in breaking off and offering, as the British instructions had it, "every assistance possible to enemy craft in distress." It was a confusing change from the desperate gallantry of the morning.

There was some doubt as to the treatment of enemy men and materials thus salvaged, but ultimately they were dealt with as captures and prisoners of war. This led later to much bitter recrimination.

The comments of these various surviving admirals, captains, and commanders, all now fatigued and overwrought men, and many of them experiencing the smart and distress of new wounds, as they set their battered, crippled, and bloodstained ships to these concluding tasks, make no part of this narrative; nor need we dwell upon their possible reflections upon the purpose of life and the ways of destiny as they had been manifested that day. Many of them were simple men, and it is said that battle under modern conditions, when it does not altogether destroy or madden, produces in the survivors a sort of orgiastic cleansing of the nerves. What did they think? Perhaps they did not think, but just went on with their job in its new aspect.

It is to be noted, perhaps, that before nightfall some of the ships' crews on both sides were already beginning what was to prove an endless discussion, no doubt of supreme importance to mankind, which side could be said to have "won" the Battle of the North Atlantic. They had already begun to arrange and to collaborate in editing their overcharged and staggering memories...

Amazement was going round the earth. Not only in London and New York, but wherever men were assembled in cities the news produced a monstrous perturbation. As night followed daylight round the planet an intense excitement kept the streets crowded and ablaze. Newspapers continued to print almost without intermission as fresh news came to hand, and the wireless organizations flooded the listening world with information and rumour. The British and Americans, it became clearer and clearer, had practically destroyed each other's fleets; they had wiped each other off the high seas. What would happen next, now that these two dominating sea powers were withdrawn from the international balance? The event was dreadful enough in itself, but the consequences that became apparent beyond it, consequences extraordinarily neglected hitherto, were out of all proportion more stupendous and menacing for mankind.

CHAPTER TWO

Facing the Storm

All life has something dreamlike in it. No percipient creature has ever yet lived stark reality. Nature has equipped us with such conceptions and delusions as survival necessitated, and our experiences are at best but working interpretations. Nevertheless, as they diverge more and more from practical truth and we begin to stumble against danger, our dearest dreams are at last invaded by remonstrances and warning shadows. And now this dream that was the life of the Lord Paramount was changing; more and more was it discoloured by doubt and adverse intimations.

He had taken hold of power with an absolute confidence. Mr Parham talking to an undergraduate had never been more confident than the Lord Paramount evicting Parliament. His task then was to have been the restoration of the enduring traditions of human life to their predominance. His role had been the god-like suppression of rebellious disorders. By insensible degrees his confidence had been undermined by the growing apprehension of the greatness and insidiousness of the forces of change against which he was pitted. The logic of events had prevailed. He was still convinced of the rightness of his ideas, but the god-like role had shrunken to the heroic.

The Battle of the North Atlantic had been the decisive accident to shatter his immediate vision of a British Empire rejuvenescent and triumphant, crowning the processes of history and recognizing him as its heaven-appointed saviour. He had to begin over again and lower down, and for a time at least at a disadvantage.

Blow upon blow rained upon him after that opening day of calamity. First came the tale of disaster from the battle itself: this great battleship lost, that cruiser on fire, a score of minor craft missing. At first both Britain and America accepted the idea of defeat, so heavy on either side was the list of losses. Then followed the relentless unfolding of consequences. The Dominions, with a harsh regard for their own welfare, were standing out. Canada had practically gone over to the United States and was treating for a permanent bond. South Ireland was of course against him; a republican *coup d'état* had captured Dublin, and there was already bloody and cruel fighting on the Ulster border; South Africa declared for neutrality, and in some of the more Dutch districts Union Jacks had been destroyed; Bengal was afire, and the council of Indian princes had gone over *en bloc* from their previous loyalty to a declaration of autonomy. They proposed to make peace with Russia, deport English residents, and relieve the Empire of further responsibility in the peninsula. It was appalling to consider the odds against that now isolated garrison.

The European combinations of the Lord Paramount had collapsed like a house of cards. The long projected alliance of Paramuzzi with Germany against France, which had failed to materialize so long as the German republic had held and so long as the restraining influence of Anglo-Saxondom had been effective, was now an open fact. For all practical purposes America, Great Britain, Russia, were all now for an indefinite time removed from the chessboard of Europe, and the ancient and obvious antagonism round about the Alpine massif were free to work themselves out. Europe was Rhineland history again. An unhoped for *revanche* offered itself plainly and clearly to the German people, and the accumulated resentment of ten years of humiliation and frustration blazed to fury. Von Barheim's once doubtful hold upon power lost any element of doubt. He was hailed as a reincarnation of Bismarck, and in a day Germany became again the Germany of blood and iron that had dominated Europe from 1817 to 1914. Liberalism and socialism were swamped by patriotism and vanished as if they had never been.

Within three days of the Battle of the North Atlantic nearly the whole of Europe was at war, and the French were clamouring for the covenanted British support upon their left wing as they advanced into Germany. The French fleet was quite able now to keep the vestiges of America's naval forces out of European waters, and there was also the threat of Japan to turn American attention westward. Hungary had lost no time in attacking Roumania; Czechoslovakia and Yugoslavia had declared for France, Spain mounted guns in the mountains commanding Gibraltar and became unpleasant to British shipping, and only Poland remained ambiguously under arms and at peace, between a threatening Russia on the east, dangerous Slav states to the south, a Germany exasperated on the score of Danzig and Silesia, and both Latvia and Lithuania urging grievances. The windows of the Polish Embassy in Paris suffered for this ambiguity.

There were pogroms in Hungary and Romania. Indeed, all over Eastern Europe and nearer Asia, whatever the political complexion of the government might be, the population seemed to find in pogroms a release of mental and moral tension that nothing else could give.

Turkey, it became evident, was moving on Bagdad, and a revolt in Damascus seemed to prelude a general Arab rising against France, Britain, and the Jewish state in Palestine. Both Bulgaria and Greece mobilized; Bulgaria, it was understood, was acting in concert with Hungary, but Greece as ever remained incalculable. Public opinion in Norway was said to be violently pro-American and in Sweden and Finland pro-German, but none of these states took overt military action.

The inertias of British foreign policy were tremendous.

"We hold to our obligations," said the Lord Paramount, sleepless, white, and weary, and sustained at last only by the tonics of Sir Titus, but still battling bravely with the situation. "We take the left wing in Belgium."

CHAPTER THREE

Overture in the Air

"We take the left wing in Belgium."

It was an admission of failure; it was the acceptance of a new situation. In the original scheme for world warfare that the Lord Paramount had laid before the Council of the British Empire, he had dismissed the possibility of fighting in western Europe. He had seen his war east of the Vistula and Danube and with its main field in Asia. He had trusted unduly to the wisdom and breadth of view of both America and the European chancelleries. And consequently, in spite of a certain insistence from Gerson, he had troubled very little about the novel possibilities of air war at home. Now, hard upon the heels of the naval tragedy, came the new war in the air.

The land war on the European frontiers made little progress after the first French advance into Westphalia. The Franco-Italian front was strongly fortified on either side, and the numerous and varied mechanisms of the reconstituted British army had still to come into action. There had been some miscalculation about the transport needed to put them across the Channel. But every power now possessed huge air forces, and there was nothing to prevent their coming into action forthwith.

The bombing of London, Paris, Hamburg, and Berlin with high explosives occurred almost simultaneously. The moon was just entering upon its second quarter; the weather all over the Northern Hemisphere was warm and serene, and everything favoured this offensive.

Night after night, for fifteen days, the air of Europe was filled with the whir or gigantic engines and the expectation of bursting bombs. The fighting planes kept each other busy; anti-aircraft guns were a disappointment, and all the great centres of population seethed with apprehensions and nervous distresses that might at any time explode in senseless panics. The early raiders used only high explosives. The conventions were observed. But everywhere there was a feeling that these explosive and incendiary raids were merely experimental preludes to the dreaded gas attacks.

There was a press agitation in London for "Gas masks for everyone" and a strong discussion of possibilities of the use of "anti-gases." The London authorities issued exhortations to the people to keep calm, and all theatres, music halls, and cinemas were closed to prevent nocturnal congestions of the central districts. Millions of masks were issued, most of them of very slight efficiency, but they served to allay panic, and indeed no alleged precaution was too absurd for that purpose.

Gerson, looking ahead, removed as much as he could of the establishment of the government headquarters to a series of great gas-proof dugouts he had prepared at Barnet, but for a time the Master clung to his rooms in the War Office and would not resort to this concealment. Gerson protested in vain. "But," said the Lord Paramount, "Whitehall is Empire. To be driven underground in this fashion is already half defeat."

One night a rumour gained conviction as it spread until it became an absolute assurance, that gas was on its way and gas in monstrous quantities. There followed a reign of terror in the East End of London and a frantic exodus into Essex and the West End. The Germans used incendiary shells that night, and there were horrible scenes as the fire engines fought their way through the westward streaming crowds. Hundreds of cases of people who were crushed and trampled upon reached the hospitals, and the bombs and the fires accounted for thousands more.

The Lord Paramount was asked to visit the hospitals. "Can't the Royal Family do that?" he asked almost irritably, for he hated the spectacle of suffering. His heart quailed at the thought of that vista of possibly reproachful sufferers. And then, changing a tone which jarred even on his own sensibilities: "I will not seem to infringe upon the popularity of the reigning house. The people will rather see them than me, and I have my hands full – full! – my God, full to overflowing."

Mrs Pinchot understood, she understood entirely, but the general public, which has no sense of the limitations of the time and energy of its leaders, interpreted this preoccupation with duty as an inhuman rather than superhuman characteristic and made its interpretation very plain and audible. It became clearer and clearer to the Lord Paramount that destiny had not marked him for a popular leader. He tried to steel his heart to that disappointment, but the pain was there. For his heart was as tender as it was great.

Gerson greeted the cresendo of the air attacks with unconcealed satisfaction.

265

"They're getting it in Paris worse than we are," he said. "Those German incendiary bombs are amazing, and nerves are all out. They're talking of reprisals on the population in Westphalia. Good! Rome got it too last night. It's this sort of thing the Italians can't stand. They feel too much. They may turn on Paramuzzi in a frenzy if we just keep on at them. But, trust me, nothing could be better to wake up our own people. They'll begin to snarl presently. The British bulldog hasn't begun to fight yet. Wait till its blood is up."

The ugly mouth closed with an appreciative snap.

"The only possible reply to these German incendiaries is Gas L. And the sooner we get to that the better. Then the world will see."

CHAPTER FOUR

The Strong Way with Mutiny

B ut the common man in Britian was not being the British bulldog of General Gerson's hopes. He was declining to be a bulldog altogether. He was remaining a profoundly sceptical human being, with the most disconcerting modern tendencies. And much too large a part of his combative energy was directed, not against the appointed enemy, but against the one commanding spirit which could still lead him to victory.

The Decree of Public Safety was now the law of the land. It might not be strictly constitutional, but the dictatorship had superseded constituionalism. Yet everywhere it was being disputed. The national apathy was giving place to a resistance as bold as it was dogged. North, east, and west there were protests, remonstrances, overt obstruction. The recalcitrant workers found lawyers to denounce the Lord Paramount's authority, funds to organize resistance. Half the magistrates in the country were recusant and had to be superseded by military courts. Never had the breach between the popular mind and the imperial will of the directive and possessing classes been so open and so uncompromising. It was astounding to find how superficial loyalty to the Empire had always been.

The distress of the Lord Paramount at these tensions was extreme. "My English," he said. "My English. My English have been misled." He would stand with a sheaf of reports from the mobilization department in his hand repeating, "I did not count on this."

It needed all the most penetrating reminders of which Gerson was capable to subdue that heroically tender heart to the stern work of repression. And yet, just because the Lord Paramount had stood aside and effaced himself in that matter of the hospitals he was misjudged, and his repressive measures were understood to be the natural expression of a fierce and arrogant disposition. The caricaturists gave him glaring and projecting eyes and a terrible row of teeth. They made his hands – and really they were quite shapely hands – into the likeness of gesticulating claws. That was a particularly cruel attack. "I must be strong," he repeated to himself, "and later they will understand."

But it is hard for a patriot to be stark and strong with his own misguided people. Riots had to be dispersed with bayonets and rifle-fire in the south of Wales, in Lancashire and the Midlands. There was savage street fighting in Glasgow. The tale of these domestic casualties lengthened. The killed were presently to be counted by the hundred. "Nip the trouble in the bud," said Gerson. "Arrest the agitators and shoot a few of them, if you don't like firing on crowds. Over half the country now time is being lost and the drafts delayed."

So those grim sedition clauses which had looked so calmly heroic on paper were put into operation. The military authorities arrested vigorously. A few old hands were caught in the net but even before the courts martial were held it was apparent to the

Lord Paramount that for the most part they were dealing with excitable youths and youngish men. Most of these younger agitators would have been treated very indulgently indeed if they had been university students. But Gerson insisted upon the need of a mental shock for the whole country. "Shoot now," he said, "and you may forgive later. War is war."

"Shoot now," said Gerson, "and the rest will come in for training, good as gold. Stop the rot. And let 'em say what they like about you."

The Lord Paramount could feel how tenderly and completely that faithful secretary of his could read the intimations of his saddened and yet resolute profile. "Yes," he admitted, "we must shoot – though the bullet tears us on its way."

The order went forth.

There was a storm of remonstrances, threats, and passionate pleas for pity. That was to have been expected. Much was fended off from direct impact upon the Lord Paramount, but he knew the protest was there. It found an echo in his own too human heart. "The will of a great people," he said, "must override these little individual stories. There is this boy Carrol from Bristol they are asking me to reprieve! There seems to be a special fuss about him. A sort of boy scholar of promise – yes. But read the poison of those speeches he made! He struck an officer..."

"Shall Carrol die?" asked an outbreak of placards along Whitehall that no one could account for. That hardened the Lord Protector's mouth; he must show he would not be bullied, and in stern response to that untimely challenge young Carrol and five and thirty associates died at dawn.

There was a hideous popular clamour at this unavoidable act of war. The Lord Paramount's secretarial organization was far too new and scanty to protect him adequately from the clamour of this indignation and, it may be, something in himself acted as an all too ready receiver for these messages of antagonism. Abruptly out of the void into which he was wont to vanish appeared Sir Bussy the unquenchable. He was now almost full size again and confident and abrupt in his pre-war style.

"This shooting of boys!" he said. "This killing of honest and straightforward people who don't agree with you! Why, damn it! we might be in Italy! It's a century out of date. Why did you ever let this war get loose?"

The Lord Paramount stood defensively mute, and it was Gerson who took the words out of his mouth and answered Sir Bussy. "Have you never even heard of discipline? Have you never heard of the needs of war? I tell you we are at war."

"But why are we at war?" cried Sir Bussy. "Why the devil are we at war?"

"What the devil are fleets and armies for if we are never to use them? What other ways are there for settling national differences? What's a flag for if you're never going to wave it? I tell you, it's not only street-corner boys and Bolshie agitators who are going against the wall. This Empire of ours is fighting for its life. It calls on every man. And you know as well as I know, Sir Bussy, what it needs to win... And at what a pace the stuff is coming in!"...

Gerson had turned to the Lord Paramount, and Sir Bussy, it seemed, was no longer present.

"Peace time you may be as soft as you like – delay and humbug have always been the rule for home politics, naturally – but you can't play about with war and foreign policy. For things of that order you need a heart of steel."

"A heart of steel," echoed the Lord Paramount.

"Gas L and a heart of steel."

"We go through with it, *mon général*," said the Lord Paramount. "Trust me."

"Time we started going through with it…"

What was far more distressing to the Lord Paramount than any other resistances or remonstrances over this business of internal discipline was the emergence from nothingness of a certain old lady, old Mrs Carrol. Against addresses, protests, demonstrations, threats of murder, and the like, the Lord Paramount could be the strongest of strong men, could show a face of steely disregard. But old Mrs Carrol was different. Her attack was different in its nature. She did not threaten, she did not abuse. Carrol, it seemed, had been an only son. She wanted him alive again.

She came like a sudden thought into his presence. She was exactly like an old woman lodge keeper at Samphore Park, near Mr Parham's early home. That old woman, whose name was long since forgotten, had had an only son also, three or four years older than the juvenile Parham, and he had worked in the garden of Mr Parham's father. Always he had been known as Freddy. He had been a very friendly, likeable boy, and the two youngsters had been great friends and allies. He read books and told stories, and once he had confided a dreadful secret to his companion. He was half minded to be a socialist, he was, and he didn't believe not more'n half the Bible was true. They had had an argument, a quarrel, for it was young Parham's first meeting with sedition, and duty and discipline were in his blood. But of course it was impossible there could be any identity between this long-forgotten rustic and young Carrol. By now he would be old enough to be young Carrol's father.

It was a little difficult to trace how this old lady got at the Lord Paramount. She seemed to have great penetrating power. His staff ought perhaps to have fended her off. But the same slight distrust of those about him, that sense of the risk of "envelopment," which made the Lord Paramount desire to be as "accessible" as possible to the generality, left just the sort of opening through which a persistent old woman of that kind might come. At any rate, there she was, obliterating all the rest of the case, very shabby and with a careworn face and a habit of twisting one hand round inside the other as she spoke, extraordinarily reminiscent of Freddy's mother.

"When people go to war and get boys shot and the like, they don't think a bit what it means to them they belongs to, their mothers and such, what have given their best years to their upbringing.

"He was a good boy," she insisted, "and you had him shot. He was a good *skilful* boy."

She produced a handful of paper scraps from nowhere and held them out, quivering, to the Lord Paramount. "Here's some of the little things he drew before he went into the works. Why, I've seen things by royalties not half so good as these! He didn't ought to have been shot, clever as he was. Isn't there anything to be done about it?

"And when he got older he had a meccano set, and he made a railway signal with lights that went on and off, and the model of a windmill that went round when you blew it. No wonder he was welcome in the works. I'd have brought them here for you to see if I'd thought they would have weighed with you. You'd have marvelled. And now he won't never make anything more with his hands, and those busy little brains of his are still as stone."

There is no record that Alexander or Cæsar or Napoleon was haunted by an old woman who kept on twisting her hands about as though she were trying to wring the blood out of a deed that was done, and who sought to temper her deadly persistence by a pose of imploration. Almost she cringed.

"You don't understand, my good woman," said the Lord Paramount. "He put his brains to a bad use. He was a mutineer. He was a rebel."

The old lady would have none of that. "Artie wasn't ever a rebel. Don't I know it? Why, when he was little I was frightened at his goodness, always so willing, he was, and so helpful. I've thought time after time, for all his health and spirits, 'That boy must be ailing,' so good he was to me...

"And now you've shot him. Can't anything else be done about it still? Can't something be done instead?"

"This crucifies me," he said to Mrs Pinchot. "This crucifies me."

That made him feel a little better for a time, but not altogether better. "All things," he said, "I must suffer in my task," and still was not completely convinced. He descended from his cross. He tried to be angry. "Damn old Mrs Carrol! Can no one make that old woman understand that *war is war?* This is no place for her. She must be stopped from coming here."

But she continued to come, nevertheless; though her coming had less and less the quality of a concrete presence and more and more of the vague indefinable besetting distressfulness of a deteriorating dream.

CHAPTER FIVE

The Declaration of Washington

The Great War of 1914–18 had not only been the greatest war in history, it had also been the greatest argument about war that had ever stormed through the human mind. The Fourteen Points of President Wilson, the vague, unjustifiable promises of Crewe House to a repentant Germany, had been more effective than any battle. And now this great war the Lord Paramount had launched was taking on the same quality of an immense and uncontrollable argument.

In the long run man will be lost or saved by argument, for collective human acts are little more than arguments in partial realization.

And now that strange mixture of forward-reaching imagination, hardy enterprise, exalted aims, and apparently inseparable cynicism which makes the American character a wonder and perplexity for the rest of mankind was to become the central reality of the Lord Paramount's mind.

The argument was given definite form by an entirely characteristic American action on the part of the President. He issued a declaration, which was to be known in history as the declaration of Washington, in which, illogically enough since his country was at war, he proposed to decline any further fighting. America, he said, was not too proud but too sane to continue the conflict. He did not add, the Lord Paramount remarked, as he might have done, that the Battle of the North Atlantic had left her quite incapable for a time of any further effective intervention in Europe or Asia. Everything she had left she needed to watch Japan. But that factor in the question the President ignored – shamelessly. And he said things fellows like Hamp or Camelford or Atterbury might have said. He said things Sir Bussy would have cheered. He was the first head of a state to come out definitely on the side of the forces that are undermining and repudiating history.

This declaration of inaction, this abandonment of militant nationalism flew like an arrow athwart the Atlantic into the hands and into the mental storm of the Lord Paramount. The document presented itself a hasty duplicate from some transmitting machine, in smudged purple lettering, and he paced his bureau with it in his hand and read it aloud to his always faithful listener. An inner necessity obliged him to read it aloud, distasteful though it was in every line. This great denial was worded with that elaborate simplicity, that stiffly pompous austerity, which has long been the distinctive style of American public utterances.

" 'There has arisen suddenly out of the momentary failure of one young airman's skill in Persia a great and terrible crisis in the affairs of the world. With an incredible rapidity the larger part of mankind has fallen again into warfare. The material of warfare stood ready to explode, and there was no other means sufficiently available to avert this collapse. All over our planet, beyond every precedent, men are now slaying and destroying. These United

States have not been able to remain aloof. Already our battleships have fought and thousands of our sons have been killed, and were it not for the ingrained sanity upon our northern and southern boundaries, all this continent also would be aflame.

" 'Yet the fortunate position of our territories and our practical community of ideas with the great dominion to the north of us still hold us aloof from the extremer carnage. That and the naval strength that still remains to us, suffice to keep our homeland untouched by the daily and nightly horrors that now threaten the civilian life in all the crowded cities of Europe and Asia. Our share in this work of devastation, as far as we are disposed to take a share, depends upon our willingness to attack. So far we have attacked and will attack only to stay the hand of the destroyer. It is still possible for the people of the American communities, almost alone now among all the communities of the world, to sleep soundly of nights, to spend days untroubled by the immediate sounds and spectacle of battle, to think and exchange thought with deliberation, and to consider the rights and possibilities of this tragic explosion of human evil. It is our privilege and our duty now to sit in judgment upon this frightful spectacle as no other people in the world can do.

" 'It would be easy – indeed, for some of us Americans it has already been too easy – to find in our present relative advantage the recognition of peculiar virtues, the reward of distinctive wisdom. I will not lend myself to any such unctuous patriotism. It is for the historians of a coming day to apportion the praise and blame among the actors in this world catastrophe. Perhaps no actors are guilty; perhaps they are impelled by forces greater than themselves to fulfil the roles prepared for them; perhaps it is not men and nations but ideas and cultures that we should arraign. What matters now is that justly or unjustly we Americans have been favoured by fortune and granted unequalled privileges. We can serve the world now as no other people can do. In serving the world, we shall also serve ourselves. Upon us, if upon any people, has been bestowed, for the second and supreme occasion, the power of decision between world peace or world destruction.

" 'Let us, in no spirit of boasting or nationalistic pride, but with thankfulness and humility, consider the peculiar nature of these United States. In their political nature they are unlike anything that has ever existed before. They are not sovereign states as sovereign states are understood in any other part of the world. They were sovereign states, but they have ceded to a common federal government that much of their freedom that might have led to warfare. Not without dire distress and passion and bloodshed did our forefathers work out this continental peace. The practical and intellectual difficulties were very great. It was hard to determine what was of local and what of general concern. To this day many points remain debatable. On the issue whether our labour should be here bound and here free, we spilt the lives of a generation. We learnt that we must make all labour free forever if progress was to continue. Not always have we been wise and noble in our career. Much that we have learnt we have learnt in suffering and through error. Nevertheless, our huge community, year by year and generation by generation, since its liberty was won, has been feeling its way towards the conception of an enduring and universal peace, has been seeking by pacts and propaganda some way of organizing a permanent peace in the world. It has become our tradition so far as we can be said to have a tradition. No other great mass of human beings has ever had so clear and active a peace disposition as our consolidated peoples. To us warfare has become a thing unnecessary and horrible, as intolerable as many another harsh and frightful custom, horrible and unpardonable now as human sacrifice and as that holocaust of victims at a chieftain's burial which once seemed integral to social life. We know, and have gone far to realize in fact, that the life of all human beings can be fearless and free.

" 'And if we have gone cautiously in our search for peace, avoiding above all things any entangling alliances with Powers organized on the militant pattern of the past, that separateness has not been because we, unmindful of our common humanity, were disposed to a selfish and sluggish isolation from the less happily circumstanced states of the Old World. It is rather because from our beginning and through the great wisdom of our chief founder Washington, we have been aware of the immense dangers that lurk in so mighty a proposition, so intricate and gigantic a project as world organization. It has been our steadfast determination that our naïve and ever-increasing strength should not be tricked into the service of Old World hates and Old World ambitions. From the utterances of President Wilson, through notes and memoranda and messages and conferences, to the days of the Kellogg Pact, the voice of America has been plainly for peace on earth and goodwill between all kinds of men.

" 'In the past twelve years we have experienced much, seen much, thought and discussed abundantly, and it becomes clearer and clearer in our minds; it is a matter now of common remark and agreement, that we must regard all states and governments of today merely as the trustees and temporary

279

holders of power for that universal conciliation and rule to which all things are tending. Here, as the elected head of your federal government, I can say plainly that no man on earth whatever owes more than a provisional allegiance to the rulers he may find above him, and that his profounder, his fundamental loyalty, is to no flag or nation, but to mankind. I say this of our constitution and of our flag as of all other flags and constitutions. The frightful suffering, bloodshed, and destruction of this present moment call to every man to turn his mind and hopes towards that federal government of the world whose creation, steadfastly and speedily, is now the urgent task before our race. Such rulers and ministers as fail to subserve this coalescence now are, we declare, no less than traitors to their human blood, the traitor slaves of dead imaginations and superannuated organizations.

" 'And so we, the government and people of the United States, stand out of this warfare just as completely as it is possible for us to stand out of it, armed and watchful, seeking some form of intervention that will bring it to an end. We issue our invitations to all such powers as remain still hesitating and neutral in this confusion of hates, to gather in conference, a conference not simply now for treaties, promises, and declarations, but for the establishment forthwith of united activities and unified controls, that shall never cease from operation henceforth. And we appeal not only to sovereign states to realize this conception of which our people has become the guardian and exponent; we appeal to every free-minded individual man and woman in the world. We say to all and sundry, "Stand out of this warfare. Refuse to be belligerent. Withdraw your services, withdraw your resources." We are honest and loyal in our endeavour, we are acting upon the accumulated resolve of a century and a half, and we call to you for a loyalty transcending flag or country. So far as we of these States can assist and support your action, without intensifying the bitterness of conflict, we will. Restrain your rulers. Give yourselves now to that possible Empire of Peace, in which we and you and all the life that stirs upon this planet may cooperate together.' "

The reader paused.

He took a deep breath, made three paces to the window, and turned. He held out the paper and patted it. "There it is," he said. "It was bound to come. There it is, plain and clear – the bolt that has been gathering force and weight – the moral attack."

He paced. "Propaganda with a vengeance. An attack on our morale more deadly than a thousand aeroplanes."

He stopped short. "Was there ever such hypocrisy?" he demanded.

"Never," said Mrs Pinchot stoutly. "It's revolting."

"They pressed us with their fleet building. They bullied and quarrelled when we were only too ready for acquiescent action. They Shylocked Europe. And then all this humanitarian virtue!"

Something seemed to twist round in the mind of the Lord Paramount, something that twisted round and struck at his heart. He could not maintain his indignant pose. This Presidential address suddenly allied itself with things that had lain dormant in his mind for weeks, things he associated with men like Camelford (and, by the by, where on earth was Camelford?) and Sir Bussy. He stopped short in his pacing, with the typed copy of the address, held by one corner, dangling from his fingers.

"Suppose," said the Lord Paramount, "it is not hypocrisy! Suppose he really means the things he has said here! In spite of his patriots."

He stared at Mrs Pinchot, and she was staring back at him.

"But how can he mean things that don't mean anything?" She stuck to it loyally.

"But they *do* mean something. They *do* mean something. Even if they don't mean it straight. Suppose this is humbug. I believe this is humbug. But humbug does not pretend to be something unless it pays to do so. There must be something to which it appeals. What is that something? What is that shapeless drive? Such history as I have ever taught or studied. A world without flags or nations. A sordid universal peace. The end of history. It's in the air; it's in the age. It is what Heaven has sent me to dispute and defeat. A delusion. A dream..."

"Where am I?" said the Lord Paramount and passed his hand across his brow. "Who am I?... A delusion and a dream? One or other is a delusion – this new world or mine?"

BOOK FIVE

QUINTESSENTIAL

CHAPTER ONE

The Spirit of the Times

"This is far more than a war between Britain and America," said the Lord Paramount. "Or any war. It is a struggle for the soul of man. All over the world. Let us suppose the President is hypocritical – and he *may* be hypocritical; nevertheless, he is appealing to something which has become very real and powerful in the world. He may be attempting only to take advantage of that something in order to turn the world against me, but that does not make that something to which he appeals less considerable. It is a spirit upon which he calls, a powerful, dangerous spirit. It is the antagonist to the spirit that sustains me, whose embodiment I am. It is my real enemy."

"You say things so wonderfully," said Mrs Pinchot.

"You see this man, entrusted in war time with the leadership of a mighty sovereign state, spits his venom against all sovereign states – against all separate sovereignty. He, the embodiment of a nation, deprecates nationality. He, the constitutional war leader, repudiates war. This is Anarchism enthroned – at the White House. Here is a mighty militant organization – and it has no

285

face. Here is political blackness and night. This is the black threat at the end of history."

He paused and resumed with infinite impressiveness:

"Everywhere this poison of intellectual restatement undermines men's souls. Even honest warfare, you see, becomes impossible. Propaganda ousts the heroic deed. We promise. We camouflage. We change the face of things. Treason calls to treason."

She sat tense, gripping her typewriter with both hands, her eyes devouring him.

"Not *thus*," said the Lord Paramount, his fine voice vibrating. "Not *thus*..."

"The jewels of life I say are loyalty, flag, nation, obedience, sacrifice... The Lord of Hosts!... Embattled millions!...

"I will fight to the end," said the Lord Paramount. "I will fight to the end... Demon, I defy thee!..."

His hands sought symbolic action. He crumpled the Presidential address into a ball. He pulled it out again into long rags and tore it to shreds and flung them over the carpet. He walked up and down, kicking them aside. He chanted the particulars of his position. "The enemy relentless – false allies – rebels in the Empire – treachery, evasion, and cowardice at home. God above me! It is no light task that I have in hand. Enemies that change shape, foes who are falsehoods! Is crown and culmination in the succession of empires ours to close in such a fashion? I fight diabolical ideas. If all the hosts of evil rise in one stupendous alliance against me, still will I face them for King and Nation and Empire."

He was wonderful, that lonely and gigantic soul pacing the room, thinking aloud, hewing out his mighty apprehensions in fragmentary utterances. The scraps of the torn Presidential address now, in hopeless rout, showed a disposition to get under tables and chairs and into odd corners. It was as if they were ashamed of the monstrous suggestions of strange disloyalties that they had brought to him.

"Curious and terrifying to trace the growth of this Adversary, the Critical Spirit, this destroyer of human values... From the days when Authority ruled. When even to question was fatal... Great days then for the soul. Simple faith and certain action. Right known and Sin defined. Now we are nowhere. Sheep without a shepherd... First came little disloyalties rebellious of sense and sloth. Jests – corrosive jests. Impatience with duty. One rebel seeking fellowship by corrupting his fellow. The simple beliefs, incredible as fact but absolutely true for the soul. That was the beginning. If you question them they go; the ages of faith knew that. But man must question, question, question. Man must innovate – stray. So easy to question and so fatal. Then Science arises, a concatenation of questions, at first apologetic and insidous. Then growing proud and stubborn. Everything shall be investigated, everything shall be made plain, everything shall be certain. Pour your acids on the altar! It dissolves. Clearly it was nothing but marble. Pour them on the crown! It was just a circle of metal – alloyed metal. Pour them on the flag! It turns red and burns. So none of these things matter...

"Why was this not arrested? Why did authority lose confidence and cease to strike? What lethargy crept into the high places?...

"And so at last the human story comes to a pause. The spirit of human history halts at her glorious warp and weft, turns aside, and asks, 'Shall I go on?'

"Shall she go on? With God's help I will see that she goes on. One mighty struggle, one supreme effort, and then we will take Anarchy – which is Science the Destroyer – by the throat. This Science, which pretends to be help and illumination, which illuminates nothing but impenetrable darkness, must cease. Cease altogether. We must bring our world back again to tradition, to the classical standards, to the ancient and, for man, the eternal values, the historical forms, which express all that man is or can ever be...

"I though that Science was always contradicting herself, but that is only because she contradicts all history. Essential to science is the repudiation of *all* foundations, her own included. She disdains philosophy. The post is a curiosity – or waste paper. Anarchism! Nothing is, but everything is going to be. She redeems all her promises with fresh promissory notes...

"Perpetually Science is overthrown, and perpetually she rises the stronger for her overthrow. It is the story of Antæus! Yet Hercules slew him!"

"My Hercules!" whispered Mrs Pinchot, just audibly.

"Held him and throttled him!"

"Yes, yes," she whispered, "with those strong arms."

The manner of the Lord Paramount changed.

He stood quite still and looked his little secretary in her deep, dark eyes. For one instant his voice betrayed tenderness. "It is a great thing," he said, "to have one human being at least in whose presence the armour can be laid aside." She made no answer, but it was as if her whole being dilated and glowed through her eyes.

Their souls met in that instant's silence.

"And now to work," said the Lord Paramount, and was again the steely master of his destiny.

"Oh, God!" he cried abruptly and jumped a foot from the ground.

There was no need for her to ask the reason for this sudden reversal of his dignity.

A whining overhead, a long whining sound, had grown louder, and then a loud explosion close at hand proclaimed that another enemy aeroplane had slipped through the London cordon. She leapt to her feet and handed him his gas mask before she adjusted her own, for one must set a good example and wear what the people have been told to wear.

CHAPTER TWO

Fantasia in Trafalgar Square

"There's no gas," he said and pointed to the clear red glow in the east. He tore off his mask, for he hated to have his face concealed. He sniffed the pervading anti-gas with satisfaction. He echoed in a tone of wonder, "*Still* there is no gas."

She too emerged from her disfiguring visor. "But are we safe?" she asked.

"Trust me," he said.

The sky was full of the loud drone of engines, but no aircraft was visible. The evening was full of warm-tinted clouds, and the raiders and the fighting machines were no doubt dodging each other above that canopy. The distant air barrage made an undertone to the engine whir, as if an immense rubber ball were being bounced on an equally immense tin tray. The big Rolls-Royce had vanished. Its driver, perhaps, had taken it to some less conspicuous position and had not yet returned.

"I find something exhilarating in all this," said the Lord Paramount. "I do not see why I should not share the dangers of my people."

A few other intrepid spirits were walking along Whitehall, wearing gas masks of various patterns, and some merely with rags and handkerchiefs to their mouths. Many, like the Lord Paramount, had decided that the fear of gas was premature and either carried their masks in their hands or attempted no protection. Except for two old-fashioned water carts, there were no vehicles in sight. These water carts were busy spraying a heavy, slowly volatile liquid with a sweetish offensive odour that was understood to be an effective antidote to most forms of gas poisoning. It gave off a bluish low-lying mist that swirled and vanished as it diffused. A great deal of publicity had been given to the anti-gas supply after the East End panic. The supply of illuminating gas had been cut off now for some days, and the retorts and mains had been filled with an anti-gas of established efficacy which could be turned on when required from the normal burners. This had the same sweetish smell as the gas sprayed from the carts, and it had proved very reassuring to the public when raids occurred.

"Let us walk up Whitehall," said the Lord Paramount, "I seem to remember an instruction that the car should shelter from observation under the Admiralty arch in case of a raid. We might go up there."

She nodded.

"You are not nervous?" he asked.

"Beside you!" she glowed.

The car was not under the arch, and they went on into the Square. There seemed to be a lull in the unseen manœuvres overhead. Either the invaders had gone altogether or they were too high to be heard or they had silencers for their engines. The only explosions audible were the deep and distant firing of the guns of the outer aircraft zone.

"It is passing over," said the Lord Paramount. "They must have made off."

Then he remarked how many people were abroad and how tranquil was their bearing. There were numbers visible now. A moment ago they had seemed alone. Men and women were coming out from the station of the tube railway very much as they might have emerged after a shower of rain. There were newsvendors who apparently had never left the curb. "There is something about our English folk," he said, "magnificently calm. Something dogged. An obstinate resistance to excitement. They say little but they just carry on."

But now the air was screaming!

A moment of blank expectation.

In an instant the whole area was alive with bursting bombs. Four – or was it five? – deafening explosions and blinding flashes about them and above them followed one another in close succession, and the ordered pavement before them became like a crater in eruption.

Mr Parham had seen very little of the more violent side of warfare. During the first World War a certifiable weakness of the heart and his natural aptitudes had made him more serviceable on the home front. And now, peeping out of the eyes of the Lord Paramount, he was astounded at the grotesque variety of injury to human beings of which explosions are capable. Accustomed to study warfare through patriotic war films, he had supposed that there was a distinctive dignity about death in battle, that for the most part heroes who were slain threw up their arms and fell forward in so seemly a way as to conceal anything that might otherwise be derogatory to themselves or painful to the spectator. But these people who were killed in the Square displayed no such delicacy; perhaps because they were untrained civilians; they were torn to bits, mixed indifferently with masonry, and thrown about like rags and footballs and splashes of red mud. An old match seller who had been squatting on the stone curb, an old woman in a black bonnet, leapt up high into the air towards the Lord Paramount, spread out as if she were going to fly over him like a witch, and then incredibly flew to fragments, all her boxes of matches radiating out as though a gigantic foot had kicked right though her body at them. Her bonnet swept his hat off, and a box of matches and some wet stuff hit him. It wasn't like any sort of decent event. It was pure nightmare – impure nightmare. It was an outrage on the ancient dignity of war.

And then he realized the column had been hit and was coming down. Almost solemnly it was coming down. It had been erect so long, and now, with a kind of rheumatic hesitation, it bent itself like a knee. It seemed to separate slowly into fragments. It seemed as though it were being lowered by invisible cords from the sky. There was even time to say things.

Never had Mrs Pinchot seen him so magnificent.

He put an arm about her. He had meant to put his hand on her shoulder, but she was little and he embraced her head.

"Stay by me," he said. He had time to say, "Trust me and trust God. Death cannot touch me until my work is done."

Nelson turned over and fell stiffly and slantingly. He went, with the air of meeting an engagement, clean through the façade of the big insurance buildings on the Cockspur Street side of the Square. About the Master and his secretary the bursting pavement jumped again, as the great masses of column hit it and leapt upon it and lay still. The Lord Paramount was flung a yard or so, and staggered and got to his feet and saw Mrs Pinchot on all fours. Then she too was up and running towards him with love and consternation on her face.

"You are covered with blood!" she cried. "You are covered with blood."

"Not mine," he said and reeled towards the streaming ruins of a fountain basin, and was suddenly sick and sick and sick.

She washed his face with her handkerchief and guided him towards a plateau of still level pavement outside the Golden Cross Hotel.

"It was the weakness of Nelson," he said – for it was one of his standard remarks on such occasions.

"Nelson!" he repeated, his thoughts going off at a tangent, and he stared up into the empty air. "Good God!"

Hardly twenty feet of the pedestal remained.

And then: "High time we made our way to these new headquarters of Gerson's. I wonder where that car can be hiding. Where is that car? Ssh! Those must be bombs again, bursting somewhere on the south side. Don't listen to them."

He realized that a number of distraught and dishevelled people were looking at him curiously. They regarded him with critical expectation. They became suddenly quite numerous. Many of these faces were suspicious and disagreeable.

"I would gladly stay here and help with the wounded," he said, "but my duty lies elsewhere."

Men with Red Cross badges had appeared from nowhere and were searching among the wreckage. Injured people were beginning to crawl and groan.

"We must commandeer a car," said the Lord Paramount. "Find some officers and commandeer a car. I must take you out of all this. We must get out of London to the headquarters as soon as possible. My place is there. We must find out where the car has gone. Gerson will know. We had better walk back to the War Office, perhaps, and start from there. Do not be afraid. Keep close to me... Was that another bomb?"

Chapter Three

War Is War

Gerson was talking to him. They were in a different place. It might be they were already in the great Barnet dugout which was to be the new seat of government; a huge and monstrous cavern it was, at any rate; and they were discussing the next step that must be taken if the Empire, now so sorely stressed, so desperately threatened, was still to hack its way through to victory. Overhead there rumble and drummed an anti-aircraft barrage.

"If we listen to this propaganda of the American President's," said Gerson, "we are lost. People must not listen to it. It's infectious – hallucination. Get on with the war before the rot comes. Get on with the war! It is now or never," said Gerson.

His grim and desperate energy dominated the Lord Paramount. "Gas L," he repeated, "Gas L. All Berlin in agony and then no more Berlin. Would they go on fighting after that? For all their new explosives."

"I call God to witness," said the Lord Paramount, "that I have no mind for gas war."

"War is war," said Gerson.

"This is not the sort of war I want."

Gerson's never very respectful manner gave place to a snarl of irritation. "D'you think this sort of war is the sort of war I want?" he demanded. "Not a bit of it! It's the sort of war these damned chemists and men of science have forced upon us. It's a war made into a monster. Because someone failed to nip science in the bud a hundred years ago. They are doing their best to make war impossible. That's their game. But so long as I live it shan't be impossible whatever they do to it. I'll see this blasted planet blown to bits first. I'll see the last man stifled. What's a world without war? The way to stop this infernal German bombing is to treat Berlin like a nest of wasps and *kill* the place. And that's what I want to set about doing now. But we can't get the stuff in! Camelford and Woodcock procrastinate and obstruct. If you don't deal with those two men in a day or so I shall deal with them myself, in the name of military necessity. I want to arrest them."

"Arrest them," said the Lord Paramount.

"And shoot them if necessary."

"Shoot if necessary," said the Lord Paramount...

Everything seemed to be passing into Gerson's hands. The Lord Paramount had to remind himself more and more frequently that the logic of war demanded this predominance of Gerson. So long as the war lasted. He began where statecraft ceased, and when he had done statecraft would again take up what he had left of the problems entrusted to him.

The Lord Paramount had a persuasion that Camelford and Sir Bussy had been arrested already and had escaped. Some time had elapsed – imperceptibly. Yes, they had been arrested and they had got away. Sir Bussy had shown Camelford how to get away.

CHAPTER FOUR

A Necessary Execution

Something obscured the Lord Paramount's mind. Clouds floated before it. Voices that had nothing to do with the course of affairs sustained some kind of commentary. Events were no longer following one another with a proper amplitude of transition. He seemed to be passing in cinematograph fashion from scene to scene. A pursuit of Sir Bussy was in progress, Gerson was hunting him, but it was no longer clear where and how these events were unfolding.

Then it would seem that Sir Bussy had been discovered hiding in Norway. He had been kidnapped amazingly by Gerson's agents and brought to Norfolk and shot. It was no time to be fussy about operations in neutral territory. And some rigorous yet indefinable necessity required that the Lord Paramount should go secretly at night to see Sir Bussy's body. He was reminded of the heroic murder of Matteotti, of the still more heroic effacement of the Duc d'Enghien by Napoleon. It is necessary that one man should die for the people. This financial Ishmaelite had to be ended in his turn. The day had come for property also to come into the scheme of duty.

The Lord Paramount found himself descending from his automobile at the end of a winding and bumpy lane that led down to the beach near Sheringham. Extravagantly like Napoleon he felt; he was even wearing a hat of the traditional pattern. He had to be muffled. He was muffled in a cloak of black velvet. The head lamps showed a whitewashed shed, a boat on a bank of shingle; beyond, the breakers of an uneasy sea flashed white as they came out of the blue-grey indistinctness into the cone of lights. "This way, sir," said a young officer and made his path more difficult by the officious flicking of an electric torch. The shingle was noisy underfoot.

On a plank, already loaded with shot to sink it into the unknown, and covered with a sheet, lay the body of Sir Bussy. For a moment the Lord Paramount stood beside it with his arms folded. The Dictatorship had lost its last internal enemy. Everyone had come to a halt now, and everything was silent except for the slow pulsing of the sea.

And in this fashion it was, though the Lord Paramount, that their six years of association had to end. It had been impossible to incorporate this restless, acquisitive, innovating creature with the great processes of history; he had been incurably undisciplined and disintegrating, and at last it had become a plain struggle for existence between him and his kind, and the established institutions of our race. So long as he had lived he had seemed formidable, but now that his power was wrested from him, there was something pathetic and pitiful in his flimsy proportions. He was a little chap, a poor little fellow. And he had had his hospitably friendly, appealing side.

Why had he not listened to Mr Parham? Why had he not sought his proper place in the scheme of things and learned to cooperate and obey? Why had he pitted himself against history and perished as all who pit themselves against tradition must perish? The Lord Paramount stood by the little spherical protrusion of the sheet that veiled Sir Bussy's head; Gerson stood at the feet. The Lord Paramount's thoughts went from the dead to the living.

Had he really killed Sir Bussy, or had Gerson killed him?

What are the real and essential antagonisms of human life? Spite of all the ruthless tumult of events that had crowded upon the Lord Paramount, he had continued thinking. At the outset of his dictatorship, he had thought the main conflict in human affairs was the struggle of historical forms to maintain themselves against the scepticism, the disregard, and the incoherent enterprise of modern life. But was that indeed so? Had Sir Bussy been his real adversary? Or had his real adversary been the wider, more systematic intellectual alienations of Camelford? It was Camelford had liberated Sir Bussy, had snatched him out of the influence of Mr Parham. It was Camelford who had given the fundamental mysteries of Sir Bussy's disposition a form of expression. Just as the Lord Paramount himself, out of the fears, prejudices, resistances, habits, loyalties, and conservative vigour of mankind, had been able to evoke the heroic insensitiveness of Gerson. If so, it was Sir Bussy and Gerson who were the vital forces of this affair, the actual powers, and he and Camelford were mere intellectualizers to this restlessness on the one hand and this obstinacy on the other. But why, if Sir Bussy embodied a fundamental human force, had it been so easy to kill him? It was absurd even to dream of killing a fundamental force. Had he indeed been killed so easily? A wedge of doubt invaded the mind of the Lord Paramount and spread out to colour all his thoughts.

"Uncover the face," he said.

He motioned to the chauffeur to turn his lamps on to the white and shrunken visage.

Amazing yet inevitable came the confirmation of his doubts.

"Yes," he said. "It is like him, but it is not him. Of course, Gerson, you will *always* kill the wrong man. It is well I came to see with my own eyes."

But Gerson was shameless.

"And now we've seen it's the wrong one," said Gerson, "it's time we set about the right one – if the Empire is to get its Gas L in time to win this war."

"I wonder who this is."

"Any old chap who got in the way. Such things have to happen in war time."

The Lord Paramount's reserves showed signs of breaking down. "But shall we ever get this stuff? Shall we ever overtake Camelford and Sir Bussy?"

"We got to," said Gerson in a wrathful shout.

CHAPTER FIVE

Interlude with a Mirror

The Lord Paramount had the impression that he was again in the great dugout at Barnet. He was in one of the small apartments that opened out of the central cavern, a sort of dressing room. He was putting on a khaki uniform and preparing to start on a desperate expedition. A young subaltern assisted him timidly.

The Lord Paramount was excessively aware of Gerson's voice storming down the passage. He was always storming now.

They were still in pursuit of Camelford and Sir Bussy, who were reported to be at those strange new chemical works at Cayme in Lyonesse. They had to be caught and compelled if need be at the point of a revolver, to subserve the political ideas from which they were attempting to escape. The issue whether the soldier or the man of science should rule the world had come to actual warfare. Strange Reality was escaping, and Tradition was hard in pursuit. Gerson and the Lord Paramount were to fly to Devonshire and then rush upon Cayme, "swift and sure as the leap of a tiger," said Gerson. Then indeed, with the chemists captive and Gas L assured, the Empire could confront all the rest of the world with the alternative of submission or death.

The Lord Paramount adjusted the complex and difficult belt before a mirror. Then he stood still and stared at the reflection before him.

Where was the calm beauty of the Master Spirit?

The man he saw, he had seen in other mirrors ten thousand times before. It was the face, just falling short of strength and serenity by the subtle indications of peevishness and indecision, of the Senior Tutor of St Simon's. And those troubled eyes were Mr Parham's eyes. And the hair – he had never noted it before – was turning grey. He knew it had been getting thin, but now he saw it was getting grey. Merely Mr Parham? Had he been dreaming of a Lord Paramount, and had there never been anyone else but himself in this adventure? And what was this adventure? Was he recovering now from some fantastic intoxication?

With a start he realized that Gerson had come into the room and heard the clear-cut, even footsteps approach him. The organizer of victory came to the salute with a clash of accoutrements. "Everything is ready, sir," he said imperatively.

Mr Parham seemed to assent, but now he knew that he obeyed.

Like the damned of Swedenborg's visions, he had come of his own accord to his own servitude.

CHAPTER SIX

Cayme in Lyonesse

The chauffeur stopped short at a word from Gerson. "Pull up by the wayside," directed the General, "and try and look like engine trouble."

He got out. "We will walk to the top of the hill. The fellow standing there against the sky is our scout. And over beyond is Cayme."

The Lord Paramount obeyed in silence.

They were perhaps a couple of hundred yards from the crest. The sun was setting, a white blaze, which rimmed the line of the hill with iridescence. For an instant the Lord Paramount glanced back at the bleakness of the Cornish landscape, coldly golden, and then turned to the ascent.

"We shall see very little until this damned sun is down," said Gerson. "But there is no hurry now."

"An air scout," said the Lord Paramount.

"Theirs. They keep it circling. And they have another out to sea. But the water is opaque enough, I hope, to hide our submarines. And besides, they keep pretty far out."

"We have submarines?"

"Five. Six we had. But one is lost. All the coast has been played hokey with. The sea bed's coming up. God knows how they've done it, but they've raised scores of square miles. Heaved it up somehow. Our submarine must have hit a lump or barrier – which ought not to have been there. They've just made all this Lyonesse of theirs out of nothing – to save paying decent prices to decent landowners. They bore down through it and take out minerals – minerals we'd give our eyes to get – that were hidden under the bottom of the sea."

The Lord Paramount regarded the huge boss of stone to the right of them with a puzzled expression.

"I seem to remember this road – that rock that sticks up there and the way the road turns round it."

"It goes to Penzance. Or it did."

"That old disused tin mine we passed, that too seems familiar. Something odd about the double shaft... I've never seen this coast since I was a young man. Then I tramped it with a knapsack. By Land's End and along here and so on to Tintagel."

"You'll find it changed in a moment."

The Lord Paramount made no answer.

"Now. We're getting into view. Stroll easily. That fellow up there may be watching us. The evening's as still and clear as crystal. No mist. Not a cloud. We could do with a little obscurity tonight."

"Why have we no aeroplanes up?"

Something like contempt sounded in Gerson's voice.

"Because we want to take your friends out there by surprise."

The Lord Paramount felt again that sense of insufficiency that had been troubling him so frequently during the last few days. He had asked a silly question. More and more was Gerson

306

with his lucid technical capacity taking control of things. There was nothing more to be said, and in silence the Lord Paramount surveyed the view that had opened out before them. Gerson was still in control.

"We had better sit down on this bank among the heather. Don't stand still and stare. It won't do to seem even to be watching them."

The land was changed indeed.

Cayme was unlike any town, any factory, any normal place that Mr Parham had ever seen. For it was Mr Parham's eye that now regarded it. It sat up against the incandescent sky, broad, black, squat, like some monstrous new development of the battleship. It was a low, long battleship magnified by ten. Against the light it had no form nor detail, only a hard, long shape. Its vast shadow veiled a wedge of unassimilable detail, that might be a wilderness of streams and rich pools, in gloom and mystery. The land came out to this place, shining where it caught the light, or cut into blunt denticulations by long shadows, alternated triangles of darkness, wherever there was a rock or ridge to impede the light.

"But this was sea," said Mr Parham.

"This was sea."

"And away there is still Land's End."

"Only it isn't Land's End any more. This runs right out."

"I came along here, I suppose, somewhere – hard now to say exactly where – and I had Tennyson's *Morte d'Arthur* in my knapsack. And I – I was a young man then – I looked across at the sunset – a great clear sunset like this one – and I dreamt of the lost cities and places of Lyonesse until almost I could see them, like a mirage, glittering under the sun."

"And Lyonesse is here, and it hasn't got any cities or palaces or knights. And it doesn't glitter. And instead of King Arthur and his Table Round, you've got a crew of Camelford's men, brewing God knows what treason... I wish I knew... I wish I knew."

Gerson sat in silence for a space, and then he talked again, almost as much to himself as to Mr Parham.

"There they've got the stuff. They've got it; they've got everything. If we can wrench that place out of their hands suddenly – we have it all. I have men who can work it all right, given the stuff. Then we shall have poison gas to scare the world stiff... And we'll scare them... But swift and sure like the pounce of a cat – we must get them down before they can lift a finger. They'll blow the place to smithereens before they let us have it. Camelford has said as much. God knows what chemists are coming to! They didn't dare say 'No' to a soldier in the last Great War."

"These coasts have changed," said Mr Parham, "and the world has changed. And it seems to me tonight as if God himself had changed to something strange and dreadful."

They sat in silence. The sun which had been a white blaze had sunk down until it touched the high line of the silhouette of Cayme, and its blinding glory had become only a blazing red disk.

"Tell me," said Mr Parham. "What are our plans?"

Gerson glanced sideways to be sure the scout was out of earshot.

"We have all the Gas L the Empire could produce before these fellows collared the material. Just about enough for this job and no more. Further in some of it lies along the road, disguised as barrels of tar. Down in the village there, which used to be a fishing village and which now grows vegetables, keeps cows, and takes in washing for Cayme, it is piled up as barrels of beer. We have cases and cylinders hidden among the rocks."

"But where are our men?"

"At Bodmin, at Penzance, waiting for the dark with bicycles, and oh! – there's a good lot about here, though you don't see them, hidden in ditches since last night, lying under heaps of dry heather, down in that wood we passed. Waiting for a noiseless rocket at one o'clock tonight. Each one ready for his job. Behind that first line is Burchell with men in every town from Plymouth to Exeter, all hanging about unobtrusively, ready to follow up. What a man he is! What energy! Like a boy, an immense clever boy. He wouldn't let this happen without him. Would there were more like him!"

"And at one o'clock?"

"Quietly we shift the gas into the great ditch they have round that place, see our masks are adjusted, and let it loose."

"Which means?"

"They'll wriggle a bit – blast 'em!"

"And then?"

"No more of them. And at dawn we go in with our gas masks on – and take possession. Like digging out a wasp's nest."

"Suppose the gas doesn't work instantly – and they blow up in spite of us?"

"Then, my Lord Paramount, we are done. We'll go back to find London selling us, and selling us, the Union Jack with us, to anyone who cares to buy. We'll go back to find patriotism over and dead from China to Peru. We'll go back to find lords and dictators, ten a penny. Or – if we respect ourselves – we won't go back. But I think we can trust Gas L."

Never had the Lord Paramount felt so utterly Mr Parham. He looked about him at that evening, and it was a golden dome of warmth and stillness in which it was very good to be alive, and far off he heard some late lambs bleating and crying to the deep answers of their mothers.

"It's quite possible the book of history will close with a bang," said Gerson; "quite possible. About one o'clock tomorrow morning. We've done what we can. We've stuck like men to our own ideas. But, for instance, Gas L is faintly visible, a thin blue-grey vapour. At night it may get past them – but if they see it before they sniff it... Or if they have an anti-gas..."

The General left the rest to Mr Parham's imagination.

"Does he keep up all night?" asked Mr Parham indicating the slowly circling plane by a movement of his head.

"There are reliefs. For all we know, we are spotted now. For all we know, every bit of our little scheme is known. For all we know, we're trying to kill a sleeping tiger with a pea shooter, and all we shall do is to wake it up."

A long silence. The ever broadening and ever reddening dome of the sun seemed to be pouring its molten substance slowly and steadily into the mysterious black receptacle of Cayme.

"How still it is!" whispered Mr Parham.

"That's the damned thing about them," said Gerson, betraying a certain irritability. "*Still!* They never give a sign. These scientific men, these 'moderns,' as they call themselves, have never made a declaration or offered a deal a proper-minded man could consider. Only vague criticisms and pointless pacificism. Science has slipped out of our hands when we weren't looking. It used to be subservient enough. Years ago we ought to have forbidden scientific study or scientific knowledge except to men under military discipline, and we ought to have put our scientific discoverers under the Official Secrets Act. Then we should have had them under control. And perhaps their damned progress wouldn't have gone on so fast. They'd have mumbled their rotten theories in a corner, and we could have treated them as a joke. And if we'd been more nippy about the traders and the moneylenders we could have kept them trading respectfully, as they used to do. But we let the scientific men and the industrialists and the bankers all run about and get notions just as they pleased, and here they are, out of control, a gang of cosmopolitan conspirators with the mask off, actually intercepting munitions that are vital to the Empire and treating for peace with enemy countries on their own account. It's kind of symbolical, sir, that we are here, conducting military operations by stealth, as it were – with even our uniforms planned to be invisible... War ashamed of itself!... *Their* doing!"

And suddenly Gerson gave way to an outburst of the obscene, unmeaning blasphemies dear to simple souls the whole world over. He consigned men of science to the most unnatural experiences and the most unseemly behaviour. He raged against the vanity of intelligence and the vileness of mental presumption.

The last acutely bright red line of the sun's disk vanished abruptly from above the black crest of Cayme as though someone had suddenly thought of it and drawn it into the building. Minute cirrus clouds that had hitherto been invisible revealed themselves as faint streaks of gold in the sky and slowly faded again. Mr Parham remained sitting very still. General Gerson turned to the waiting scout with directions for him to get the rugs and hamper out of the car and send it on to Penzance. He and the

Lord Paramount would wait here among the stones until it was time to begin the attack.

It seemed to Mr Parham that the time passed very quickly before the attack began. An intense blue evening with a westward glow deepened through twilight into a starry night, which had fewest stars and a brighter edge to the north-west. He supped from the hamper and lay under a rock while Gerson, imitating and answering the sounds of improbable birds, made mysterious visits along the ridge and athwart the moor. Then when darkness came they started off, after much whispering and creeping about, blundering down the long slopes towards the erstwhile cliffs that marked the boundary of the old land and the new. Then a crawling forward with great circumspection and every possible precaution against noise. Then abruptly the startling discovery that he was not alone with Gerson, but one of a numerous line of furtive figures and groups, dimly visible against the sky line, some of them free handed and some bearing burdens.

Gerson handed Mr Parham a gas mask. "Don't make any mistakes with it," he said. "It's Gas L. Get the edge *sucking* against your face."

An interval of waiting in which one heard one's heart beating, and then the noiseless rocket like a meteor across the sky. Another interval for which there was no measure, and then the stealthy release of the Gas L.

The Gas L was plainly visible; it was as if it had a sort of grey luminosity. It crept along the ground and then slowly rose like swans' necks, like snakes, like the letter S, or like the top of a manuscript L, craning forward and down again towards the looming masses, now close at hand, of the mysteries of Cayme. It reached them and seemed to feel its way up their steep sides

312

and slowly, slowly reached the crest of the walls and poured over...

"At dawn we go in," said Gerson, his voice made Lilliputian by his mask. "At dawn we go in."

Mr Parham shivered and made no reply.

He felt cramp for a time, he was tickled and worried by his mask about his ears, and perhaps he slept for, at any rate, the hours again passed very quickly, and almost abruptly the scene was warm with the sunrise. Seen closely and with the light of morning on them, the walls of Cayme were revealed as a hard greenish substance with a surface like dulled metal, and they rose, slanting backwards out of this ditch without any windows or loopholes, towards the sky. The ditch was unexpectedly deep; it made one a little giddy to come upon it suddenly, and in it there was no water at all and no bottom visible, but very far down something cloudy, a sort of heavy yellowish smoke that writhed and curled about and did not rise. One had to move cautiously and peer because of the difficulty of seeing in a gas mask. One saw in a series of clipped pictures. The attack was lined out all along the edge of the ditch, a series of slouching cynocephali, with snouted white heads who turned about with cautious and noiseless movements and nosed and made gestures one to the other. Everyone carried a rifle or a revolver in his hand.

For a time the line was like a slack string along the edge of the ditch, uncertain of its next step. Then some common impulse had turned them all to the left, and they were following the edge of the ditch in Indian file as if to seek some point at which to cross it. The wall bent away presently and, rounding the bend, Mr Parham came into view of a narrow drawbridge of open metal work, about the end of which a number of the assailants had halted in a cluster.

Leadership he realized was needed.

He found himself with Gerson at the foot of the drawbridge and the others standing as if awaiting a decision. At the far end of that slender strip of open iron-work was an open doorway without a door. It gave into the darkness of an unlit passage. The nothingness in that passage was extraordinary. Not a living thing was to be seen and not a sound broke the immense silence of Cayme. Mr Parham wished that the word "mouse-trap" had not come into his head.

"Well?" came faintly from within Gerson's mask.

"If they are dead it is all right for us," said Mr Parham. "But if they are not dead, then it does not matter what we do, for even here we are completely in their power. One rifleman up there could pick us off one by one."

"Why did they leave that door open?" asked Gerson.

"I don't know. But I feel I have to go in."

"All or nothing," said Gerson.

He turned and gestured for six men to accompany them.

Mr Parham in a state that was neither abject nor arrogant, a new Mr Parham, puzzled and filled with wonder and dread, crossed the little bridge. He entered the passage. Gerson paused behind him to scrutinize the frame of the doorway. He made a comment that was inaudible. He looked up and dodged suddenly.

A door guided by grooves fell swiftly, stopped short with a metallic impact, and cut them off from the daylight and all support.

Gerson swore and tried to shove it up again. Mr Parham saw the thing happen without astonishment and remained quite still. They were not in darkness. A few small electric lamps seemed to have been switched on by the falling door.

CHAPTER SEVEN

The Adversary Speaks

M r Parham was astounded by his own fatalism. He who had conceived he held the mastery of the world in his shapely hand was now an almost apathetic spectator of his own frustration. He saw Gerson battering at the trap with a feeling – it was almost akin to gratified malice.

Gerson, he realized, had always been the disagreeable aspect of his mastery; always Gerson had spoilt things; always he had touched the stages of the fine romance of this adventure with an unanticipated cruelty and horror. Mr Parham was traditional and ready to be traditional, but Gerson he saw now was ancestral and archaic. Mr Parham realized now as he watched those simian fists hammering with furious gestures on the thick metal and pausing for the answering blows of the men outside, that he had come at last to detest Gerson almost as much as he detested Sir Bussy. He knew that this violence was futile, and he despised it as much as he hated it.

He put out his arm and touched Gerson.

Gerson sprang round, manifestly in a state of intense irritation and his mask did not completely stifle his interrogative snarl.

"That door may have fallen automatically," said Mr Parham. "For all we know yet – everyone here may be dead."

Gerson thought and then nodded and made a gesture for Mr Parham to precede him.

"And indeed," said Mr Parham to himself, "for all I know they may be dead."

In another moment he knew better. The little passage opened out into what seemed to be a large circular space and at the further side of this they saw two figures, unmasked and regarding them. Gas L was as if it had never been. They were men clad in the white overalls dear to chemists and surgeons. They made signs as if for Mr Parham and Gerson to move softly. They pointed to something hidden as yet from the newcomers. Their forms were a little distorted and their gestures a little exaggerated by some intervening transparent substance.

So they had had an anti-gas for Gas L.

Mr Parham advanced, and Gerson came close behind.

They emerged upon a circular gallery.

The place made Mr Parham think of the inside of the reservoir of a coal-gas works. Such a place would surely look like this place if it had electric lights inside it. It was large – it might have been a hundred yards in a diameter – and shaped like a drum. The little gallery on which they stood ran round it, and in the central pit and occupying most of it was a huge glass bulb, a vast retort, in which a greenish-white liquid was boiling and bubbling. The shining curvature of the glass rose before them, reflecting them faintly with a certain distortion. It shortened and broadened them. It robbed Mr Parham of all his natural dignity and made Gerson look incredibly squat and filthy and evil. The liquid in the retort was not seething equally; it was traversed and

316

torn here and there by spurts and eddies of commotion; here it was mysteriously still and smooth, here with a wild rush came a drive of bursting bubbles. They stormed across the surface and raised eruptive mounds of ebullient liquid. And over the whole whirled and danced wisps of filmy vapour. But this held Mr Parham's attention only for a moment. He realized that he was in the presence of Camelford and Sir Bussy, and he forgot everything else in that confrontation.

Both these men were dressed in the same white overalls as the assistants across on the other side of the rotunda. But they had the air of having expected Mr Parham and his companion. They seemed to have been coming to meet them.

With a gesture of irritation Mr Parham wrenched off his mask and Gerson followed suit.

"The Lord Paramount of Britain," said Camelford and bowed with manifest irony.

"Looks uncommonly like my old friend Parham," said Sir Bussy.

"This other gentleman, if I'm not mistaken," said Camelford, "is that master strategist, General Gerson."

"It's a loyal Englishman, Mr Camelford," said the General, "who has done his best to save a great Empire."

"You lost a good lot of it to begin with," said Camelford.

"Because we were shot at from behind."

"How's your war going now?"

"The war's gone to pieces. Mutiny. Disorder. London is in revolt and crying for peace. American peace propaganda has done us in – with treason at the back of us. It's the story of the poor old Kaiser over again. Beaten on the home front. No fair soldiering. If we could have made enough of Gas L – if we could have got all we had reasonably thought we should get... God! There was nothing wrong in my plans. Except that you've made a corner in Gas L. While we fought the enemy, you, you dirty sneaks, cornered our munitions. And now you've got us, and may Hell take you for it!"

Camelford turned to Sir Bussy. "He speaks with heat, but I think we may admit his facts are sound. You've always had the buying-up instinct." He smiled blandly at Gerson. "We've got the stuff, as you say. We don't pretend we haven't. Sir Bussy has been amazing. But it isn't for sale. We thought it a pity to waste it on Gas L, and so we are making use of it in another way. Our way."

A faint memory of the Lord Paramount reappeared in Mr Parham. He made the old familiar gesture with his hand. "I want that material," he said. "I demand it."

Sir Bussy's nether lip dropped. "What for?" he asked.

"To save the Empire. To save the world from chaos."

"There ain't going to be no chaos," misquoted Sir Bussy.

"What are you going to do? Where do you think you are driving? Are you going to sit here and barter your stolen goods to the highest bidder?"

"Cornered, perhaps, but not stolen," Sir Bussy corrected.

"Well?"

"We're going to take control," said Sir Bussy.

"*You!* A handful of financial and technical scoundrels!"

"*We're* not going to take control," said Camelford, "if Sir Bussy will forgive me. Something else *has* taken control. And there are more men coming into this business of creation than you or Gerson dream."

Mr Parham looked about him, at the smooth circular walls about them, at the monstrous glass retort, at the distant figures of the silent attendants in white. Their number had now increased to six, and they all stood watching noiselessly It was extraordinarily still and large and clean and – queer. It was not like industrialism. It was profoundly unhistorical. It was the new thing coming. And at his side stood Gerson. He, on the contrary, was like all the heroes of all the faint hopes that have never succeeded. That never very attractive little figure in its uniform of soiled khaki suffered enormously by the contrast, looked brutish, looked earthy. Crawling through the darkness over rough ground usually given over to rabbits and an occasional goat had not improved his never very meticulous appearance, and his native physical vigour, the natural strength of his dark hair, made it very evident that he had had no time for a shave for a couple of days.

Mr Parham, who had always had a reasonable care for his own costume, experienced a wave of profound disloyalty to his sturdy colleague. This latter looked a pig of a creature, he looked as toughly combative with anything and everything as a netted boar. He was more than half an animal. Yet surely for all his savagery he had the inflexible loyalty of a great hero, he had a heart of ruthless, inexorable gold. Surely?

Mr Parham's thoughts came back to the last sentence Camelford had uttered and to this strange place into which he and Gerson had blundered. "Something else had taken control?" Not Gerson but something else? What was the issue that had brought them to this confrontation? Gerson hot and dirty, versus this Something Else? Which was not this group nor that group. Not the nation nor the Empire. Not America nor Europe. Which was a sort of emanation from the released and freely acting intelligence of mankind.

A trace of the Master Spirit was still in Mr Parham's manner, but behind the mask of his resolute bearing he felt his mind had fallen open and lay unprotected against new strange heretical assailants.

"What is your aim here?" he asked. "What do you imagine you are doing? My ideas are still the common ideas of humanity. They are the forces of history. They are the driving power that has brought civilization to its present pass. Tradition. Discipline. Obedience. What are your ideas? Why have you raised this land out of the sea and made this place?"

"We never raised this land out of sea," said Camelford. "We never made this place. And we learn our aim as we get to it."

"Then who the devil – ?" said Gerson.

"This place came. No single man planned it. No single man foresaw it. It appeared. As all the great inventions have appeared. Not out of individuals but out of the mind of man. This land with its hidden stores of strange minerals lay under the sea, ready for anyone who fulfilled the conditions fixed for raising it. And these works and the gas we are making, those also depended on the fulfilling of conditions. We individual men of science and men of enterprise do no more than observe the one supreme condition – which is that the human intelligence should have fair play. Now that these things have realized themselves, we look for the next thing we have to do."

"Ugh," said Gerson.

"The old face of human life is passing away. In that obedient fashion to which our science has trained us we observe the coming of the new. The age of war and conquest is over. War is done with but with war a thousand other once vital things are done with also. The years of restraint are at an end. The patriots and warriors and masters, the flags and the nations, have to be rounded up now and put away forever. Powers and empires are over. The loyalties that served them must die. They matter no more. They become a monstrous danger. What was it Sir Bussy said? 'The ideas of an old buck rabbit in the reign of Queen Elizabeth.' Shut the book of national conflicts and conquests now and hand it over to the psychologists. We are the workers of a new dawn. Men of no nation. Men without traditions. Men who look forward and not back. Men who have realized the will and the intelligence that we obey and possess in common. Our race has to organize the whole world now, a field for this creative energy that flows through and uses and guides us."

"But you are brewing a gas here!" said Mr Parham. "It is a gas – a dangerous gas. What is it?"

"It takes some brewing. If a crack in that retort let in the air – well, somewhere else this thing would have to begin over again. Here it would be finished. This stuff you see here is only a stage in a long string of processes. Before our product is ready to use there have to be corrosive and destructive phases. It is unavoidable that there should be these phases of corrosion and destruction. What is adventure if it has no danger? But when we have done, the gas we shall have here will not be a poison gas at all. Instead we shall have a vapour to enter into blood and nerve and brain and clean the mind of man as it has never been cleaned before. It will allow his brain, so clogged and stifled still by old rubbish, so poisoned and cramped and crippled, to free itself from all that holds it back now from apprehending and willing to the utmost limits of its possibility. And that points to a new world quite different from the world to which your mind is adapted. A world beyond your dreaming. You don't begin to imagine yet a tithe of the things a liberated human brain can do. All your poor old values will be mislaid and forgotten. Your kingdoms and empires, your morals and rights, all you find so lovely and splendid, the heroism and sacrifices of battlefields, your dreams of lordship, every romantic thing, the devotion of servants, the subjugation of women, and the deception of children – all the complex rigmaroles of your old world will be washed out of men's thought. We are brewing a new morality here and a new temerity. Instead of distrusting each other, killing each other, competing with and enslaving and consuming one another, we go on to a world of equals, working together under the guidance of realized fact, for ends too high for your imagination..."

"But this is the voice of Satan himself," interrupted Mr Parham. "This is the Sin of Pride defying Heaven. This is Babel come again."

"No," said Camelford, and it seemed to Mr Parham that he began to grow larger and tower over his hearers. "It is the way of escape from our narrow selves. Forward to the new. Cling to this traditionalism of yours a little longer, cling still to what *you* call history, with all these new powers and possibilities we are pressing into your hands – and there can be only one end – Catastrophe."

The word Catastrophe reverberated in Mr Parham's mind. Then his attention was caught and riveted on Gerson's attitude. The General's one serviceable eye, dilated and intent, was fixed on Camelford, his lips were pressed together, his bulldog face was set in an expression of stern indignation. A deep Indian red had

invaded his complexion. He was rigid except that his right arm
was moving very slowly. His hand gripped the butt of his
revolver and was tightening on it and drawing it out.

A strange conflict prevailed in Mr Parham's mind. He found
this talk of Camelford's antagonistic and hateful, but he did not
want to interrupt it; he wanted to hear the man out; above all, he
did not want to have the talk interrupted by Gerson in Gerson's
fashion.

And besides, what was Gerson doing here? He had not been
asked to this party. But was it a party? This was not a dinner
party. It was a séance. But no! What was it? Where were we?
Cayme?

Within the now frightfully confused soul of Mr Parham
intellectuality grappled with reaction. Not yet, at any rate, must
things come to this. He made a weak movement of his hand as if
in restraint of Gerson's intention.

Instantly Gerson had whipped out his weapon. "Stand off,"
he said in an aside to Parham, and then to Camelford, "Hands
up!"

Camelford did not seem to realize his danger. "Put that old
thing up," he said. "Give it to me. You'll break something."

He came, hand out, towards Gerson.

"Keep back!" said Gerson. "I'll show you if this sort of thing
is over. It's only beginning. I'm the real Lord Paramount. Force
and straight shooting. Do you think I care a damn for your gas or
you? Catastrophe! A fig for your old catastrophe! Which is always
coming and never comes... Hands up, I tell you. Put up your
hands, you damned fool! *Stop!*"

He fired. Then very swiftly the blue steel barrel under Mr
Parham's nose sought Sir Bussy.

Vainly. Gerson's shot hit the metal door that closed upon that elusive being. Mr Parham felt an instant pang of exasperation with both these uncontrollable spirits. He still wanted Camelford to go on. His mind flashed back to Camelford. But Camelford was staggering with his hand on his throat.

Then it was catastrophe, as Camelford had said.

A crash and a splintering of glass. Camelford had fallen through the great glass retort, carrying down a transparent shattering triangle, had splashed into the liquid and now lay far below, moving convulsively on the curve of the nether glass. For a moment the air about them was full of ascendant streamers of vapour made visible as they changed to green and mingled with the air. They eddied and whirled. They spun faster and faster.

Gerson had turned his weapon upon Parham. "You too! *You* to talk of war! With the wits of a prig and the guts of a parasite! Get out of my world!"

The vituperating mouth hung open arrested. No shot came.

But now everything was moving very swiftly. One last flash of frantic perception closed the story. The rotunda yawned open as though some mighty hand had wrenched it in two, and through the separating halves of the roof appeared the warm glow of sunrise. A universe of sound pressed upon and burst the drums of Mr Parham's ears. An immense explosion which seemed to have been going on for some moments caught him and lifted him backward and upward at an incredible speed, and Gerson, suddenly flat and bloody, flashed by, seemed to be drawn out longer and longer until he was only a thread of scarlet and khaki, and so vanished slanting up the sky, with his revolver spinning preposterously after him...

CHAPTER EIGHT

Postmortem

The world and all things in it vanished in a flash of blinding light.

The word "extinction" sang like a flying spark through the disintegrating brain of Mr Parham. Darkness should have swallowed up that flying spark, but instead it gave place to other sparks, brighter and larger. "Another life or extinction? Another life or extinction?"

With a sort of amazement Mr Parham realized that experience was not at an end for him. He was still something, something that felt and thought. And he was somewhere.

Heaven or hell? Heaven or hell?

It must be hell, he thought, surely, for it was pervaded by the voice of Sir Titus Knowles, if one could call that harsh, vindictive, snarling sound a voice. The very voice of Gerson. Hell – and in the company of Sir Titus! But surely hell would be something fuliginous, and this was a clear white blaze.

The words of Sir Titus became distinct. "*Got* you!" he bawled. "*Got* you! There's the ectoplasm! There's the mighty visitant's face! Painted bladder, as I said. Clever chap, but I've got you. Sham dead if you like for as long as you like, but I tell you the game is up."

It was the upstairs room in Carfex House, and Carnac Williams was lying in a dishevelled heap upon the floor. Hereward Jackson was holding back Knowles, who was straining out his leg to kick the motionless body.

Mr Parham staggered up from his armchair and found Sir Bussy doing likewise. Sir Bussy had the flushed face of one roused suddenly from sleep. "What the devil?" he demanded.

"I don't understand," said Mr Parham.

"Exposure!" panted Sir Titus triumphantly and tried another kick.

"A foul exposure, anyhow," said Hereward Jackson and pushed him back from his exhausted victim. "Spare the poor devil!"

"Le' go!" cried Sir Titus...

A manservant had appeared and was respectfully intervening between Sir Titus and Hereward Jackson. Another came to the assistance of Carnac Williams.

A tremendous wrangle began...

"Gaw!" said Sir Bussy when it was all over.

CHAPTER NINE

The Last Straw

"I 'm going to walk up to Claridge's," said Sir Bussy. "This affair has left me stuffy. You go that way?"

"As far as Pontingale Street, yes."

"Come on to Claridge's. My nieces are having a great dance there... That ectoplasm fairly turned me sick... I've done with this spook business for good and all."

"I always wanted to keep out of it," said Mr Parham.

The two men set out side by side, and for a time each pursued his own thoughts. Sir Bussy's led him apparently to some conclusion, for suddenly he said, "Gaw" – as if he tapped a nail on the head.

"Parham, were you awake all through that séance?"

"No. I was bored. I fell asleep."

"*I* fell asleep." Sir Bussy reflected. "These séances make you sleep – and dream. That's the trick of them."

Mr Parham looked at his companion, startled. Had he too dreamt? And what had he dreamt?

"I dreamt about the things those fellows, Camelford and Hamp, were saying the other night."

"Curious!" said Mr Parham, but he felt the thing was much more curious than his voice betrayed. What if they had had the same dream?

"I seemed to see their arguments in a sort of realized kind of way."

How poor the man's powers of expression!

"You and I were on opposite sides," he added "Daggers drawn."

"I hope not."

"There was a war. Gaw! I can't tell you. Such a war! It was like trying to plug a burst steam pipe." Sir Bussy left his hearer to imagine what that meant. And Mr Parham was able to imagine.

"I cornered the chemicals," said Sir Bussy. "I and Camelford. We kind of held it up. We did our best. But at last the natural lunacy in things got loose and – everything seemed to blow to pieces. There was a nasty little toad of a sojer. *Bang!*"

"That was the waking up?"

"That was the waking up."

Then Sir Bussy went off at a tangent. "We rich men – I mean we big business people – we've been backing the wrong horse. We've been afraid of Bogy Bolshevik and all the new things, and damn it! it's the *old* things that mean to bust up affairs. We're the new things ourselves. What did J. C. say? No good putting new wine in old bottles... The world's rising and splashing over. The old notions and boundaries won't hold it... I wish I could describe my dream to you. Extraordinary it was. And you were in it somehow all through... And Camelford... Hamp was American ambassador. Crazy, it was..."

Now this was getting more and more remarkable. But no – it was not the same dream – similar, perhaps. It was impossible that it could have been the same...

A dream, as everyone knows, can happen with incredible rapidity. It may all have happened in a second. The sounds of Sir Titus Knowles turning on lights and bumping about with the medium and snarling at him had no doubt provided the gunfire and flashes and evoked warlike images in both their awakening minds. And the rest had arisen from what lay ready in their antagonistic attitudes.

Sir Bussy went on with conviction: "If we don't see to it, these Old Institutions of yours and all that – these old things that ought to be cleaned up and put away now – will upset the whole human apple cart – like some crazy old granny murdering a child. Foreign offices, war offices, sovereignty, and clutter like that. Bloody clutter. Bloodstained clutter. All that I got as clear as day. They can't hold things any longer. They've got to be superannuated, shoved away in the attic. I didn't realize. We've got to do something about it soon. Damn soon. Before another smash. We new people. We've just floated about getting rich and doing nothing about it... Buying and selling and amalgamating and monopolizing isn't enough. The worst thing in life is to have power and not use it to the full... There wasn't a thing in my nightmare that might not happen."

Mr Parham waited for what might come next. It was extraordinary, this parallelism, but still his reason insisted they could not have had the same identical dream.

"Was there," he said, "by any chance, a sort of Lord – Lord Protector in your dream?"

"No," said Sir Bussy. "There was just a damned pig-headed patriotic imperial government and a war. Come to think of it, there was something – a sort of dictatorship. They put Labour out of business. I thought the chap was Amery. A sort of lofty

Amery. Amery drawn out elegant – if you understand me. He didn't amount to much. What mattered was the ideas behind him."

"And where did I come in?"

There was a catch in Mr Parham's breath.

"You were on the side of the government and we argued. You were for the war. In this dream I seemed always to be meeting you and arguing. It made it very real. You were some sort of official. We kept on arguing. Even when the bombs were bursting and they tried to shoot me."

Mr Parham was to a certain extent relieved. Not completely but sufficiently. There had been a dream, evidently, a similar dream; a clearly similar dream. It is a distinctive feature of the séance condition that people should have similar dreams; but his dream and Sir Bussy's had not been the same dream. Not exactly the same dream. They had visualized the expectation of a possible war that haunted both their minds, but each in his own fashion – each with his own distinctive personal reference. That was it. The brief and tragic (and possibly slightly absurd) reign of Mr Parham as Lord Paramount could be locked forever in his own breast.

But what was Sir Bussy saying?

He had been telling something of his dream that Mr Parham had missed.

"We've got to give people a juster idea of what is going on and give it 'em quick. Or they'll fall into unutterable smash-up. Schools – you can't. You can't get the necessary *quality* in teachers. Universities lock themselves against us. Yes, they do. We've got to snatch the new generation out of the hands of doddering prigs and pedants and tell 'em, tell 'em, tell 'em.

330

Catch the oversplash of life. In new ideas, in new organizations. The way out is through books, newspapers, print, talk... 'Light, more light,' as old Gutty said." (Did he mean Goethe?)

"I'm coming into the newspaper world, Parham, I tell you. You've often suggested it, and here I am doing as you said. You know a thing or two. This sort of war drift can only be stopped by a big push the other way. Bigger than anything done so far. Crowds of people in earnest. The Big Push for the new world! What of a big Sunday paper – that's the day they read – to give 'em science, give them the drift and meaning of the new world that – was it Camelford said it? – the new world that's trying to get born... Or was it that chap from Geneva?... Warn them how Granny still mutters and messes about with the knives... A great big powerful paper."

At these words a queer irrational excitement made Mr Parham tingle from head to foot. His sense of antagonism to Sir Bussy faded and vanished. Hopes long cherished and long suppressed arose in him with such a strength and violence that his orientation was lost. He could see this only as one thing, a proposal to himself. The proposal was coming in a manner he had never thought of, it was coming with a strangely twisted look, but surely it was coming. He was going to have his paper. At last. He might have to take rather a different line from the one he would have preferred before his dream, but his dream had twisted and turned him about a lot, and his awakening still more. And anyhow – it was a paper!

"Isn't a Saturday weekly perhaps a better medium?" he asked in a strained, ill-controlled voice. "Smaller circulation, perhaps, but more real influence."

331

"No, I want this paper to go out to the main public by the hundred thousand. I want to go behind all those clever fellows. They cut no ice. I want to go out with pictures and vulgar noise and all that, and tell 'em and tell 'em and tell 'em, week after week, that these old things of yours are played out and dangerous and – oh, damnable!"

"*These old things of yours?*" Something chill blew upon Mr Parham. But still the poor desperate soul hung on. For six expectant years he had desired this thing.

"I don't quite see myself doing that," he said. "I'm not a Garvin, you know. I doubt if one can be both copious and fine."

Sir Bussy stopped short and regarded his companion with amazement, his mouth askew, for a couple of seconds or more. "Gaw!" he said at last. "I wasn't thinking of *you*."

Mr Parham was now very pale. The incredible was happening. His mind refused to accept it. "But the paper!" he gasped.

"I'll have to do it with the right sort of fellows," said Sir Bussy, speaking slowly. "It would be up against every damn thing you are."

He was staring at Mr Parham in manifest amazement. As though he realized something for the first time. Six years they had been together, and never had it entered his head that the ideal editor of anything was Mr Parham. And he meant, he really meant, this illiterate Cockney! to conduct his paper himself. Out of a dream he had got this crazy confidence. Some fantastic dream in the heavy and charged atmosphere of that séance. That infernal séance! That ten thousand times accursed séance! It had put everything awry. It had shattered everything. It had been a vat of mental fermentation. Out of its tedious tensions these hypnotic revelations had arisen. It had dispersed the decent

332

superficial controls of both their minds and laid bare things that should never have been laid bare. It had revealed the roots of their imaginations. It had exposed the irreconcilable. How true and sound had been the instincts of Mr Parham, when he had resisted the resort of these darkened chambers and these irrational expansions of expectation which are the inevitable consequences of séance conditions!

A paper – a great paper, financed by Sir Bussy! And not to be his! A paper *against* him!

Six years wasted! Slights! Humiliations! Irritations! Tailors' bills!

Never in his life had he screamed, but now he was near screaming. He felt with his fingers inside his collar and had no word to say. Something had broken within him. It was the back of that poor weary camel of hope which for six long years had carried him so far and by such winding tracks, uphill and downhill, across great spaces, into strange continents, in pursuit of Sir Bussy.

They stopped short at the corner of Pontingale Street. Mr Parham glared, speechless, at his companion. Here indeed their ways diverged.

"But come on," said Sir Bussy. "It's hardly midnight yet. Come on and see if my nieces aren't setting Claridge's afire. Everyone will be there – drabs and duchesses – Gaby – everybody."

For the first time in their relationship Mr Parham declined an invitation. "*No*," he said recovering the power of speech.

Sir Bussy never took a refusal without a struggle. "Oh, *come!*" he said.

Mr Parham shook his head. His soul was now brimming over with hate for this bilking, vulgar little scoundrel, this treacherous and incurable antagonist. His hate may have looked out of his eyes. They may have revealed the spite of devil within the don. For the first time, perhaps, in this long intercourse Sir Bussy may have seen all that Mr Parham could feel about him.

For twenty seconds of stark revelation the two men confronted each other, and then Mr Parham, recovering his discretion, was catching his soul back from its windows and drawing down the blinds. But Sir Bussy did not repeat his invitation to Claridge's.

"Gaw," he said, and turned away towards Berkeley Square. He did not even say "Goodnight."

Never before had Mr Parham heard a "Gaw" so fraught with derision and dismissal. It was an entirely unanswerable "Gaw." It was abandonment.

For a minute, perhaps, he stood quite still as Sir Bussy receded. Then slowly, almost submissively, he turned his face towards his lodging in Pontingale Street.

It seemed to Mr Parham that all reality had deserted him. Not only had Sir Bussy gone off with all his dearest hopes, but it was as if his own substance had gone from him also. Within, the late Lord Paramount was nothing now but a vacuum, a cavernous nothingness craving for reassurance.

Had he no future? Some day, perhaps, when old Waterham died – if ever that old bit of pemmican did die – the Mastership of St Simon's. That – and a pose of smiling disdain. With a little acid in the smile.

His mind swayed uncertainly and then came round with the quivering decision of a compass needle towards the dusky comfort and intimacy, the limitless understanding and sympathy of little Mrs Pinchot. She would understand him. She would understand. Even if all that had made history for him went to the dust destructor, even if a new upstart history that took no heed of Princes and Powers, Persons and Policies and was all compact of biology, economics and suchlike innovations, ruled the earth in its stead. He knew she would understand – whatever there was to understand, and see it, whatever it was, in a light that would sustain and help him.

True indeed that the chief proofs of her devotion and understanding had come to him in this dream, but there is an element of revelation in every dream, an element of good in every disaster.

Happily he had her telephone number...

And so, showing a weary back to us, with his evening hat on the back of his head, our deflated publicist recedes up Pontingale Street, recedes with all his vanities, his stores of erudition, his dear preposterous generalizations, his personified nations and all his obsolescent paraphernalia of scholarly political wisdom, so feebly foolish in their substance and so hideously disastrous in their possible consequences, and his author, who has come to feel a curious unreasonable affection for him, must needs bid him a reluctant farewell.

H G Wells

The History of Mr Polly

Mr Polly is one of literature's most enduring and universal creations. An ordinary man, trapped in an ordinary life, Mr Polly makes a series of ill-advised choices that bring him to the very brink of financial ruin. Determined not to become the latest victim of the economic retrenchment of the Edwardian age, he rebels in magnificent style and takes control of his life once and for all.

ISBN 0-7551-0404-8

H G Wells

In the Days of the Comet

Revenge was all Leadford could think of as he set out to find the unfaithful Nettie and her adulterous lover. But this was all to change when a new comet entered the earth's orbit and totally reversed the natural order of things. The Great Change had occurred and any previous emotions, thoughts, ambitions, hopes and fears had all been removed. Free love, pacifism and equality were now the name of the game. But how would Leadford fare in this most utopian of societies?

ISBN 0-7551-0406-4

H G WELLS

THE INVISIBLE MAN

On a cold wintry day in the depths of February a stranger appeared in The Coach and Horses requesting a room. So strange was this man's appearance, dressed from head to foot with layer upon layer of clothing, bandages and the most enormous glasses, that the owner, Mrs Hall, quite wondered what accident could have befallen him. She didn't know then that he was invisible – but the rumours soon began to spread...

H G Wells' masterpiece *The Invisible Man* is a classic science-fiction thriller showing the perils of scientific advancement.

ISBN 0-7551-0407-2

H G WELLS

THE ISLAND OF DR MOREAU

A shipwreck in the South Seas brings a doctor to an island paradise. Far from seeing this as the end of his life, Dr Moreau seizes the opportunity to play God and infiltrate a reign of terror in this new kingdom. Endless cruel and perverse experiments ensue and see a series of new creations – the 'Beast People' – all of which must bow before the deified doctor.

Originally a Swiftian satire on the dangers of authority and submission, Wells' *The Island of Dr Moreau* can now just as well be read as a prophetic tale of genetic modification and mutability.

ISBN 0-7551-0408-0

H G WELLS

MEN LIKE GODS

Mr Barnstaple was ever such a careful driver, careful to indicate before every manoeuvre and very much in favour of slowing down at the slightest hint of difficulty. So however could he have got the car into a skid on a bend on the Maidenhead road?

When he recovered himself he was more than a little relieved to see the two cars that he had been following still merrily motoring along in front of him. It seemed that all was well – except that the scenery had changed, rather a lot. It was then that the awful truth dawned: Mr Barnstaple had been hurled into another world altogether.

How would he ever survive in this supposed Utopia, and more importantly, how would he ever get back?

ISBN 0-7551-0413-7

H G Wells

The War of the Worlds

'No one would have believed in the last years of the nineteenth century that this world was being watched keenly and closely by intelligences greater than man's...'

A series of strange atmospheric disturbances on the planet Mars may raise concern on Earth but it does little to prepare the inhabitants for imminent invasion. At first the odd-looking Martians seem to pose no threat for the intellectual powers of Victorian London, but it seems man's superior confidence is disastrously misplaced. For the Martians are heading towards victory with terrifying velocity.

The War of the Worlds is an expertly crafted invasion story that can be read as a frenzied satire on the dangers of imperialism and occupation.

ISBN 0-7551-0426-9

HOUSE OF STRATUS

Internet:	www.houseofstratus.com including synopses and features.
Email:	sales@houseofstratus.com info@houseofstratus.com (please quote author, title and credit card details.)
Tel:	Order Line 0800 169 1780 (UK) 800 724 1100 (USA) International +44 (0) 1845 527700 (UK) +01 845 463 1100 (USA)
Fax:	+44 (0) 1845 527711 (UK) +01 845 463 0018 (USA) (please quote author, title and credit card details.)
Send to:	House of Stratus Sales Department House of Stratus Inc. Thirsk Industrial Park 2 Neptune Road York Road, Thirsk Poughkeepsie North Yorkshire, YO7 3BX NY 12601 UK USA